Tempest in a Teapot

Tempest in a Teapot

JUDY BAER

Guideposts

New York, New York

Tempest in a Teapot

ISBN-13: 978-0-8249-4803-0

Published by Guideposts
16 East 34th Street
New York, New York 10016
www.guideposts.com

Distributed by Ideals Publications, a division of Guideposts
2636 Elm Hill Pike, Suite 120
Nashville, Tennessee 37214

Library of Congress Cataloging-in-Publication Data has been applied for.

Cover by Deborah Chabrian
Design by Marisa Jackson
Typeset by Nancy Tardi

Printed and bound in the United States of America

10 9 8 7 6 5 4 3 2

For Val Swedberg and Beverly Fosen Hanson, thank you.

You know why!

GRACE CHAPEL INN

A place where one can be
refreshed and encouraged,
a place of hope and healing,
a place where God is at home.

Chapter One

*I*t can't get much better than this," Sylvia Songer said as she leaned against an old oak tree, with her eyes closed and a blissful smile tipping the corners of her mouth. Her fair skin was mottled by sunlight and shade as the canopy of overhead branches moved in the breeze. "Like the Garden of Eden."

Jane Howard laughed quietly and, unbeknownst to Sylvia, added a few more freckles to the watercolor she was painting of her friend. "The Garden of Eden after the fall, I'm afraid. Imagine what the original must have been like." Her own dark, thick hair, pulled back and tied with a piece of string she'd discovered in her painting supplies, gleamed in the afternoon light. A breeze rustled the leaves again and a mockingbird sang joyously somewhere near the pond on this lovely Saturday in late June. It was difficult to imagine a setting more perfect than this one.

"Thanks for bringing me here. I love it when you ask me to tag along while you paint." Sylvia yawned and stretched like a contented cat in the sun.

Jane was spending more and more time at Fairy Pond, it seemed. Although the inn she ran with her sisters Louise and Alice was warm and welcoming, it wasn't always the ideal place to sketch and paint. Usually too much was happening there, and Jane, who ran the kitchen, was often up to her elbows in some sort of dough or other. Fairy Pond was her escape, her haven from the outside world.

"Looks like you've been fairly creative yourself," Jane commented as Sylvia held up the piece of hand quilting she'd been stitching. It was a colorful baby quilt covered with ducks, bunnies and balloons.

"A sample for the store." Sylvia ran Sylvia's Buttons, a fabric store in the center of Acorn Hill. "If I don't come out here with you, I don't sew any hand-quilted samples for my customers to see. Being able to sit here, visit with you and sew in this lovely place is pure bliss."

"It is, isn't it? When I first came to Acorn Hill from San Francisco, it was the place I came to when I needed to regroup." Jane thought about the sometimes challenging adjustments she'd had to make when she first arrived to live and work with her two older sisters. "Fortunately, now I just come here because I love it."

A gust of wind shivered the leaves above them as the trees stood like sentinels around them. The rocks were covered with moss so soft and green it looked like velvet, and the handsome plants that clung to the earth made Fairy Pond feel like the safest, most enduring and ageless place on earth.

"I hope it never changes," Sylvia commented, as she returned to her meticulous stitching. "I want to come here to quilt until I'm so old that I can barely get my walker around those big rocks over there. Or maybe I'll have to hire your little friend Josie Gilmore to push me here in my wheelchair."

"That's a visual," Jane said with a grin. "And here's another." She turned the piece she'd been working on so that Sylvia could see it.

"Oh my," Sylvia breathed, "it's beautiful. Far prettier than I merit."

"Give yourself a little credit." Jane handed Sylvia the painting. "Hang it where you can see it to remind yourself how pretty you really are."

"You do know just the right things to say, don't you?" Sylvia looked amused. It had always amazed her how easy it was for Jane to make friends and to delight them with her outgoing manner.

"Not always. I recently put my foot in my mouth."

"How so?"

"I was telling Alice about a horrible dream I'd had the night before. I didn't hear Aunt Ethel come in, and she heard the whole thing before I realized she was standing there."

"What's so awful about hearing someone's dream?" Sylvia snapped a piece of thread in her teeth and began to change to another colored spool. "I think it's interesting. Joseph's dreams in the Bible are fascinating."

"They didn't always win him friends, though," Jane pointed out. "Eleven sheaves of wheat representing Joseph's brothers bowing down to him? It didn't exactly make him the most popular kid on the block."

"His interpretations of dreams didn't make him a favorite with others either."

"Telling the baker he'd lose his head in three days? No, I suppose that wasn't a hit." Jane stretched. "There's a lot of action in Genesis, that's for sure. But this wasn't a Joseph-type dream, a foretelling of the future." Jane frowned and shuddered at the thought. "At least I hope it wasn't. It was about poor Lloyd."

"There's not much 'poor' about Lloyd," Sylvia pointed out. "He's mayor of Acorn Hill, he loves what he does, he drops in frequently for a great meal at the inn or at your Aunt Ethel's, he has Ethel as a…dare I say it…girlfriend…"

Sylvia scrunched her nose and frowned, thinking about the vivid red hair the elderly Ethel sported. "Maybe Lloyd doesn't have it so great after all, that Ethel part..."

They both laughed out loud. They loved Jane's aunt, who was dear, devoted and kindhearted . . . and could sometimes drive a person to distraction with her inquisitive nature. She lived next to the inn, so the Howard sisters often got the brunt of her sometimes misguided enthusiasm.

"I shouldn't laugh," Jane said. "It was a very strange dream I had. Aunt Ethel didn't like it one bit. You know how protective she can be about Lloyd."

"Even protective of him in *your* dreams? Isn't that going a bit far? What on earth did you dream about anyway?"

"I suppose it started because Lloyd and Aunt Ethel had been over for dinner. We had a lasagna with meat and nearly two pounds of cheese in it, garlic toast slathered in garlic butter, an ambrosia salad made with sour cream, and fresh cookies for dessert—macadamia coconut cookies. Let's just say that Lloyd ate more than his share of the cookies, but they are among his favorites."

"Eat cheese, sour cream and cookies, apply fat directly to arteries. Is that what your dream was about?"

"Actually, no. I dreamed that I was in New York City watching the Macy's parade, and Lloyd was in it."

"Marching? Or was he riding a float?" She held up her hand. "Don't tell me he was grand marshal. This *is* a unique dream."

Jane felt herself flush even now. "No. Lloyd was one of those gigantic colored balloons the parade is famous for. He was all pumped up with air and huge as the rest of the balloons, but he was smiling and waving his hands. He even yelled 'Hi, Jane' to me."

"You must dream in Technicolor," Sylvia commented. She'd forgotten about her quilting and her full attention was now on Jane.

"Actually, I do. Lloyd was wearing a black tuxedo, a white shirt, a little red vest, a top hat and spats. He reminded me of that funny figure you see in the Monopoly games."

"I'm impressed," Sylvia commented. "Your dreams are interesting, unlike mine. Last night I dreamed I was a hundred dollars short when I closed my till for the day."

"Anyway, there he was, floating above the crowd, waving, smiling and having a wonderful time when suddenly, *pop*, he exploded and disappeared. Nothing was left of him but bits of rubber, floating down from where he'd been only moments before."

"Lloyd *exploded*?" Sylvia started to laugh. "That's the craziest dream I've ever heard!"

Even Jane had to smile. "I know. That's what Alice and

I thought too, and we laughed as well . . . until we realized that Aunt Ethel was standing by the kitchen door looking very upset. I don't know what came over her, but she was angry. Surely she knew we weren't laughing at Lloyd, but at the crazy dream. Still, she acted like it was Lloyd we were chuckling at."

"Weird!" was all Sylvia could say.

"Aunt Ethel's face turned red and she sputtered in that mad-little-wet-hen way she has and then she started to weep."

Sylvia's head snapped up. "But why?"

"We haven't been able to figure it out. Both Alice and I apologized profusely, assuring her that it was just a wacky dream, but it didn't help much. She still looked like she wanted to cry, but she said it wasn't our fault. Then *she* apologized, for what, I'm not sure, and headed back home."

"How odd." Sylvia scraped her strawberry blonde hair away from her face and tucked it behind her ears.

"Aunt Ethel's been acting funny the past few days. I think I'll stop by her place on my way home and see if I can sort it out. That's part of why I'm glad to be out here, regrouping. There's such . . . tranquility . . . here."

"Is Grace Chapel Inn busier than usual?" Sylvia asked sympathetically.

"Yes, and no. All our current guests are checking out

today and tomorrow, and there's a whole new crop checking in. Apparently we're getting some positive recommendations among businesspeople. We've been getting more
and more people for a night or two when they have
business to conduct in the area. We even have a few regu-
lars like Ned Arnold." Ned, the fill-in pharmacist, came
and went regularly, a semi-permanent fixture around the
inn.

"I'll bet that makes Alice and Louise happy—more
income to offset expenses."

"Money's never been abundant for us, but the situation
is getting better. Speaking of money, Alice said we had a
banker checking in this week. Someone from the West
Coast, I think."

They worked quietly for a while, comfortable with the
silence and with each other.

Then Jane spoke again. "I like having repeat guests
because we get to have familiar faces at our breakfast
table."

"I'll bet your cooking is what makes them come back,"
Sylvia teased. "Grace Chapel Inn's rooms are fabulous, of
course, but I've had your sour-cream raisin muffins and
maple-pecan coffee cake often enough to know I'd drive a
long way for food like that."

"Thanks." Jane groaned and patted her flat stomach. "For the first time in all my years as a chef, I think I've put on weight eating my own food."

"And just where did you pack on that extra ounce?" Sylvia inquired sweetly. "On an earlobe? Or is your little toe feeling pudgy?"

Jane grinned. "Oh, I didn't keep it. I just started running longer in the morning. But if I keep eating the way I have been, I'll have to run all the way to Pittsburgh to work it off. I pulled out some low-calorie books only yesterday."

"The guests won't like that."

"I'm not going to put them on a diet—just the rest of us."

"Smart idea. Maybe I should take up hiking. I was an avid bird-watcher once, you know."

"I didn't."

"I carried bird and plant books everywhere I went and tried to figure out if I was looking at a wood duck, a Northern shoveler or a plover. I did the same for plants, but gave it up because I didn't learn to recognize poison ivy until it was too late."

"Well, then," Jane said. She dropped her brushes and watercolors into the small kit she carried and began to pack up. "Maybe we can come out here sometime and leave our paints and thread behind. I haven't gone bird-watching since I was ten years old."

"I could stay here until dark. It's such a peaceful place," Sylvia murmured.

When Jane got to the inn, the delivery truck from Craig Tracy's Wild Things florist shop was parked out front. Alice and Louise were standing on the front porch. As she watched, Craig, who was making his own deliveries today, handed them a huge and colorful bouquet of flowers. Alice smiled broadly, and Louise also looked pleased.

"What's this?" Jane dropped her things onto a rocking chair on the porch. "Does one of us have a secret admirer?" She grinned at Craig, who was watching Alice fumble to open the card.

"Wait and see," Craig said. "Maybe you all do."

"Well, isn't this nice?" Alice blurted out as soon as she got the tiny card out of its envelope.

"Let me see." Louise playfully snatched the card away and read it. Her neck and cheeks pinked even more. "My, my."

"Isn't anyone going to tell me who it's from?" Jane protested, knowing full well that she'd hear soon enough. "And who it's for?"

"All of us!" Louise waved the card. "And it's from that group of gentlemen who stayed with us last week."

"The bank examiners?" Jane took the card and read it.

> Thanks to the three most gracious host-esses we've met in a long time. We'll be back.
>
> Best wishes,
> The Bank Spies

> P.S. Jane, we'd like to put in a special request for country-style hash with eggs and raspberry cheesecake muffins.

"Isn't that nice," Alice said, pleased.

"How thoughtful," Louise agreed.

"I wouldn't mind tasting those muffins myself," Craig offered. "They sound great."

"Anytime you want," Jane said with a smile. "I've got some in the freezer right now. Coffee?"

"Can I take a rain check? Everybody seemed to think today was a good day to order flowers. I still have several deliveries to make." He waved good-bye.

After Craig had driven away, Alice, inhaling the fragrance of the bouquet, asked, "How was Fairy Pond?"

"Lovely, as always. You should come with me sometime,

Louise. You have been to Fairy Pond in the summertime, haven't you?" Jane, considerably younger than her sisters, had not always been privy in their school days to what the "big girls" thought or did. Louise and Alice had often been more mothers than sisters.

"Oh, a time or two," Louise said vaguely. She smiled faintly as if she hadn't thought about it in a very long while.

Chapter Two

After dinner, Jane looked out the window toward the carriage house where her Aunt Ethel had lived for the last ten years. "The light's on. I think I'll run over and say hi to Aunt Ethel. I feel bad that she was so upset over that silly dream of mine."

"It couldn't have been about the dream," Alice commented. "Maybe something else was troubling her."

"Then that's all the more reason to talk to her. She hasn't mentioned that anything is wrong, has she?"

"Not at all. You are making a mountain out of a molehill, Jane," Louise said briskly. "Besides, I thought you had planned to bake tonight. We have a full complement of guests for several days to come."

"I won't be gone that long. See you in a few minutes." With that, Jane headed out the door.

What is with me, anyway? Jane mused. She stopped at Ethel's often but she had rarely felt compelled to go there as she did tonight. She walked across the lawn, stepping on the stones that linked Grace Chapel Inn with the carriage house.

There were lights burning in the window. It was a cozy little scene with, among other things, a pot of geraniums on the front step and an iron lawn ornament of a bunny in the grass.

Jane smiled. She had been obliged to talk long and fast to convince Ethel that she wanted that bunny rather than an obese, bug-eyed frog with his tongue out to catch a passing fly. Ethel's tastes tended toward the unusual—and that included her startling, bottle-red hair.

She knocked on the door as she turned the knob and stuck her head inside. "Aunt Ethel, it's me, Jane."

Ethel stepped out of her bedroom decked out in pink—pink sponge rollers in her hair, pink nightie, fuzzy robe and furry slippers. "Hello, dear. Come in."

"You should probably lock your door when you're getting ready for bed," Jane commented, "so no one walks in and surprises you—like I just did."

"Here? Oh my, I never think of it. Acorn Hill has always been so safe..."

"Times change. Even here, I'm sad to say."

"I suppose you're right. There is more traffic going through all the time." Ethel's expression turned wistful. "Sometimes I wish things could just be the way they used to be."

"You mean when you were on the farm and Uncle Bob was alive?"

"Of course that! Or even just a few years ago when there was no doubt in anyone's mind that Acorn Hill was just a sleepy town. Everyone knew everyone else, and we never locked a door, and we left our cars running in the winter when we ran in to pick up a few groceries or the mail. Things were simpler then."

Jane plopped into the overstuffed armchair she'd sat in so many times when she was a little girl. Ethel had reupholstered it a few times, but it always gave Jane a sense of being embraced by the past. "Is there a problem, Aunt Ethel? You haven't seemed quite yourself recently."

Ethel fluttered a hand in the air as she put a kettle on to heat water for tea. "Don't pay any attention to me, dear. I've just been a bit tense the past few days." She put graham cracker sandwiches made with a white frosting filling on a plate and brought them to Jane. "When I was younger, I could have blamed this on hormones, but now I suppose I have to fault old age."

"What do you mean?" Jane picked up a frosting-filled treat, bit into it and sighed blissfully. These were the delicacies of her childhood. Whenever she and her sisters went to the Buckley farm as children, Ethel would serve graham crackers stuck together with powdered sugar frosting, a treat Jane had considered an exotic concoction. Now she realized that they had been probably quick, inexpensive sweets for the band of children who could have eaten the Buckleys out of house and home. Jane still loved the treats for all the memories they brought back for her, and Ethel still made them when her nieces or her grown children came to visit.

The teakettle started to whistle, and Ethel poured water over tea bags in china cups and carried one to Jane. "It's a faster world now, isn't it?" Ethel said enigmatically. "So much hurry and flurry. So much paperwork and so many meetings."

Jane did a double take. She never would have described Ethel's life that way. Her "paperwork" was limited, and most of the hurry and flurry in being a member of the Grace Chapel Church Board was of her own making.

"I didn't know you felt that way. Maybe you should pull back a little. You do work very hard at the church. Or perhaps you could enroll others to help you…"

"Oh, I'm not troubled by that," Ethel blurted, seeming surprised that Jane would even mention such a thing.

"Then what are you talking about?"

"Running Acorn Hill, of course. Permits to issue, meetings to chair, too much mail, too many complaints. I know Bella is very competent, but even she can't get all that done, you know."

Ah, Bella Paoli, the mayor's secretary. This was Jane's

first actual clue as to what they were talking about. "You mean *Lloyd Tynan* is too busy."

"Didn't I say that? Of course I mean Lloyd. Do you know that only two days ago he got a letter from the Chamber of Commerce in Potterston about joining them in a campaign to draw more tourists to this area? Why, I've rarely seen Lloyd so upset. His face got red and and he just glowered. You know how he is about keeping Acorn Hill just the way it is."

Of course. Everyone who had ever met Lloyd—and a lot that hadn't—knew that.

"Is that why you were so upset overhearing Alice and me talking?"

"That horrible dream of yours? About Lloyd popping like a big balloon? My dear, such a violent image. How could I help it?"

Jane could think of a lot of ways for Ethel to avoid getting upset, none of which she was inclined to suggest to her. Not eavesdropping might be the first of them.

"I'm sorry I ever mentioned that silly dream."

"It might sound silly now, but I'd just been to Lloyd's office, and he was very upset at the officials in Potterston. I worry sometimes, that's all. It appears they expect him to go along with their plans without protest or input. Well, Lloyd has a thing or two to say about that."

Jane nibbled on a cracker and sipped her tea. "Maybe he shouldn't take it all so seriously, and we should continue to urge him to work at a slower pace."

Ethel nodded and then frowned. "But he has always maintained that Acorn Hill has a life of its own away from the outside world, and that's the way we like it. With that position he won by a landslide, you know. And he feels he has a responsibility to stand by that platform."

Wrong tactic, Jane thought. Lloyd and Ethel were as passionate about what was best for the town as any two people could be. And, she suspected, Ethel's rampaging emotions and teary state over the dream were about her concern for Lloyd.

Jane often caught herself thinking about "Lloyd-and-Ethel" as one word, one being, these days. They were a close pair, and Ethel was concerned about her precious "special friend."

Hoping to change the subject, Jane commented, "Sylvia and I went to Fairy Pond today. She did some hand quilting and I did a watercolor portrait of her as she sat. It was very enjoyable."

Ethel chuckled a little. "When I was young, Fairy Pond was a very popular place for picnics. We considered it romantic, you know. When I think back now, I realize that the trees were young and there was not nearly the foliage there is now. Why, it was just a tad of water and some shrubbery compared to how beautiful it is now." She averted her eyes. "But we liked it."

Jane sat a little straighter in her chair. "You and Bob Buckley, you mean?"

A rosy glow began to rise in Ethel's cheeks. "Well, yes, we did go there a lot." An expression of consternation flitted across her features. "Not *alone*, of course. Always as part of a group."

Jane forced herself not to grin. Ethel had always been very concerned about propriety. It's a wonder Uncle Bob ever got her alone long enough to propose.

Now Ethel was on a reminiscing streak. "It was quite the spot. Even our teachers at school planned a picnic for us there. At one time, someone built picnic tables and benches. It's all gone now, of course." Her eyes grew unfocused as she looked toward her past.

"So it's a multigenerational landmark as well."

"Lloyd's parents got engaged there. He told me so. And your mother and father used to picnic there in the early days of their marriage."

No wonder she liked Fairy Pond, Jane thought; it was a place rich with sweet memories from the last hundred years.

"Who owns Fairy Pond and the land around it?" Jane

asked idly as she debated whether or not to eat another cracker sandwich.

"Who? Why, it's the same people who have always owned it," Ethel said as if that made everything perfectly clear.

"And they are . . . ?"

"The Jones family, of course. Adam and Etta Jones had it first." Ethel began to tick off the lineage on her fingers. "When they died, their two sons inherited it." Her pink spongy rollers bounced as she talked.

Jones. Jane tipped her head back against the soft round chair and closed her eyes. *Jones.* She couldn't recall ever having met the people Ethel had just named, but she did recall hearing about a Casper Jones when she was very small. She recalled it because it was an unusual name and she had assumed Casper was a ghost, just like the one she had seen in cartoons.

She noticed Ethel giving a big yawn, one so large that Jane could see all her molars.

"I'd better go. I can see you're tired. I just wanted to make sure I hadn't upset you." Jane pushed out of the chair.

"You're such a blessing to me, dear." Ethel shuffled over to Jane on her pink fuzzy slippers. "You and your sisters." Her eyes misted. "Sometimes I forget that you three aren't my own children. With mine spread out over the country, I miss them terribly. Why, without you, I'm not sure what I'd do." Ethel frowned. "I'd probably have to go live near one of them, but that would mean leaving Acorn Hill." She paused to consider. "I am a lot like Lloyd," she said. "I like it that Acorn Hill seldom changes. You can count on it, like a reliable old friend."

Jane bent to gather her aunt into her arms. "We do love you, you know. And we probably don't tell you so nearly enough." She felt her aunt's chuckle.

"Dear, every time you invite me for dinner and welcome me into your home, I'm reminded that you love me. Why, even the food you serve is a labor of love."

Touched, Jane gave her aunt another squeeze. "You're a little honey sometimes, you know that?"

"Yes, yes. Lloyd says the same thing…" Ethel began to blush again.

Too much information, Jane thought. She had skirted the edge of her aunt's relationship with Lloyd enough for one night. It was time to go home.

"Have you been at Aunt Ethel's all this time?" Alice asked when Jane returned.

"We had a lovely chat. I'm glad I went. It's good to be reminded that she's not being nosy or a fussbudget all the time. She really is a dear woman."

"Two new guests arrived while you were gone, business-men, both of them. Not very talkative, either."

"One fellow's name is Philip Crane, I think. Both wore fancy suits and carried lovely leather briefcases."

"My, my. We are attracting more businesspeople. These guys probably aren't quite as sociable as vacationers." Most of those who stayed at the inn were open and friendly, and it seemed as though the sisters often found themselves involved in their guests' lives in one way or another.

"No, but they'll be just as hungry."

"I suppose they will. I'd better start baking and getting things set out for tomorrow."

Alice followed her into the kitchen. "And a couple who have been sightseeing are arriving soon, so plan for them as well."

"Dishes, silverware, napkins, oatmeal, jams and jellies, homemade granola, fruit…" Jane ticked off the list of things that could be placed on the buffet tonight for early-rising guests.

"Viola Reed stopped by today with the new recipe books you ordered." Alice looked doubtful. "Are you sure we have room for any more? Every spare shelf in the study is full."

"Are you hinting that I should clean a few out?" Jane grinned. "I do have a few that I could give away. Who's a deserving cook?"

"Josie's mother Justine has certainly shown an interest. Every time she helps serve for one of the inn's teas, she copies down new recipes to try at home."

"Good choice. I'll pick out some for her tomorrow." Jane filled trays with her items. "How is Viola doing?"

"Fine. She's excited about the next reading she's planning. She's suddenly decided that Ben Franklin has been badly overlooked in the past few years. She's ordered practically everything that's ever been written by or about him and is planning to reeducate the populace about him."

"Poor Ben." Jane loved quoting Ben Franklin herself, but in the hands of the Acorn Hill bookseller, who knew what might happen to him when he wasn't here to defend himself?

"She thinks it will be good for us. Viola is quite proud of her extensive knowledge concerning the history and notables of Pennsylvania."

"'He who falls in love with himself will have no rivals,'" Jane quoted Franklin. "I suppose we should be glad that Viola cares so much about helping us improve ourselves and learn our history."

"And," Alice added slyly, "she's thinking of asking you to do a mural depicting significant places in Acorn Hill. She wants it painted in her store."

"Oh no! No way! No, no, *no*! I'm spending the next few months tending to my own business. Please tell her I want to develop some new candy recipes, sketch, make jewelry and take care of the inn. And be firm. Ever since I moved back to this quiet, sleepy little town I've run myself ragged. The idea of painting to Viola's standards sends chills up and down my spine."

"So there's nothing outside the inn that you're willing to get involved in for a while?"

"You've got that right. I came here to slow down after the pace of my life in California. Seems to me that so far, all I've done is press my foot harder on the gas pedal."

Chapter Three

I usually prefer a lighter brew of coffee . . ."

Some guests are just more difficult than others, that's all. Love them all—that's what Grace Chapel Inn is all about.

". . . so bitter, don't you think?"

They're checking out in a few days.

". . . of course, not everyone has a palate as delicate as my own . . ."

I hope.

Jane could hear the whiny, complaining voices of one of their guests even through the kitchen door. She gritted her teeth and gave thanks that she would soon be listening to Rev. Kenneth Thompson's sermon on loving one's neighbor at Sunday service. She was also grateful that all the guests had either gone to early services in the area themselves or slept in late. That in itself was a miracle. No one, so far, had made an appearance to share the breakfast table with the present diners.

". . . We've stayed at a lot of bed-and-breakfasts. Haven't we, Harold?" the bleating, disembodied voice continued, speaking to the hapless gentleman who had innocently wandered in for breakfast with his opinionated wife and was getting not only a stomach-full but also an earful.

Poor Harold didn't get a chance to reply.

"Why, we really are experts on bed-and-breakfasts. I keep a notebook to grade them in five categories—cleanliness, mattress comfort, service, attractiveness and food. I also keep a list of things we've done in the area so we'll know which ones were in the most interesting locations."

The voice lowered conspiratorially. "It's pretty boring here, isn't it? Oh, the quilt shop and the antique store are adequate, as is the bookstore—if it weren't for all those books on cats. That hardware store is something like I've never seen before. One of everything, including every useless tool and gadget. But you don't like gadgets, do you dear?"

Again, Harold was denied an opportunity to express an opinion. Jane was positive his life was completely void of thingamabobs, doohickeys and widgets. His wife must see to that. *Harold and Genevieve Thrumble . . . Harold and Gen. Gen, such a cute nickname*, Jane thought, *for such an . . . uncute— if there is such a word—woman.*

"The store that sells all the teas is interesting, but other than that . . . Fortunately, the drive to Potterston is nice. And west of town, such green farmland—the Amish still turn over the soil with horse and plow. You'd think a place like this would be desperate for more business, but they don't seem to be trying very hard. Why, they could have hundreds more people like us visiting if they'd develop some attractions."

The best reason I've ever heard for keeping things the same. Jane punched a lump of bread dough into submission. *Go, Lloyd!*

What's more, although Mrs. Thrumble hadn't seemed to notice, Lancaster County was full of places for tourists to visit—pageants, buggy rides, Amish farms, art exhibits, music, fishing, boating and golf. There were dozens of brochures available for the inn's guests, telling them where to find covered bridges, quaint restaurants, mills, farmers' markets and museums. Acorn Hill was actually an anomaly, a self-sufficient little town with commerce burgeoning all around it.

". . . Maybe we should have spent more time in Philadelphia. There's so much more history there. Do you think this place has any history . . . ?"

Jane closed her eyes and fought back a groan. Mrs. Thrumble was standing in living history and completely oblivious to it.

At that moment, Louise sailed into the kitchen. Her lips were pursed so tightly she looked as though her face were sucking in on itself. Her eyes were flashing and Jane noticed that her hands were actually trembling.

"That . . . woman!" Louise scowled. "Did you hear what she said about the inn?"

"'Only adequate,' were her words, I believe."

"Or your muffins?"

"They should have been warmer—and more streusel on top."

"And the way you decorated the downstairs bath?"

"She never was much for fish and the like." With each answer, Jane grinned a little wider.

"How can you be so calm?" Such agitation was highly unusual for the usually unflappable Howard sister.

"Not much I can do, Louie. Maybe I'm more accustomed to complainers than you are. I spent a lot of years working in restaurants, you know. We got complaints for the oddest things. One time I had a gentleman order bouillabaisse and then complain because it had seafood in it. I'm not sure what he expected, but it's a little like asking for clam chowder and then refusing to eat it because it has clams in it. And there was the time a lady ordered borscht and sent it back with a complaint that it tasted like beets and cabbage. And I can't even tell you how many times gazpacho came back to be heated."

"You are a better woman than I," Louise pronounced. "I am beginning to realize that I don't take criticism very well, especially where Grace Chapel Inn is concerned."

"That's because it's so close to your heart, Louie, but you have to remember, you can't please everyone all of the time." Jane smiled tightly. "And in certain instances, you can't please some folks *any* of the time. Maybe we should have remembered Ben Franklin's wise words before we started this venture."

"And what were they?"

"'Guests, like fish, begin to smell after three days.'"

Louise uttered a little groan. "It's a test. There's something I'm supposed to learn from this."

"I think patience is one of God's hardest lessons, don't you?"

Louise moved to Jane's side and gave her a hug. "You're such a ray of sunlight here. You're so steady and so optimistic."

Jane hugged back. "Oh, my emotions can get stirred up, that's for sure, but I usually save such a reaction for the things I feel most passionate about—social justice, the environment—that kind of stuff."

"And your passion for God."

"Well, that goes without saying. So let's each say a private prayer for the Thrumbles and hope they have a wonderful time here in spite of themselves."

"Then I am going upstairs to do my Bible study. It is on Galatians 5:22—the fruits of the Spirit."

"Ah 'But the fruit of the Spirit is love, joy, peace, patience, kindness, goodness, faithfulness, gentleness and self-control.' God's right on target as usual. And while you pray about the particular fruit of patience, I'm going to sit down with our guests and see if I can rescue our other new guest from the onslaught. I heard him enter the dining room a short while ago."

"Oh, good idea. His name is Peter Gowdy. We didn't talk very long, but he said he works for the state of Pennsylvania. He seems very nice."

As Louise escaped, Jane headed into the lion's den or, in this case, Genevieve's lair.

"How's everything?" she asked cheerfully, keeping one eye on the peevish couple.

"Great! Just great!" Peter Gowdy, a balding man in his early forties, said hurriedly. He was obviously relieved to have additional company in the room. "Excellent. Love that granola."

Jane liked him immediately. "Thanks, I make it myself."

"No kidding? If you make it to sell, I'd like to take some home with me. It's super."

Mr. Thrumble looked straight down into his cereal bowl, and Mrs. Thrumble pursed her lips. "Is that legal? To sell food out of a place like this, I mean?" she asked.

"Well, I'm sure Mr. Gowdy can check on that for us," Jane said sweetly, trying to divert this from becoming a legal discussion. "My sister Louise says you work for the state government."

"That's right."

"Are you a politician?" Mrs. Thrumble asked. "If you are, there are a few things I'd like to discuss with you—"

"No," Mr. Gowdy hurried to say. "I'm a biologist."

Mrs. Thrumble sniffed at the disappointing discovery.

"So tell me about your work, Mr. Gowdy," Jane said as she poured herself a cup of coffee.

"Come on, Harold, we need to get going." Mrs. Thrumble stood up and tugged her husband's sleeve. "I want to go antique shopping in Potterston. The prices in the store here are very high. I'm sure I can get better deals somewhere else."

To Jane's relief, Mrs. Thrumble towed her husband out of his chair and toward the stairs. Mr. Thrumble looked back pleadingly, as if he would actually *like* to know what a biologist did for the government.

After they had disappeared, Peter Gowdy pretended to mop his brow with a napkin. "Just so you know," he ventured, "the coffee is great. And the breakfast was fantastic. I don't want you to think I concurred with—"

"Thanks, but you don't have to worry. Chefs begin to grow thick skins after a while."

"It occurs to me that running an inn can be very challenging."

"And rewarding." Jane winked. "You just happened to have breakfast with the challenging. Now tell me what it is you do, exactly. If you have time, that is."

He reached for another piece of coffee cake, and Jane refilled his cup.

"I'm a plant-and-critter detective, basically. My job varies. I often work with highway engineers to design roads and bridges that will do the least damage to the ecology of an area. I consult with the Department of Conservation and Natural Resources on a number of issues. Currently I'm on the trail of slug slime."

Jane did a double take. "Excuse me, what did you say?"

"Slug slime. Glamorous, I know, but try to curb your enthusiasm." When Mr. Gowdy smiled, laugh lines crinkled in the corners of his eyes.

"Slug slime is actually the mucus trail a snail leaves behind as it moves. I'm studying how slugs and snails interact with the rest of the ecosystem, and trying to discern how the recent low humidity is affecting them."

"I can imagine hundreds of people standing in line waiting for *that* job," Jane teased.

"It's more interesting than you think." Mr. Gowdy eyed her. "How much do you actually know about slugs?"

"Just that cayenne pepper keeps them out of my garden."

Mr. Gowdy nodded sagely. "Those imported European slugs give our native varieties a bad name."

"European slugs? *We* have European slugs? Now you're pulling my leg."

"No, believe it or not, I'm not. Most people don't even know that slugs are merely snails without a shell. How could they know that native slugs don't enjoy gardens? They prefer more forest-like conditions."

"Who would have guessed?" Jane teased again.

He grinned. "My point exactly. No one has ever really thoroughly studied slugs and snails. If they begin to disappear in an area, for example, something else in the ecosystem suffers as a result."

"The departure of slugs and snails causes suffering?"

"Snails need calcium from the earth. If the soil's calcium is depleted, and snail numbers decline, then bird numbers also begin to decline."

"Not enough food for the birds?"

"They are important to the food chain, but if snails lack calcium, that means birds will lack it too, their egg shells won't be strong enough, and their reproduction will not be as successful as it would normally be."

"I'll never sprinkle cayenne pepper in the garden again. Who knew that those creatures were such charitable givers to the universe?"

"We live in a miraculous world, that's for sure. It's designed to work harmoniously. It's when we humans get in and mess around that we start to have trouble."

"That I'll agree with." Jane glanced at her watch. "I have a hunch we could sit here for hours discussing the merits and challenges of the snail, but you'd probably prefer to be out looking for them than in here talking about them."

"Fascinating as snails are, you're even more so."

Jane put her hand to her cheek and said, Scarlett O'Hara style, "Why you sweet-talkin' man, you!"

He chuckled as he pushed away from the table. "That's how women always react to me in social situations. I don't always talk about slugs and snails, though. I can carry on a rather stimulating conversation about the pearlymussel, pimpleback, pink mucket and small whorled pogonia as well. And don't even get me started on the bog turtle."

"It didn't even cross my mind." Jane liked this new guest. His dry sense of humor almost made up for the Thrumbles—or at least one of them. "Are you staying long?"

"No. Just a night or two more. Since snails travel only a few inches a minute at best, it doesn't take long to catch up with them. Especially not for a long-legged guy like me.

Besides, I have several other stops around the state before I can complete my report."

"I know already that we'll miss you when you leave. Would you like to take a couple of muffins and a thermos of coffee along on your hunt?"

Mr. Gowdy took the offer of food and went off happily on his snail safari.

Chapter Four

*A*lice and Louise had left early for church, and Jane was about to leave for services as well when a sleek, black Mercedes pulled up in front of the inn. Before she could get to the porch to greet its driver, he had stomped up the steps, flung open the door and burst inside. The screen door slapped shut behind him.

"Hello—"

"Sam Horton. My business associate Philip Crane and I stayed here last night. We had to go out early. Is there any breakfast left?"

"Sure. I'll brew a fresh pot of coffee. Have a seat in the dining room."

Sam Horton and Philip Crane were matter-of-fact and a bit stuffy.

They should have loosened their ties, Jane mused, as she refilled the plates with breakfast items. *It's a miracle they can even swallow, tight as those collars are around their necks.* Still, they managed, finishing off all that Jane had planned for the meal. She felt suddenly glad that Mrs. Thrumble had seemed obligated to complain. It meant she and her poor husband couldn't eat as much or act as if they were enjoying it, and that now there was enough for these two guests.

Sam and Philip spoke to each other in staccato undertones, as if whatever they were discussing was not for Jane's, or any other stranger's, ears. That was fine with Jane, who didn't like to eavesdrop on her guests' conversations. The only word she heard repeated often was the name Raymond. Likely it was their boss.

She was surprised to find them still at the table when she passed through to drop off a replacement for the morning's tablecloth. They had now decided to be chatty and jovial. Unfortunately, both were so somber that jovial for them seemed more like the artificial cheerfulness one pretends in a doctor's office just before some invasive medical test.

"So, Ms. Howard, have you lived around here long?" Sam's voice had an interrogative quality even when he was trying to be friendly.

"I was born and raised here. I left when I was eighteen for a number of years and have only recently come back."

"So your sisters are originally from here too?"

"Yes. Alice has been here forever except for college and travel. Louise came back around the time I did, although she visited here more often than me. Why?"

"Just wondering. Curious about the history of the place. I suppose your sister Alice could really give us some information ... er ... background."

"All three of us know the history of Acorn Hill in general, but for relatively new information my sisters could be more helpful." Jane felt uneasy but couldn't put a finger on the reason why. This man just didn't seem very sincere about learning about this place. So why was he asking?

"Is there anything in particular that I might be able to answer for you?" Jane inquired.

Sam leaned forward, his elbows on the table, and stared fixedly at her. He was swarthy and had intense, hazel eyes that were disconcertingly and unwaveringly directed at Jane. "I don't know. I'm just wondering about the people around here. I guess you'd say I'm a student of human nature."

And I'm a student of brain surgery. "Any particular human's nature or just in general?" *Who is this guy kidding?* Jane wondered. *I wouldn't want to be a bug under his microscope.*

He looked annoyed but pressed on. "You know, the

old-timers around here, the families that have been here since the early days, that sort of thing."

"I'm really not the best one to ask about that," Jane admitted. "But there are people around here who could answer your questions. Viola Reed at Nine Lives Bookstore is a student of the area. Fred and Vera Humbert know every person in town and could probably tell you a lot about the old-timers. Our mayor, Lloyd Tynan, knows a great deal too."

"The lady at the bookstore, you say? Thanks for the information." He shoved back from the table and tipped his head toward the front door. "Hear that, Phil? Tomorrow we have some reading to do."

After they had left, Jane stood in the dining room, baffled. Weird. Those two were the last people she'd have guessed were enamored of history, at least not history for its own sake. What was behind this puzzling show of curiosity?

Jane was glad that her interlude with Sam Horton and Philip Crane hadn't made her late for church. The service at Grace Chapel had given Jane a chance to relax and find peace, a peace that was not disturbed later that afternoon when Craig Tracy arrived at the door. He rang the bell and walked in as he always did. Craig delivered a lot of flowers from his shop to the inn as people were often there to celebrate marriages, anniversaries and birthdays.

"Can I cash in my rain check for a cup of coffee?"

"Sure, let's visit in the kitchen," Jane suggested. "I've got a new breakfast quiche I'd like you to try out before I offer it to my guests."

The kitchen was particularly bright and cheery with the sun streaming through the windows like floodlights. Every counter and surface gleamed. Craig studied Jane in her casual khakis and sleeveless denim shirt. Her dark hair was secured with a bright red claw clip she had decorated with leftover bits from her jewelry making. She wore red flip-flops and had bright red nail polish on her toes. She had painted a yellow smiley face on each of her big toes.

"Do those people have any idea how fortunate they are to have found this place and this food—and you?" He sat down at the table and crossed his arms over his chest. He was wearing a lightweight, slightly subdued Hawaiian shirt that was soft yellow and smattered with palm trees. Both Craig and Jane looked slightly exotic for Acorn Hill.

"People are very gracious. We get a lot of thank-you notes and return visits. Something's working."

"This is marvelous." Craig said after a bite of the quiche.

"I hate to admit it," Jane said, sitting down across from him, "but my pride has been tweaked and I'm trying to out-do myself for a hopeless cause." She took a sip of coffee. "We have a very critical guest staying here right now. I told Louise I didn't mind, but actually criticism for me is like waving a red flag in front of a bull. It's like a go-ahead to prove it wrong. I've dragged out the big guns, my favorite cookbooks and innovative recipes." She went to run her fingers through her dark hair but remembered she had it tied back as she always did when she worked in the kitchen. "Tell me to snap out of it, please."

"Snap out of it, please," Craig parroted. "Or just accept the fact you're human," he added. "No one likes criticism, Jane. Even if it's unwarranted. I can't tell you how many times customers have said some little thing about a bou-quet like 'It's beautiful, but I was wondering why you used that particular shade of pink' or 'I thought it would be big-ger for what you charge' or even 'You arrange flowers almost as well as my neighbor—of course, she's been at it for years . . .'"

Jane nearly choked on her coffee. "You don't simply arrange flowers, Craig. You create art."

"I'm glad someone appreciates that." He smiled widely at her and reached for the sugar.

He and Jane had talked more than once about his being an artist who didn't use paint and brush. Many people just didn't "get" it.

"Maybe I should send my exacting guest to your store. I'm sure she'd give you the same rave review I got—'adequate.'"

"Thanks but no thanks."

"I apologize for venting to you, Craig. I've always been one to accept people as they are and believe that they're as they are for a reason, but that old perfectionist in me made an unexpected appearance."

They sat quietly for a moment, enjoying each other's company and the sun through the window making the kitchen glow. Then Jane spoke. "Maybe it's just my week for unique personalities here at the inn, but we have another odd pair here inquiring about the old-time residents of Acorn Hill. I couldn't help them. In fact, I've begun to realize how little I really know about my own hometown. When I was a child, I wasn't all that interested, I suppose. Now that I'm back, it's time to learn."

"I've felt that way about my own childhood," Craig admitted. "Children are very self-centered. Their world revolves around them because they really aren't mature enough to see beyond the tips of their noses. Some grow out of that more slowly than others, and some never do."

"I've realized that I spent a lot of time pitying myself for not growing up with a mother. It was terribly sad, of course, but God gave me two nurturing sisters I didn't fully appreciate." She sighed. "And now I have the Thrumbles to teach me again to appreciate the other guests who pass through our doors. I'll learn to be grateful eventually."

"Don't you have any 'normal' guests right now?" Craig shifted his slender frame on the chair and reached for a muffin. His appetite certainly did not match his flat belly, as Jane had observed in the past.

"As a matter of fact, there's a lovely man here who works for the government."

"What does he do for the government?"

"Right now he's hunting for snails and slugs. I believe he is quite charmed with them."

"Ah, yes, a government worker who loves slugs and chases snails," Craig said with mock gravity. "You can't get much more normal than that." He smiled and rose to leave.

Sylvia didn't have a much higher opinion about the distinctive group of guests at the inn than Craig did. "If these men want to know about Acorn Hill, why don't they tell people *why* they want to know? Sounds suspicious to me. Do you think they're checking us out? Maybe they aren't businessmen at all—maybe they are casing the joint."

"You've been watching too many detective show reruns," Jane said. "Or did Viola let you spend too much time in the mystery section of Nine Lives? Tell me what joint in Acorn Hill is worth casing?"

"There's probably a lot of cash at the antique store some nights. They do a good business, and their things aren't cheap."

Jane smiled to herself, remembering that Gen Thrumble had said the very same thing about the store's prices.

"Petty thievery? What does that have to do with the history of Acorn Hill?"

"Well, it's got to be something."

"You aren't cut out to run a bed-and-breakfast, Sylvia. You'd want to make up stories about every single guest."

"I suppose you're right. I'd better stick to creating quilt patterns." Her eyes brightened. "Did you know that I've been thinking of compiling all my patterns and, as I add to them, creating a book?"

"What a great idea!"

"Well, it's only an idea right now, but who knows?"

Wendell, the house cat, took that moment to leap into Jane's lap and purr contentedly. He circled twice and then lay down and began to knead his paws on her leg.

"Wendell obviously likes the idea," Jane commented. "More tea?"

Alice ducked into the house in a breathless flutter.

"Why, what's the rush?" Jane asked. "I thought you were walking with Vera." She was sitting at the dining room table creating a piece of jewelry, a pin. It was a whimsical-looking snail that was surprisingly beautiful. Their guest Peter Gowdy might enjoy knowing that he was the inspiration for one of her creations. She held up the pin.

"Cute," Alice marveled. "Who'd think a thing like that could be attractive? And we finished our walk." Alice pushed her bobbed, reddish-brown hair away from her face. "I was hurrying because I saw the Thrumbles walking—or maybe it's more like stalking—down the street toward the inn. After what you told me about them, I wanted to make sure everything is in tip-top shape and to give you a heads-up."

So even Alice is suffering a pride attack, Jane mused.

"I suppose it's silly," Alice continued, "but I feel closer now than ever to this house and to our past. I want everyone to enjoy it as much as I do. When I'm afraid someone doesn't, I feel like I've failed as their hostess."

"We've set high standards for ourselves, haven't we?" Jane observed.

"'Do everything as unto the Lord.' That's the Howard motto."

Jane tucked her equipment into the box that held her tools and materials. "Then it's time to ask ourselves exactly what the Lord wants us to do with Mrs. Thrumble."

Only the Lord could handle Genevieve Thrumble.

Jane, Alice and Louise all agreed on that just before bedtime, the time they took together around the kitchen table to share their days and spend time in prayer.

"We will just have to give her over to Him," Louise concluded. "Why, even my most schoolmarmish glare did not keep her from telling Mr. Gowdy and those other two gentlemen to make sure the screens in their windows didn't have holes."

"The way she went on about that ladybug in her room,

you'd have thought that a vampire bat had come for a visit," Jane commented dryly.

"And she insinuated that our towels were not completely fresh." Alice's face flushed at the humiliating thought. "I had a mind to tell her that we use environmentally safe laundry products, and they aren't supposed to be heavily perfumed."

"She doesn't like the taste of our drinking water either," Jane said. "And she says we should put rice in the salt shakers so the salt doesn't clump up."

"Did you hear her say that she wondered how often we dusted?" Louise looked indignant. "As if we would let our home be unclean!"

Suddenly Alice bowed her head. "We need to pray. We aren't being very kind about Mrs. Thrumble."

"Kinder than anyone else, most likely, but you're right, Alice," Louise admitted. "We've always believed God steers our guests here for a reason. I've been wondering all day why this inn was their choice—unsatisfactory as it is—but no doubt God has a plan."

"Dear Lord," Alice began, "forgive us for having such thin skins and reluctantly loving hearts … and for our personal pride in what we do. All we do is for You and about You. Help us not to forget that and to continue to do what You would have us do despite criticism or pettiness..."

"And thank you for these guests," Jane picked up the prayer, "and teach us what we need to know to serve and love all those You send to our door..."

"Also, Lord," Louise added, "about those bills we owe..."

On her way upstairs to bed, Jane ran into Mr. Thrumble in the hallway.

"Hi, there. Can I help you?" Jane inquired. Mr. Thrumble didn't look any happier than usual. She wondered idly what he must look like when he was at home working and wasn't out having fun.

"Do you have ice for this carafe of water?" He thrust out the glass decanter from their room. "Gen doesn't like water without ice."

"I'll run right down and get you some." Jane headed for the kitchen. It took a moment to realize that Mr. Thrumble was following her.

She put ice into the carafe and filled it with bottled water. There. She couldn't do much better than that. When she turned around, she realized that Mr. Thrumble was staring longingly at the remainder of the breakfast muffins in a glass cake stand on the counter.

Tired as she was, she heard herself say, "Would you like one?"

"Well, ah, sure." He glanced at her out of the corner of his eye. "*I thought they were wonderful.*"

So they don't speak with one voice, Jane thought with amusement. "How about a glass of milk with it? Tea? Decaf?"

"Milk would be fine. We ate a late lunch and Gen said we'd get along until morning but..."

"No need to explain." Jane put her hands on her slender hips. "In fact, I'd be happy to make you a sandwich. And there's pasta salad and a slice of pie left from our supper."

"Now you're talking!" Suddenly Mr. Thrumble and Jane were best friends.

She put the food on the table and eyed the salad. "If you don't mind, may I join you? I'm a little hungry myself."

Before they knew it, half a dozen items from the refrigerator were spread on the table and they were concocting sandwiches that would have delighted Dagwood.

The more Mr. Thrumble ate, the more he talked—about his childhood, the fact that he had been a grocer, the car he drove, his two children, who "didn't come to visit very often," and a miniature poodle mix named Cutie Pie who'd been sentenced to the kennel while his owners were traveling. The more he talked, the more he laughed and the more relaxed he became. By the time he ate his pie, he was downright jovial.

"I'm glad we had this visit," Jane said as she put the last of the dishes into the dishwasher after their midnight banquet. "It's nice to know you better."

He smiled and then the smile faltered. "I know my wife can be ... challenging ... sometimes, but there's a lot of good in her. I just want you to know that. And, even if she'd never tell you in a million years, she loves your cooking and your inn. It's hard for her to be ..." He struggled for a word. "... to be nice."

Jane waited.

"She grew up in a very critical family. It's what she heard and saw all her life. I know in her heart of hearts she wants to be better liked by people, but she doesn't seem to know how." He hung his head and Jane could see gray wisps of hair circling over a developing bald spot. "I just love her in spite of herself."

After he'd gone, dutifully carrying the carafe of ice water—better late than never, Jane hoped—she stood in the kitchen shaking her head. Amazing, absolutely amazing. Here, in the most unlikely of places, her kitchen at midnight, and with the most unlikely of people, Genevieve Thrumble's husband, she'd heard something profound. "I just love her in spite of herself."

Just like God loves us in spite of ourselves. *If it's a challenge to love Gen Thrumble, imagine what it must be for God to love us*, Jane thought, *in all our weakness and sin*. Mrs. Thrumble had an unkind manner, but what about those who steal and kill and betray? What about herself? How did that look through the eyes of a perfect God?

So that's why the Thrumbles are here—to teach this lesson. A feeling of gratitude overwhelmed Jane and then she felt humbled. *Oh, Lord, thank You. Forgive me when I forget what love You've shown to me.*

Chapter Five

Monday had been a quiet day, Jane observed as she made meatballs for dinner. She had been hungry for spaghetti for some days, and when Louise told her that she had invited Lloyd, Ethel and Viola Reed to eat with them, Jane decided it was a good excuse to make a huge pot of sauce with fresh tomatoes and to use some of that Italian sausage in the freezer.

The Thrumbles had gone off early—Harold Thrumble carrying a snack of fresh fruit and macadamia nut cookies—to scope out a series of historic sites Mrs. Thrumble had chosen. He had not looked happy about it until Jane slipped him the emergency food rations, and then his face was wreathed in smiles. Sam Horton and Philip Crane, the businessmen with noses for history, hadn't been around all day, nor had Peter Gowdy, who was off on his slimy search for snails.

"Smells good in here," Louise said as she came in carrying a stack of music in one arm.

"Practicing at the church?"

"I'm playing for a wedding this coming weekend. Pastor Thompson just asked me."

"That's sudden."

"They'd planned to be married in Potterston in a very small wedding, but the pastor was taken in for emergency surgery. When Pastor Thompson agreed to do the ceremony, they decided to move the entire event here. They were disappointed to hear that the inn was almost full. They would have requested the entire place had it been available."

"A nice problem for us to have—too many demands rather than too few."

Louise sat down and gave a big sigh. "Yes, it is. Every guest helps." She paused. "Even the crotchety ones, I suppose."

Jane suppressed a smile. There had been days when she would have called Louise crotchety too. They had sometimes bumped heads after Jane's return, but now she viewed Louise as one of her dearest friends.

"Are you referring to anyone in particular?" Jane asked, and she told Louise about her experience with Harold Thrumble the night before.

"A good lesson for all of us. Don't judge, refuse to take things at face value and love people in spite of themselves." Louise took the cup of tea that Jane handed to her.

"Speaking of which," Jane said with a smile, "what time are our guests coming for dinner?"

"Ethel said it could be as late as seven tonight."

"Really? Won't Lloyd be afraid of starving to death?"

Louise chuckled. "You'd think so, but it was his idea. Apparently he has his hands full with paperwork, despite our pleas for him to slow down, but Bella agreed to stay late tonight to help him wrap up some last things. He told Ethel to come over early and said he'd join us as soon as he can."

"He's no youngster. He should listen to those who advise him to take care of himself."

"Lloyd's idea of taking care of himself is taking care of Acorn Hill," Louise reminded Jane. "If Acorn Hill isn't okay, neither is Lloyd. We all know that."

"Then I'm especially glad he's going to spend time with us, because we can coddle him. Now put your music away and wash up. I have tomatoes and mozzarella that I want you to cut up for a salad."

The doorbell rang promptly at five and Ethel hurried in, face flushed, bosom heaving.

"What happened to you?" Alice inquired. "Are you all right?"

"Of course. I just didn't realize what a vigorous walk it would be to town and back when I was in a rush. I went to the store to get you these." She held out her hand. In it was an assortment of candy, including Blackjack gum and Chic-O-Sticks, sweets sold forty years ago and just now coming back as novelty items for the new generation.

"It certainly makes me feel old when the candy I ate as a child is now considered retro," Jane said. "I hope I'm keeping up with the times." She reached for a glass bowl for the candy.

"You're ahead of them, dear," Ethel assured her. "Why, look at all those confusing modern art pieces you paint. I'm sure that someday someone will even like them."

"Shades of Gen Thrumble," Alice murmured to Jane. "Gotta love 'em."

"Thank you, Aunt Ethel. Since we're not eating until seven, I have some crudité and other finger food for appetizers. Would you like—"

The doorbell rang.

"Viola!" they chimed in unison.

"Come in," called Ethel.

Viola entered the house in a wave of color, her scarf displaying bands of scarlet and orange.

"How wonderful to be asked to dinner," Viola pronounced. "Positively delightful! I can't wait to see what you've cooked, Jane!"

"Simple but filling, that's it. Appetizer?"

Ethel and Viola filled their plates with finger food and retreated to the study to talk about the day's pressing issues, primarily Viola's cats and Ethel's opinions. Ethel was obviously delighted to have someone's company for dinner, and soon the conversation deteriorated into a list of "helpful" suggestions for ways that the inn could attract more guests. That led to a discussion of thread count in percale sheets, and they were off and running on the state of the entire home décor industry.

"Contemporary art! Child's finger paintings if you ask me." Viola's distinctive voice was easily heard, and Jane and Alice smiled at each other in the kitchen. "And those ridiculous modern chairs! They are so low to the floor that if a person managed to fall into them, they'd never get out again. And they are uncomfortable besides. Why, I went to a store in Harrisburg once that sold that kind of thing, and when I sat down, it took two sales clerks and my cousin to pull me back out. They are traps, I tell you, traps!"

Giggling erupted in the kitchen.

"*Shhhh*," they heard Ethel say. "Don't let Jane hear you. She likes that modern stuff, you know."

"At least she doesn't try to push it on people. Picasso—bah! Now Mary Cassatt, *there* was a painter!"

"Those two are a hoot," Jane chuckled. "I love it. And they entertain each other beautifully."

Alice snapped her fingers. "Entertain... That reminds me. We've got to put another plate on the table. I saw Sylvia in town and invited her as well. You don't mind, do you?"

"Absolutely not. I'm just sorry I didn't think of it myself. I've been more focused on when we'll squeeze out time to spend at Fairy Pond together."

At that moment the doorbell rang again. Another guest had arrived.

"Have everyone sit at the table," Jane instructed Alice and Louise, who had just entered the kitchen. "I've set the tomato and fresh mozzarella salads out. By the time we say grace and everyone eats that, the pasta will be ready to serve."

"What about Lloyd?" asked Alice.

Ethel waved a hand in the air. "We shouldn't wait for him. He'll be late."

As she watched her friends eat, Jane felt a warming inside her chest. These sweet, funny people were dear to her heart. Idiosyncrasies and all, they were part of the treasure of a place like Acorn Hill.

Conversation became animated around the table. Sylvia had found a new fabric company that had great promise, Alice's youth group at church was making plans for a sleepover, and Louise had received another grateful call of thanks from the bride in whose wedding she would play on such short notice.

"Thirds, anyone?" Jane inquired when everyone seemed to grow quiet. "There's plenty more in the kitchen."

Viola finished a last strand of spaghetti and smacked her lips. "No thanks, dear, I'd better save room for dessert."

Just then the front door opened and Lloyd strode into the dining room. His face was flushed and his bow tie askew, his sleeves rolled up. That surprised Jane. Lloyd was usually meticulous about his dress and grooming. *He must be very busy*.

"Anything left for me?" he asked, half joking, half concerned.

"All you can eat," Jane assured him.

He made his way to the table and sat down, bowing his head in a private grace before he took his first bite. When his plate was empty, he loosened his tie and sighed. "*Ahhh*. First thing I've eaten since breakfast. Thank you, Jane. I needed that."

Lloyd hardly looked starved, but it did surprise Jane that he hadn't taken time to eat for most of a day.

"I told you to stop for lunch," Ethel chastised. "I worry

about you. You just aren't taking good care of yourself these days."

Aha, Jane thought. *That confirms my hunch about Aunt Ethel's preoccupation of late. She's been worrying about Lloyd. At least that question is answered.*

"No time, honey bunch. Business to attend to, meetings to chair and people to see. It's a mayor's job."

Surely a little spot like Acorn Hill doesn't have all that much business, Jane reflected, *but Lloyd is in his seventies. It probably feels like a lot to him.*

"Jane," Louise asked, "have you spent any time visiting with the two gentlemen who registered? I have only seen them once in passing."

"Not much. They aren't the greatest conversationalists I've ever met. That seems odd, too, since they're such history buffs."

"History?" Lloyd's ears perked. "What kind of history?"

"Mostly of this region, I think. I wish our father were here. He could have regaled them with stories."

"Those must be the two men who came into the bookstore," Viola said. "First they asked for books on the history of the region, and then we started talking about the people in the area. They seemed very interested in who had once owned the land around here. They were particularly curious about some land just outside of town, especially the area around Fairy Pond."

"Fairy Pond, did you say?" Ethel asked.

"Yes."

That aroused Jane's curiosity and Ethel's sentimental side. "I love Fairy Pond."

"You do?" Sylvia sounded surprised. "I didn't know that you went out there, Ethel."

"Oh, not now, dear. I used to though." Ethel's expression grew dreamy and her color heightened.

"What are you thinking, Aunt Ethel?" Alice inquired. "You have a very odd look on your face."

"Oh, nothing…"

Viola made a chastising clucking sound. "It was fifty years ago, Ethel. Your nieces are grown women. They can hear that sort of thing now."

Louise and Jane exchanged smiles. "What sort of thing?" Louise asked.

Ethel actually tittered.

Viola took charge. "Your aunt is being demure, which might have been fine when you girls were young, but now—"

"Now that we're old," Jane completed the sentence, smiling.

"What Ethel is too bashful to say is that when she and

Bob Buckley were courting, they used to spend a lot of time at Fairy Pond. It was quite a hot spot for young people in love at that time."

Aunt Ethel and Uncle Bob at Fairy Pond. Young people in love. Jane remembered Ethel's comments about Fairy Pond from their earlier conversation, and when she looked at her aunt and saw her eyelashes fluttering demurely and her skin warming with pleasure at the memories, she could see that at one time Ethel Buckley must have been a very attractive young woman.

"Unchaperoned?" Alice asked mischievously.

Ethel shook her finger at Alice. "We never went alone of course. Fairy Pond was what young people today call a hang-up. No, no, not a hang-up, a hangout. Old Mr. Jones always made sure there were picnic tables in good repair and that it looked nice on his property. He's the one that planted so many of the trees in the area."

"Jones? Someone named Jones owned Fairy Pond? Why haven't I heard about this family before?" Sylvia asked.

"Oh, the Joneses were always an odd family. They kept very much to themselves. Each generation seemed to grow more and more private about their affairs. As far as anyone can tell, the remaining Joneses are practically hermits," Viola said.

Jane was itching with curiosity about this family that

she had learned about only days before. "Tell me more," she encouraged. That was all it took for Viola to get started. Lloyd and Ethel soon followed.

"Adam and Etta Jones were a lovely couple, really. He owned a lot of land around Fairy Pond. They liked their privacy, though, so they were perfectly happy to live right in the middle of all those woods and keep the rest of the world away."

"And they never came out?" Sylvia asked.

"Of course they did." Viola looked over at Sylvia as if she weren't paying attention. "But only on their terms."

"They always went to church. That's how they knew Daniel and Madeleine," Ethel said. "In fact, Adam Jones and my brother Daniel were friends of a sort. If Adam shared confidences with anyone, it was with my brother."

"Fascinating," Jane murmured. "I had no idea."

"Both Adam and his wife loved nature. They must have had a dozen birdfeeders surrounding their house. They'd sit in the window and count the types at the various feeders. In his later years, Adam joined the Audubon Society."

Jane turned to Louise and Alice. "Did either of you know about these people?"

The sisters looked at each other and then at Jane. "We did," said Alice, "but you were so much younger, and both

Mr. and Mrs. Jones had passed away by the time you might have met and remembered them."

"Did they have any children?" Sylvia asked.

"Two," Viola supplied happily. Dispensing information was right up her alley. "Boys. Casper and Orlando. Both odd, just like their parents."

Jane, sitting back to listen to and observe the people at the table, noticed Alice looking at Louise with a strange, questioning look. So close to imperceptibly that Jane almost missed it, Louise shook her head.

"Now what did you say we were having for dessert?" Lloyd asked suddenly, apparently bored with the speculation about the unusual Jones family.

"I didn't say. How about a little spumoni? I always love it after an Italian meal."

Lloyd looked disappointed, obviously having planned on something more substantial than ice cream.

"Lloyd," Alice said, a loving firmness in her voice, "are you sure you want to eat anything more? Your face was getting quite pink as you were eating. Are you all right?"

Lloyd harrumphed and Ethel blushed.

"So you noticed, eh? I probably downed quite a bit of food, but I need to eat those carbs tonight."

"Carbs?'" Alice echoed blankly.

"Sure. Isn't that what athletes eat before they compete? I'm sure I read that somewhere."

"My goodness, Lloyd!" Viola said as she threw her slipping scarf back over her shoulder. "What on earth could you be competing in? A geriatric triathlon?"

Ethel giggled.

Lloyd looked at her. "I suppose we have to fess up, huh, honey bunch?"

Fess up? What on earth for? Jane wondered. *And Lloyd has called Aunt Ethel "honey bunch" twice tonight.*

"Ethel and I signed up for a little class, didn't we, Ethel?"

A flush of red colored Ethel's neck. "I suppose we have to tell them sometime."

Louise sat straight in her chair, wearing her best, most proper look. "What have you two done now?"

"Justine Gilmore is trying to make a little extra money," Lloyd explained.

"And there isn't a really good paying job for her right now—other than odd jobs like filling in for Sylvia or helping Jane serve here at the inn for special teas—so she's started her own business," Ethel added.

"Why haven't we heard about this?" Louise demanded.

"She probably thought you were too young to be interested."

Louise looked shocked and then amused. "That's not been an excuse for ignoring me for a very long time, Lloyd. What is Justine up to?"

"She's going to lead an exercise group for people seventy and over. A number of senior citizens have expressed an interest," Lloyd explained.

"Ohhh ..." Louise sounded doubtful.

"Justine came to speak to us last week. She said that she enjoyed exercising and was familiar with a lot of exercise tapes and the like. She wondered if any of us would be interested in starting a little class. Said she likes older people and knows how hard it is for us to get started exercising alone. She's also studied the special needs of people our age. Well, to make a long story short, several us agreed to join her. I contacted Rev. Drew Rogers at the Methodist church, and he said we could use the church basement for our classes. He was quite excited about the prospect. I hadn't known until now that he's quite the health enthusiast. He played football in high school and college. He even has a weight set in the parsonage."

"Another 'no pain, no gain' enthusiast," Viola said without enthusiasm.

Lloyd ignored her comment and smiled with satisfaction. "Another little enterprise going on right here in

Acorn Hill without having to involve any outsiders. And," he added ominously, "there are a few people in the senior group who could use a little exercise."

Lloyd and Aunt Ethel in an exercise class? It was almost beyond imagining. The image of Ethel in a leotard and Lloyd in gym shorts glimmered in Jane's mind. By the stunned expressions around the table, others were probably thinking the same thing.

"I am . . . speechless," Louise finally proclaimed. "I had no idea that was what Justine was up to."

"Smart cookie, that girl. And good with old folks too." Lloyd turned to Viola with a sly smile. "Are you joining our class?"

Viola shook her finger at Lloyd. "You know very well, Lloyd Tynan, that I'm not nearly old enough to qualify. Besides, rolling around on the floor, trying to put my elbow in my ear and my foot behind my head? No, thank you. It doesn't sound quite right for me." She turned to Ethel. "Have you thought this through? Really?"

Ethel looked flustered but unyielding. "We could all stand to lose a few pounds. I'm all for it."

Ethel's pronouncement seemed to put a cap on the evening's conversation. Full of good food and good intentions, one by one, the guests expressed their thanks for the sisters' hospitality, bid one another good-bye and began their journeys home.

After the other guests had gone, Jane and Sylvia stood on the front porch talking.

"Can you believe it? Lloyd and your Aunt Ethel, I mean?" Sylvia still looked as though she had been zapped by a stun gun.

"Not if I hadn't heard it for myself." Jane leaned against the rail and breathed in the night air. "But it's kind of cute. I wish I could be there to watch."

"Not me. I'd rather go to Fairy Pond and quilt. Even thinking about Lloyd and Ethel trying to get in shape makes me sweat."

"How does tomorrow afternoon look to you? I'd like to do a little painting. Want to join me?"

"If Justine can watch the shop for me, I'll be there. She's been so helpful, willing as she is to come in on a moment's notice to cover for me. In the weeks since she's agreed to do so, she's been an absolute delight to have around. I wish I could hire her full time, but the fabric and quilting business isn't *that* good."

Before either woman could say more, a man taking long, loping strides came up the walk. "Hi, ladies. Enjoying the beautiful weather?" Peter Gowdy was wearing jeans and a sweatshirt and carried a backpack, which, no doubt, contained his day's work of slug hunting.

"Yes, indeed." Jane made introductions and then asked, "How was your day?"

Mr. Gowdy's big smile flashed in the porch light. "Great. I got everything I need and then some. I was planning to stay another day, but I think I'll be leaving tomorrow instead. Hope that's not a problem for you." He looked intently at Jane.

"Only that we'll miss you at our breakfast table. Maybe you'll have to come back and do more research one day. Just think of us."

"Without a doubt." He glanced over his shoulder. "Did the Thrumbles have a good day? Did they get cheered up?"

Sylvia smiled at the question.

"I didn't hear them come in. We had company for dinner." Jane frowned. "I hope we didn't make too much noise."

Mr. Gowdy chuckled. "No need to worry about it. If you did, you're sure to hear about it in the morning. Good night, ladies."

Chapter Six

Alice was already up when Jane entered the kitchen the next morning. The coffee was brewing and the oven was preheating for the coffee cake that was on the Tuesday morning menu.

"And how are you this fine morning?" Jane asked with a smile. She poured a cup from the first pot of coffee for the day, strong enough to get herself awake and going.

"I thought I'd have another cup of tea before I left for Potterston." Alice yawned. "Unfortunately, I didn't sleep very well. I kept thinking about Lloyd. I've been wondering if I did the right thing mentioning his weight last night. He didn't seem to mind, but maybe I went too far."

"Alice, you are a nurse. You know what obesity can do to a person—heart attack, diabetes, stroke, the list goes on. Lloyd must be aware of it himself if he joined Justine's exercise class."

"And that! He can't just start exercising like he was twenty years old again. He needs a physical, good warm-up exercises—"

"You can check with Justine, but I'm sure she's thought of those things already."

"I hope so," Alice said gloomily. "Imagine, Lloyd and Aunt Ethel prancing around, kicking, high-stepping, waving their arms."

Jane grinned. "Oh, what I'd give to be there with a video camera."

"By the way," Alice said, "I had a nice visit with those two gentlemen staying here, Mr. Horton and Mr. Crane."

"Really? I haven't found them all that friendly."

"I was looking at some old photo albums in the study and they came in. Pretty soon I had one on each side of me enjoying the photos right along with me."

Hmmm, Jane thought. *That doesn't sound like the dour pair I've dealt with.*

"I suppose I got carried away, telling them stories about our father and Grace Chapel. They asked a lot of questions, though, so they must have been interested."

"What kind of questions?"

"They were curious about the businesses here, how people like the area, how much traffic from Potterston comes through here. Those kinds of things."

"Did you think for even a moment that those were odd questions for them to ask?"

Alice looked startled. "No, not really. Are they odd?"

Maybe in Alice's book they weren't, but they were plenty odd to Jane.

"Anyway, I basically told them this was a wonderful place to live."

"No harm in that," Jane commented noncommittally.

"I should say not."

As Alice went to her room, Mr. Gowdy came down the stairs. He put his luggage by the front door and joined Jane in the dining room. "Smells great," he said. "Cinnamon streusel?"

Jane nodded, poured him coffee and then handed him a plate of the still-warm cake.

"Nice little place you run here." Mr. Gowdy took a bite of the coffee cake and closed his eyes. "And the best food I've ever tasted."

"So you'll remember us next time you come to Acorn Hill?"

"I certainly will, although I don't know when that might be. I've wrapped up what I'd planned to do here and don't expect the snail population to move any time soon."

"And if they did move, you could probably catch up with them."

"Got that right."

After breakfast, Jane saw him out. "I hope our paths cross again, Mr. Gowdy."

"I'm going to give you some glowing recommendations. You may find some of my friends coming here someday. Thank you."

He smiled at her and Jane noted what kind, sympathetic eyes he had. Too bad he was leaving. She would have enjoyed sketching him and trying to capture that quality of compassion and caring on paper. But he, like all the guests, was on a schedule far apart from her own.

She watched him drive away with a twinge of sadness. So many hellos and good-byes here at Grace Chapel Inn. It was hard getting glimpses into the lives of the fascinating people who stayed here but rarely getting to know the people themselves.

Her melancholy didn't last long, however. Within minutes her work in the kitchen had captured her full attention. She was frying bacon when she heard ranting in the dining room.

Gen Thrumble had arisen in an especially foul mood. "Poor Harold," as Jane had begun mentally referring to him, wore an expressionless mask. Wisely, his lips were clamped as tightly shut as an oyster protecting a pearl.

"Pillows like rocks … lavender bath soap … I've never liked

lavender...makes me smell like my grandmother...or was that rose water she used ... didn't like it ..." Mrs. Thrumble muttered as she made her way to the breakfast table. "Better be protein today ... need protein." Then she lifted her head and eyed Jane, who stood in the dining room doorway. "Well, what are you waiting for? We're here."

Resisting an urge to salute, Jane headed for the kitchen, where Alice had returned and was waiting.

"Thrumbles on the warpath?" Alice inquired.

"Singular. Only one Thrumble at war. Mr. Thrumble, once properly fed and listened to, is a nice man," Jane said as she thrust a plate of sausage and bacon into Alice's hands. "Serve this please, and I'll bring the rest."

When Jane entered the dining room, Mrs. Thrumble had her nose in the air. Harold looked miserable and Alice looked helpless. "Mrs. Thrumble wants apricot juice for breakfast," Alice said.

"Orange is too acidic for my delicate stomach."

"I told her we didn't have any—"

"No apricot juice in the refrigerator," Jane said smoothly. "But I do have some in the pantry. Is there anything else you need?"

Jane wasn't sure, but she thought she saw a flicker of disappointment in Mrs. Thrumble's eyes.

Back in the kitchen, Alice looked unusually ruffled. "Pray for me, Jane. I'm thinking very uncharitable thoughts."

"I think I'll pray for Mrs. Thrumble instead. What must it be like to be so unhappy all the time?"

"I hate to say it, but I think she *enjoys* it. Some people just love to cause trouble." Alice sank into a chair. "I'm sorry. I have no right to be critical. I'm just tired."

"Is it still busy at the hospital?"

"Yes. Lots of patients checked out but just as many checked in. I don't think I sat down at all on my last shift except to eat half a sandwich." The corner of Alice's lip twitched. "I think I'll prescribe a nap for myself after work today."

"Good idea. What's Louise up to?"

"She told me she was practicing for that wedding and giving piano lessons. That woman could live at a keyboard, I think." Alice looked at Jane. "Louise is so talented."

"And you?" Jane raised one eyebrow. "Don't you call healing, counseling and loving talents?"

Alice flushed. "That's easy to forget when I'm listening to Louise play or watching you paint. By the way, did I hear you mention something about sketching at Fairy Pond again?"

"Sylvia called. She can't go today like we planned, so

we're going tomorrow. Want to come? I thought I'd pack a picnic lunch."

"It sounds lovely, but since I'm not scheduled at the hospital, I'll stay here and mind the fort so you can get away and relax."

"Thank you." Jane said, eyes on the door to the dining room. "I'll check on the Thrumbles."

The Thrumbles, however, had already left the dining room. Gen Thrumble's linen napkin was also missing, as were several pieces of coffee cake. Despite being dissatisfied with everything at the inn, she seemed to be tolerating the food rather nicely.

Jane heard voices coming from the porch and was surprised to find the Thrumbles there, visiting with the two gentlemen who had been so interested in Acorn Hill's history. Mrs. Thrumble was giving her own version of the current state of the town. Jane stood in the doorway and listened.

"Not much shopping here. A dress shop, a quilt shop, antiques, flowers, tea—a dull kind of place. No variety, really. No choices. The gentleman at the hardware store told me that you could get one of everything here in town, which may be true, but I like choices. One of something is hardly enough."

"What would you like to see?" Sam asked. "What would make this town a better place?"

"Frankly, I think a little shopping center would do it, some of those chain stores that are everywhere. I like things that are familiar. All these quaint little shops are so . . . unpredictable."

"A shopping center? Is that it?"

"I'm sure that sounds far-fetched to you, seeing how small and sleepy this place is. Why, even Harold noticed. Even the gas station closes at night here. Have you ever heard of such a thing? What if people need to leave town after dark?"

"Fortunately there are places down the road toward Potterston," Harold said. "Otherwise Genevieve and I would have run out of gas the other night."

"Interesting," Mr. Horton said. Mr. Crane bobbed his head enthusiastically, and Jane wondered what on earth could be interesting about that.

"So what are you fellows doing here?" Mr. Thrumble asked jovially, obviously glad to have company other than his wife's.

"Checking it out. I know someone who had relatives here once. I'm doing some business in the area."

Really. Jane took that in. *Why didn't he mention that when he talked to me or to Alice?*

❧

The mysterious Sam Horton and Philip Crane were the farthest things from Jane's mind when she and Sylvia reached Fairy Pond the next day at lunchtime. Jane carried a tote that held not only her drawing and watercolor supplies but also tuna salad sandwiches, cut-up fruit and chocolate chip walnut cookies.

Sylvia spread a thin blanket on the floor of the glade so they could set out lunch.

"You remembered everything," she commented as she discovered plates, napkins, forks and two cans of iced tea.

"I have done my share of toting food around for meals," Jane said with a laugh. "I might forget my shoes, but I'll never leave behind the dessert."

"You're wonderful to have as a friend for a lot of reasons, but it certainly doesn't hurt that you're the best cook in Pennsylvania."

"All of Pennsylvania? I don't think so. But thanks anyway."

As they ate, they listened to the birds in the trees and commented on the squirrels that were entertaining them by racing up and down the trunks.

"Why don't we do this more often?" Sylvia asked after they had eaten. She lay on her back looking up into the shifting, smoothly cruising clouds overhead. Occasional sunlight dappled her face. "Every time I come here with you, I am reminded how much I love it. Then, when I'm at the shop working, I keep telling myself I don't have time for this."

"You know how often I come here," Jane said. "You can join me any time you want." She tossed bits of bread to a bold sparrow at the edge of the clearing.

Sylvia scooted into a sitting position and picked up her sewing. "Did Lloyd and Ethel start their exercise class last night? I heard at the Coffee Shop that Justine was very excited. I hadn't realized that she'd been going to Potterston for training."

"They did. In fact, I took Ethel to class so that she didn't have to be seen in her exercise gear."

"Ethel has *gear*?" Sylvia might as well have been asking if Ethel had started playing the drums, so amazed was her tone.

"She and Lloyd are taking this exercise business very seriously. They drove to Potterston yesterday for physicals and to shop for the appropriate clothing. She told me about everything last night."

"And what might that clothing look like for someone who is seventy-something and pleasantly roly-poly?"

Jane thought back to the night before, when Ethel had scooted across the grass and into the car as if she were a fox at a hunt. She had worn a large, ankle-length raincoat that must once have belonged to her late husband Bob. It was pulled up at the collar, buttoned top to bottom and belted at the waist. Ethel hung onto the collar with both hands as if to shield her face, but her hat, a floppy straw thing she usually wore in the garden, did that for her. Only pristine white tennis shoes, so bright that they almost hurt one's eyes, gave away the fact that Ethel was going to exercise rather than to initiate some covert activity for the CIA.

"Aren't you going to be warm in that thing?" Jane had asked.

"It's just until I get to the class. I appreciate this ride, Jane. Otherwise I wouldn't have been able to dress at home in my exercise clothing. There's no good place to change at the church, and I certainly couldn't be seen walking down the street in my leotard."

No, she certainly couldn't. At least Jane had not been able to imagine it last night. Ethel had admitted to purchasing a pair of tights to wear under some shorts and a T-shirt to match because she didn't want to be "immodest."

Jane was eager to get to the Methodist church. The exercise adventure was getting more surreal by the moment. Ethel in a leotard. And Lloyd?

Ethel answered before she could ask. "Lloyd purchased some sweatpants, and he insisted we get matching sweat-shirts." Ethel's brow had furrowed. "I hope, despite the name of all this clothing, I don't have to sweat too much. When I was young, girls weren't all that fond of sweating. Times certainly change, don't they?"

They certainly do.

That was even more apparent in the side room, where oldies music was playing loudly and Justine, slender as a willow, had been helping another senior, in a vivid purple velour outfit, to warm up.

Josie was there as well and danced up to Jane. "You came! Are you going to exercise too?"

"No, honey. I just brought my Aunt Ethel here in my car."

"If she wants to exercise, then why doesn't she just walk here?"

Out of the mouths of babes. "Good question, sweetie. I think she was afraid she might be late to exercise with your mommy, that's why."

"Oh." That had seemed to satisfy Josie, who immediately danced off to greet someone else.

Jane was surprised to see how many people Justine had attracted to her class. Jane wasn't even sure she knew the names of some of them. Impressive. Now she said as much to Sylvia.

"I agree. I think it's wonderful what Justine is doing," said Sylvia.

"I know what you mean. Odd as it seemed at first, the longer I was there, the more excited I became. Those people are so young at heart and interested in life. I loved it." Jane giggled. "You should have seen Ethel and Lloyd in their sweatshirts. Both were bright orange and had 'Athlete-in-Training' emblazoned across the front. It reminded me of a costume party and gym class all rolled into one. There's a lesson in this, Sylvia."

"What's that?"

"God gave us lives to live and we should live them with passion and enthusiasm. I loved that everyone there wasn't willing to sit down and call themselves old. As a matter of fact, Ethel said, 'Why Jane, I do believe I'm a teenager with wrinkles.'"

"Do you think about growing old?" Sylvia asked, her voice more serious.

"Me? No. I'm having too much fun to think about that —or to let it happen either. In many ways I feel more whole and youthful now than I did when I lived here at eighteen."

"Do you think sometimes about how differently things might have turned out?"

Jane shot her friend a sharp glance. "Differently? What are you getting at, Sylvia?"

Sylvia let her shoulders slump and she tipped her head to one side. "Sometimes it makes me sad that I never married."

"So, Sylvia, if you were to get married now, what attributes would you look for in a husband?"

It occurred to Jane that she missed girl talk like this.

"As opposed to when I was eighteen or twenty, you mean?" Sylvia picked up one of the cookies that Jane had tucked into their lunch. "They'd probably be like two different species. When I was young, what mattered to me was looks. Is he handsome? Popular? Athletic? Does he drive a nice car? Those were the questions I usually asked myself back then."

"I notice you didn't mention that he had to be smart," Jane observed with amusement.

"Who cared about smart? Not me! I grew up poor. I dreamed about having an attractive, well-to-do, football quarterback sweep me off my feet and show everyone that I was special enough to be loved by a guy like that." Sylvia's expression was sad when her gaze met Jane's. "Pathetic, huh? All I wanted to do was make the other girls, the ones who didn't treat me well, jealous."

"You aren't the only girl in the world who felt that way."

"I'm sure not, but I feel embarrassed for the person I was then. I hadn't gotten to know Christ personally." She smiled. "But since I have, a lot of things have changed, including my priorities."

"So tell me what qualities you'd look for in a partner now."

"Let's see…" Sylvia made herself comfortable and gazed off into space as if contemplating a complex philosophical question.

"Solid faith, trustworthiness, compassion, kindness, gentleness, faithfulness…"

Sylvia laughed. "See what I mean? What was important to me as a girl is so insignificant now." She sighed. "I suppose that is one good thing about seeing forty in the rearview mirror, isn't it?"

They were laughing when they heard the sound of something crashing through the underbrush.

Chapter Seven

Sylvia gave Jane a startled glance. They had been at Fairy Pond nearly an hour and it had been exquisitely quiet until now.

"Just a deer, probably."

"Are there bears out here?"

"I don't think . . ." Jane's voice trailed away as she saw Sam Horton and his cohort Philip Crane clomp through the underbrush and stumble into the clearing. They were still in business suits and looked ludicrously out of place. Sam Horton had burrs clinging to his pant legs below the knees, and Philip Crane's hair was decorated with stray leaves and part of a spider web.

"Ray's right—he should have his head examined. Only a real nutcase would want to live in a primitive spot like this, that's for sure . . ." Mr. Horton glanced up and saw Jane and Sylvia staring at him.

"Wha . . . oh . . . ah . . . hello, ladies." He brushed the front of his suitcoat as if that would help his rumpled condition.

Mr. Crane hurriedly straightened his tie, oblivious to the bird's nest starting in his hair.

"What are you doing out here?" Jane asked, after introducing Sylvia to the pair. Strange as it seemed, she felt that the men had intruded upon them here. She usually loved bringing people here to show off the beautiful spot, but these two, in their suits and wingtips, didn't fit. They were interlopers in one of her precious little secrets.

Feeling remorseful for those uncharitable thoughts, she mustered a smile. "I certainly didn't expect to see you here. Aren't you a little far from the business world?"

Sylvia stared at them as if they had materialized out of thin air.

Mr. Horton's face flushed a dark, unhealthy red. Mr. Crane spoke up. "Actually, this is business...in a way..." He turned to look at his partner. "Right?"

The look Mr. Horton shot him was daggered.

"Well, sort of... I mean, maybe not..."

"Just looking around," Mr. Horton concluded briskly. "And, although this has been a nice, uh, break, we have to move on. Good to see you." And, acting as though there were nothing odd about their appearing from the underbrush, and as if they weren't bizarrely out of place, they nodded and walked off, Sam Horton leading, Philip Crane hurrying to catch up.

"What on earth was that about?" Sylvia gasped. "Those two just appeared out of the trees like they went walking in a forest every day. Is there even a path back there?"

Sylvia pushed the branches aside and peered into the thickening trees and bushes.

"Well, is there?"

"There's a lot of undergrowth. I can't even imagine how those two got through."

"Where there's a will, there's a way, I guess." Jane picked up a pencil but didn't feel much like sketching any more. The unexpected visit had been unnerving.

"Maybe we should just go home now and come another day," Sylvia suggested. "After those two have checked out of Grace Chapel Inn and left Acorn Hill."

Jane laughed. "I'm sure they're fine. Although they are certainly engrossed with Acorn Hill. They've been asking questions ever since they arrived. I suppose I shouldn't be surprised that they'd go hiking around here."

"Seems like they would have dressed for it." Sylvia stared at her friend. "Jane, are you thinking what I'm thinking?"

"That this is highly unusual behavior? Yes, and something odd is motivating it."

Sylvia nodded. "But what?"

"It's all very strange." Jane began to pack her art supplies. "And, although we're consumed with curiosity, it's probably none of our business. After all, Fairy Pond doesn't belong to us."

"You're right. I do feel protective, though. Fairy Pond is so ... delicate."

"Just like fairies?" Jane asked, amused. "Beautiful and fragile and hard to find?"

"Something like that."

Later, as they walked away from Fairy Pond, Jane felt a churning feeling in her stomach. Nerves? No. Indigestion? Not likely. Instinct? Maybe that was it, she thought. Her instinct was telling her something was amiss. Unfortunately, she had no clue as to what it might be.

They were halfway to the public road when Sylvia said, "What is this place today—Grand Central Station?"

Jane glanced up to see a man walking on the path toward them.

She guessed that he was in his sixties. He wore brown corduroy trousers and a neat, red-plaid flannel shirt. His brimmed hat was tilted back a bit, allowing a lock of gray hair to cross his forehead. Below the hat brim was a pleasant face graced with a gray mustache. He held a walking stick in one hand and what might have been a bag of nails in the other.

He hesitated when he saw them. After studying the women briefly, he seemed to give them a stamp of authorization, if not approval. It was as if they had passed muster and could be trusted to walk on the path.

In a courtly fashion, he lifted the brim of his hat in a gesture of greeting. Then he walked by them without a word, heading toward Fairy Pond.

Jane and Sylvia didn't speak until they were on the paved road leading back to Acorn Hill. Then Sylvia turned to Jane, big-eyed. "Who was that?"

"I have no idea. I don't think I've ever seen that man before. He was kind of cute, though."

"This is creepy. Businessmen and strangers at Fairy Pond? I'm just dying to know what's going on."

"Heavy traffic day in the woods, that's all," Jane said more lightly than she felt.

Sylvia's brow furrowed. "Those men are staying at the inn. Couldn't you ask them what they were doing?"

"Hardly. We respect our guests' privacy. Besides, if they weren't willing to tell us before, they certainly won't be now."

$\backsim$

After the friends had parted company and Jane had returned to the inn, she greeted her sisters and told them that she was going to take a nap. They encouraged her to do just that. When she awoke, Louise was setting the table for their evening meal, and Alice was removing dishes from the refrigerator. "We were hungry and decided to eat as soon as you came down. I hope that is okay with you."

"Fine. Sylvia and I didn't have much for lunch." Jane moved to pour herself a glass of iced tea. Distracted by her thoughts concerning recent events, she paid very little attention to her sisters as they finished what they were doing and didn't even seem to hear Alice when she asked Jane to say grace.

"What? Oh, the blessing? Of course." Jane bowed her head and was silent for a long moment before beginning. "We thank You for this food, Lord, for the abundance You provide for us every day. Thank You for my sisters and for the opportunity to serve You here at Grace Chapel Inn. And…I give to You whatever mysteries seem to be circling around us this week. I know that You are in control, and I ask that things work for Your good. In Jesus' name we pray. Amen."

When she lifted her head, both Alice and Louise were staring at her as though they were quite concerned.

"Jane?" Alice said anxiously.

"What is wrong?" Louise demanded. "Your prayer—"

"It's a feeling I've been having, that's all. There's something about two of our guests…"

"Mr. Horton and Mr. Crane, you mean?"

"They seem so secretive."

Alice went to the front desk and returned with the registry in which she recorded information about all their guests. She pulled a card from beneath a paper clip. "Here is a business card. I asked for it when they checked in."

Jane felt a rush of embarrassment. She had been enjoying all this crazy speculation, and one of her answers had been in the registry all along. She reached for the card.

Sam Horton
Horton & Crane
Developing the Future
Development of Commercial Properties Is Our Specialty

Developers? Jane tucked the card into her pocket. She was going to have to think about this.

"That's the mystery you were praying about?" Louise asked.

"One of them. Maybe my imagination is working overtime. Something odd did happen as Sylvia and I were leaving

Fairy Pond this afternoon. We crossed paths with a mysterious, gray-haired gentleman who was heading toward the pond. He tipped his hat to us but didn't say a word."

"How was he dressed?" Louise asked.

"He wore corduroy trousers, a plaid shirt and a straw hat, and he carried a walking stick. He can't be local, or Sylvia or I would have recognized him."

Louise and Alice exchanged a strange look, much like the one they had exchanged at dinner on Monday night.

"What?" Jane said. "Why are you two looking at each other like that? Do either of you know who this fellow is?"

"We might have an idea, but nothing for certain . . ." Alice stumbled on the words and looked ill at ease.

"What idea? If you know, tell me. It's not like it's a big deal or anything."

"It could be Casper Jones."

"Jones? As in the family that owned the land around Fairy Pond? I didn't know there were any Joneses still in the area."

Louise sat ramrod straight in her chair, lips pursed, a flush moving up her cheeks.

Jane tried to ready herself for a revelation. "What happened to them?"

"Orlando died a couple of years back." Alice dug deep

into the purse of her mind. "The obituary was in the newspaper."

"And the other one—Casper?"

Alice and Louise stared at her in astonishment. "You don't know?"

Jane shrugged helplessly. "Know what?"

"He still lives on the land near Fairy Pond."

Jane looked puzzled. "He lives where?"

"About a quarter mile past the pond," Alice said. "The dirt driveway to his house enters from the west, and the house is shrouded in trees. He's been there all along."

"Why haven't we seen or heard of him?"

"Few people see him other than the postman and delivery people. He even has groceries delivered."

"Rumor has it," Alice said, "that he leaves a check in the mailbox and doesn't even come out to get his things until the deliveryman has gone. Maybe he's gotten strange over the years."

At that moment, there was a knock on the front door and Ethel's voice drifted to where they were seated. "Yoo-hoo! Anybody home?"

Before anyone could get up, Ethel walked toward the kitchen. She was wearing a fuchsia-colored velour jogging suit with glittery rhinestones on the collar and pockets. She had managed to negotiate a matching fuchsia headband into her Titian red hair, no doubt for an après-exercise look. Other than being so brightly colored that she was almost noisy, she looked rather cute in a round, gaudy sort of way.

"I didn't mean to interrupt your dinner, but I thought I'd just pop in to say hello. Viola is going to meet me here and we're going walking."

"You're really into this exercise thing, aren't you? And now you have Viola going for a power walk." Jane was tickled by the idea.

"We're not getting any younger. And I really believe I have a bit more spring in my step since class. Exercise is very good for a person. Maybe Viola will be inspired."

Aunt Ethel was springy even without exercise, Jane thought. She would be downright bouncy pretty soon. She stood, got Ethel a cup of coffee and set a tray of cookies in front of her.

"Oh, I couldn't!" Ethel looked at the sweets in horror. Then she looked again, a little more closely this time. "Macadamia chunk? And frosted molasses cookies? Oh, and macaroons! Maybe just one…"

Three cookies later, she turned back to her nieces. "I didn't mean to interrupt when I came in. You looked as though you were having a serious discussion. Don't let me stop you."

"I ran into someone walking toward the pond today," Jane said. "I'd never seen him before so I was asking my sisters if either of them might know who it could be. He was a gray-haired gentleman. Dignified looking and wearing a—"

"Oh, that's probably Casper Jones," Ethel said lightly. "Fred said he was in the hardware store today. I'll bet I haven't seen him myself in two or three years."

"Does he have someone he visits in Acorn Hill?"

"Oh no. He's always at home in that little house of his. He never leaves it unless he's desperate for something, the basics—nails, sugar, salt. Otherwise he just lives off his own land as far as I know. He's Acorn Hill's very own hermit, you understand."

Jane understood nothing of the kind. She looked stunned. "I lived here eighteen years before I left and—"

"He wasn't such a recluse then. You were a youngster back then. You probably saw him then and just didn't recognize him." Then the wheels turned in Ethel's head, and she looked at Alice and Louise. "Of course you *must* have seen him. He was at the house with Louise a good deal. He was in love with her, you know."

"*What?*" Jane heard her own voice rise nearly an octave.

"He was in love with …" She turned her head to look at her sister. "*Louie?*"

Louise was looking decidedly uncomfortable. Her color was high, and her expression alternated between mortification and fond reminiscence.

"Why haven't I heard about this?"

"Oh dear," Alice fussed.

"Oh dear, oh dear," Aunt Ethel echoed. "I have put my foot into it this time, haven't I? I had no idea that Jane didn't know …"

"She was just a child, Ethel, fifteen years younger than Louise. By the time she was old enough to discuss such things, that was ancient history."

"It was hardly an interesting topic of discussion then anyway," Louise interjected. She was fidgeting nervously with the chain around her neck that held her glasses. "And it is not interesting now either."

"I suppose you're right. All that happened a long time ago," said Alice.

"Speak for yourself, Alice," Jane said. "I'm interested. *Very* interested."

"Jane, you were not more than six or seven years old when Casper …" Louise blushed as she spoke the name, "went into the Army and left Acorn Hill."

"And you'd already graduated when he moved back permanently," Alice added. "He had a couple of tours of duty and went to college before he came home."

"And he's stayed here ever since," Ethel concluded grandly. "Tucked away in that little house in the middle of his property, just beyond Fairy Pond."

"So Casper Jones owns Fairy Pond?"

Alice and Ethel exchanged confused looks. "I'm not sure what he owns out there. His father left the land to Casper and Orlando," Alice said.

"And Orlando . . ."

"Is the one who passed on. So sad." Ethel shook her head sympathetically. "But that was years ago. I suppose no one has ever asked Casper how much of the land he owns now. He's not much for people and conversation, you know."

Obviously, Jane thought.

"In fact," Ethel continued, "sometimes he's gone so long that Fred Humbert or Lloyd—they see him the most because they're usually in town when he does come—go out to check on him."

"Really?" Louise sounded startled . . . and interested.

"What is it like out there?" Alice asked. "I've wondered sometimes if he's been living in a hovel."

Jane looked from one face to another in amazement. Here they were, talking matter-of-factly about a hermit who had once loved her sister Louise and had spent the last years of his life living in a small house in the woods. Of course, she reminded herself, none of this information was a surprise to anyone but her. Apparently one could even become accustomed to having hermits hiding in the woods outside of town.

"Louie!" Jane said forcefully. "If you were in love with this man and the whole town knew it, the least you could do is tell your own sister."

Chapter Eight

*J*ane's words hung in the air, only to be broken by Viola's bursting through the front door and announcing in a pained tone, "Acorn Hill is finished, ruined! It will never be the same again." She sank into the nearest chair, her head in her hands. "Our poor, lovely town. Gone forever."

When Viola had read the death scene from Shakespeare's *Romeo and Juliet* for an audience at her Nine Lives Bookstore, she hadn't had as much emotion in her voice.

"Whatever do you mean, dear?" Ethel asked as she patted Viola's shoulder. "An explosion? A fire?"

"Worse!"

"An outbreak of the Black Plague," Jane offered unhelpfully. She wanted to get back to Louise and her story about Casper Jones.

"If only it were so simple."

Alice put her hand over her mouth and giggled. "Plague's not all *that* simple, Viola. Take it from a nurse."

But Viola was oblivious to all but her own alarm. "Speeding cars. Strangers everywhere. Burglars. Stoplights. I can see it all now."

"Burglars and stoplights? Viola, what are you talking about?"

"You haven't heard?" She mopped at her eyes. "Of course not. You weren't there to hear the dreadful news. I only went to the city council meeting to ask that they consider paving the alley behind my store. It's so dusty as it is, that I can't keep my door open without soiling the books. In winter it's fine but—"

"Viola!" Louise said sternly. "Please get on with it."

Viola tossed her head. "I had no idea that those…people …would be there." She said the word people with such disdain that Louise's eyebrows arched upward. "And," Viola looked accusingly at Louise, "you allowed them to stay in your inn."

Jane whistled under her breath. Surely not the Thrumbles. She had packed them off only today. Mrs. Thrumble had "helpfully" handed Jane a list of suggestions for improving the inn on her way out the door.

Change your alarm clocks. The digital numbers are too bright and the clock made a humming sound.

Leave two truffles per person instead of one on the pillow when you turn down for the night—you don't want to look miserly.

More sweet items at breakfast—brownies, perhaps.

But even Genevieve Thrumble wouldn't take her complaining as far as the city council. Then a sick feeling began to grow in Jane's stomach. *Sam Horton and Philip Crane. Horton & Crane, Developing the Future. Development of Commercial Properties Is Our Specialty.*

"Was it our businessmen?"

"The same." Viola looked accusingly at Jane. "Did you know what they were up to?"

"I still don't know for sure. What is it they want?"

"Why don't you tell us, Viola," Alice urged gently.

"They are commercial developers, and they've been skulking about looking at a location for a gas station and convenience store." Then her voice wavered. "With six pumps."

"What on earth for?" Ethel asked. "We're just a dot on the map compared to Potterston, and they have a perfectly nice highway to use."

"Alternate routing," Viola said gloomily, as if she were diagnosing a fatal disease. "Apparently the state is considering improving some roads, and one is the road that intersects

Chapel Road north of town. You are just lucky that the inn won't be directly affected by these changes."

"So it's not definite?" Louise asked.

"No, but these two men told the council that they are speculators and are banking on the road's being enlarged. They think this is a good business move and that it's a potential moneymaker for the entire town if there's a state-of-the-art gas station and convenience store in place."

"How hideous!" Ethel gasped.

"They're counting on Acorn Hill's becoming a"—Viola shuddered—"'profitable little tourist trap.'"

"Well, that is just plain nonsense," Louise said calmly. "I cannot believe that anyone in town would sell them property to do such a thing."

"They already have someone willing to sell and the land has been chosen." Viola said mournfully.

"Where?" Alice said, "I can't imagine—"

"Fairy Pond!"

"Casper Jones would never sell," Louise said firmly. "He loves that place."

"He may not have any voice in this," Viola said. "He doesn't own all the land out there."

"But of course he does," Louise said. "Who else? His parents lived there long before he was born."

"When the elder Joneses died, the land was divided between Casper and his brother Orlando. Casper was given the half that included the family's house, and Orlando's half included Fairy Pond."

"But Orlando is no longer living."

"No, but his son is. Apparently he owns what had been his father's share."

Suddenly, Jane realized, everything was beginning to fall into place. Mr. Horton and Mr. Crane's being secretive, asking questions.

"So Casper doesn't own all the land?" Alice sounded surprised. "I've never heard of Orlando's son visiting either Casper or Acorn Hill."

"It wouldn't be that difficult to hide, would it?" Jane asked. "Especially since Casper Jones rarely shows his face in town."

"True, but it's pretty difficult not to be noticed in Acorn Hill."

That, Jane had to admit, was true.

"I am not sure that the young man would visit Casper anyway," Louise said softly. "I have seen Casper since I moved back to Acorn Hill. He was in Fred Humbert's store one day, and seeing him reminded me of how different he was from his brother."

Four pair of curious eyes turned her way, but Louise was not about to go any further.

"Casper and Orlando were like night and day," Ethel said. "Casper was always a gentle, compassionate person. Younger students at school loved him because he was always kind to them. He always had beautiful manners."

"That's true," Alice agreed. "Our father always liked Casper."

Jane could not believe that she was listening to her sisters talk about an individual who had once been so important in Louise's life and who was completely unknown to her. "What was his brother like?" she blurted.

Louise and Alice exchanged glances, as did Ethel and Viola. It was Ethel who finally spoke. "He was a bully, plain and simple. Orlando was always making mischief."

"Sometimes more than mischief," Viola added. "He's the one who opened a faucet in the church basement and left it running. It caused considerable damage, and when they confronted Orlando, he thought it was the funniest trick he'd ever played."

"He set fire to a manure pile on the outskirts of town and it smoldered for weeks," Viola added.

"I often wondered how their parents could raise two boys with such different personalities." Ethel shook her head as she pondered the question. "No one was too sorry when Orlando left Acorn Hill."

"Not even Casper," Louise added.

"Where did Orlando go?"

Louise spoke. "To California, I think. Orlando always had a way with his hands. He said he was going to be a carpenter and build homes for rich people in California."

"A noble ambition," Jane said with a hint of sarcasm in her tone.

"Oh, he did very well, I heard," Viola said. "He became a builder. Eventually he began buying land, building houses on it and then selling them for outrageous sums of money." She shook her head sadly. "And all the while his brother was content to live in the house where he grew up."

Another note of alarm rang in Jane. "Whatever happened to this son of Orlando's?" she asked.

"I've been told that he followed in his father's footsteps," Viola said.

"Then it's likely he wants to do some development of property in Acorn Hill," Alice added.

"A gas station is hardly big development," Jane pointed out, "but if the highway is improved, I'm sure that things could change."

"Then why didn't he come himself?" Ethel fumed. "He sent those two sneaky men in his place!"

"Probably because he wants to keep this a secret," Jane surmised. "If his father told him anything at all about Acorn Hill, he would know that the people here wouldn't like it."

"And I'm sure he knew Casper would hate it," Louise added. Her expression darkened. "It would be just like Orlando to do this to his brother only out of pure meanness. He probably filled his son's head with this or made a deathbed request or something just to remind his brother that he still had power, even after he was gone."

"He sounds like a horrible man." Jane frowned.

"No two brothers were ever more unlike," Louise agreed.

"But we're just speculating," Alice reminded them. "We shouldn't jump to conclusions."

"She heard this at the city council meeting, Alice. It sounds like some conclusions have been made already."

At that moment, Ethel clapped her hand on her chest and looked stricken. "Oh, poor Lloyd! Can you imagine what this is doing to him?"

For a man whose favorite words were *status quo*, this could be quite upsetting.

"How did he handle it at the meeting, Viola?" Jane asked.

Viola looked thoughtful. "I was so stunned myself that I didn't look around much, but come to think of it, he seemed stricken. I've never really known what the statement 'green around the gills' meant, but he did look a little green while those two men were being interviewed."

"I should go to him," Ethel said. "I'm sure he's terribly upset by this."

Jane recalled how concerned about Lloyd her aunt had been even before this unsettling news. "Why don't I go with you?" Jane stood quickly. As she did so, she glanced at Alice and Louise.

"I think I'll go too." Alice also rose.

"I'll join you," Louise said, her tone brooking no argument.

Viola, who had left the meeting to spread the news, looked confused for a moment before saying, "I'll go too. I know they had a lot to discuss about other matters, so I'm sure everyone is still at the meeting."

The five of them marched down the street in an odd little parade formation with Viola, the bearer of the bad news, leading the troops. Louise and Alice walked side by side, talking and gesturing. Jane matched her step to that of Ethel.

"No need to hurry, Aunt Ethel. According to Viola, they'll all still be there when we arrive. No use getting winded."

Ethel, red-faced already, said, "Justine was right. I am out of shape. Lloyd and I both thought she worried too much about us at her exercise class, but by the end of the evening, we both agreed she was right." Ethel waved a hand in front of her face to cool herself off. "I don't know why we haven't taken better care of ourselves. On the farm I got all the exercise I needed . . . oh, dear . . . I have to stop and rest."

The others went on ahead, not even realizing that Jane and Ethel had stopped for a breather. Viola was slowing down too, so it wasn't hard to catch up with them before the group reached Town Hall.

From outside the meeting room, they could hear raised voices. Inside, though Philip Crane and Sam Horton had already left, there was a spirited conversation going on.

"Don't be ridiculous," Fred Humbert was saying. "We can't just let this happen without even making a protest. Can you imagine what would happen if fully loaded semis were bearing down on the center of Acorn Hill? There are noise, safety and pollution issues to address even before we get to the fact that this is a lovely place just the way it is."

"Don't be so quick to jump to conclusions, Fred. We can't just say no without doing our own research."

"I don't see why not."

The women tiptoed inside the meeting room door. Fred Humbert, in denim jeans and a checked shirt, was pacing at the side of the room. His brow was deeply furrowed, and his troubled expression surprised Jane. Fred was usually a rock of a man, composed, cool in a crisis. But tonight he was upset and showed deep concern. Jane glanced around to see who had spoken after Fred and was surprised to see Joseph Holzmann standing on the other side of the room. "For one thing, it wouldn't be right. They came to us with a proposal. We're duty-bound to examine it."

"Even if we already know we don't want it?" Fred's lips turned down in a scowl.

"Are you so sure about that, Fred?" Joseph said it mildly, but the words spread an electric shock through the room.

"What do you mean 'am I sure'? Of course I'm sure! I've lived in Acorn Hill all my life, raised my children here, run a business, and I know I don't want it."

"But you aren't everyone," Joseph said, standing his ground. "Maybe others should have some input into this. We could send out a survey—"

Fred turned suddenly toward Joseph. "How would you vote? How do you feel about having Acorn Hill—" Fred sputtered. "—*violated* like this?"

"Those are pretty strong words."

"They match a strong feeling."

Joseph was silent for a moment, obviously weighing his words. "I think Acorn Hill is the finest little community in Pennsylvania. Rachel and I love it here."

"So there's your answer!" Fred interrupted triumphantly, looking pleased. Several others in the group nodded.

"Not entirely. We also make our living here, as do all of you. I can't speak for everyone else, but if I'm honest, I have to admit that more traffic through town would benefit my antique store, just as it would the Coffee Shop and the—"

"My hardware store is just fine without a bunch of newcomers demanding services. We don't have the infrastructure to allow major developments to go in here."

"No? Maybe not. But we do have enough for a second gas station."

"One oversized, modern-looking monster of a station," someone shouted.

"One gas station," Joseph reiterated. "You people are acting like we're going to be swamped with newcomers if those developers build anything at all. Maybe traffic won't come this way, and they'll be out of luck. But we'll get their taxes in the coffers."

"Money? You'd betray Acorn Hill for money?" Lloyd stood on the platform at the front of the room. His expression revealed dismay. "Joseph, what are you saying?"

"I'm just saying that we'd better take a poll and make an informed decision. Nothing more."

Hands waved in the air and voices blended into a

cacophony, most directed at poor Lloyd. When all was said and done, Fred and Joseph were to head up a committee to speak with citizens and report back to the council.

The scraping of chairs against wood and the shuffling on of jackets signaled that the meeting was in adjournment until next week.

"Frankly, I don't see how we could stop them anyway," Viola said morosely. "If they can't build exactly where they want, they'll find another place." Her shoulders sank. "The likes of them would probably fill in Fairy Pond and build on top of it."

Jane felt sick to her stomach. From the looks on her sisters' faces, she knew they felt the same. Where had this eruption come from, anyway? Just today she had learned that Casper Jones had had a relationship with her sister, and that he had a brother named Orlando, a nasty fellow who had apparently fathered a chip off the old block. And now this. What were the ramifications for Acorn Hill?

Jane had no idea, and nothing that came to mind comforted her in the least.

Chapter Nine

The women walked back to Grace Chapel Inn in atypical silence, each processing for herself what this all might mean for Acorn Hill. While the others gathered around the large dining room table, arranging a chair here and there, Jane went to the kitchen and brewed coffee and boiled water for tea. She collected a large plate of the simple but hearty oatmeal cookies and brownies that she often put out for guests.

In a crisis, Jane always felt compelled to feed people. The words *comfort food* were not meaningless for her.

When she walked back into the dining room, people were pulling more chairs toward the table and others were filtering through the front door. Not to her surprise, some of those at the meeting had found their way here to talk. Fred and Vera Humbert, Craig Tracy and Ned Arnold, and, Jane was pleased to note, Rev. Ken Thompson, Grace Chapel's pastor.

Lloyd was the last to arrive, and none of them had ever seen him quite so worked up.

Suddenly no one seemed to know what to say. Jane broke the awkwardness. "Coffee or tea?" Soon the room erupted into a cacophony of chatter.

"Have you ever heard the likes of it?"

"What nerve!"

"Who does he think he is?"

"Can't somebody *do* something?"

"A gas station by Fairy Pond? Contemptible!"

"If they think they can bully us around, they've got another thing coming."

"What about Joseph? What did you think of him standing up like that?"

"I had no idea he was dissatisfied with his business."

"A traitor in our midst!"

"I can't believe—"

Pastor Thompson cleared his throat so loudly that everyone turned to look at him.

"Shall we give thanks for this food Jane has prepared for us?"

Quietly, those around the table bowed their heads.

"Dear Father," he began, "we thank You for this food set before us, for the welcoming table we have gathered around and for Your presence with us now. We seem to have come to one of those forks in the road, Lord, that only You can help us see our way through. We ask Your hand on the councilmen, the concerned citizens and our mayor, and that whatever happens, You are glorified. Amen."

Heads around the table nodded. Fred spoke. "More than once over the years I've come here to hash one thing or another out with Pastor Howard. He always told me it was, as he called it, a 'place of peace and thoughtful discussion.'"

"'Place of peace.'" Jane tried the words on for size. "I like that."

"And that it shall remain," Louise added. "No bickering here." She sighed. "I think there will be plenty of that to go around as it is."

"I'm not bickering," Fred said, "but those guys sure have a lot of nerve."

"It's Orlando Jones who had the nerve," Viola muttered. "He was bad, that one, very bad."

"No use speaking ill of the dead, dear," Ethel ineffectively patted Viola on the arm, doing absolutely nothing to soothe her.

"Then let's speak ill of the living. That son of Orlando's has never even been here to see the spot, and now he's selling some of the most beautiful land around Acorn Hill for a gas station. Have you ever heard of such a thing?"

It happens all the time, Jane thought to herself. *Daily in this push for growth, nature is forced to take a back seat to "progress." But for these people, and for the first time here in Acorn Hill, it is personal.*

Pastor Thompson cleared his throat again. "I agree with Louise. There should be no bickering here."

Every pair of eyes turned to look at him in astonishment.

"But Pastor Ken," Fred said, "we're not bickering. We all agree."

Jane hid a smile. It was true. Bickering required opposing views.

Pastor Thompson caught her smile and rolled his eyes as if to say, "I tried."

"Let them vent," Jane mouthed.

He nodded, grinned and sat back to listen.

Jane kept one eye on Lloyd, and she noticed that Ethel kept looking at him too. His face was growing ruddier by the moment. It was as if every comment or complaint voiced added to his considerable distress.

Fred turned to Lloyd. "You haven't said much since you got here. You're the mayor. What do you have to say about this?"

Lloyd opened his mouth, and Jane braced for an eruption, but none came. Instead, reining in his temper, he said slowly, "I've got lots to say, but before I do, I think that I'd better find out what the rest of you have to say first."

"Don't take what Joseph said as an attack," Pastor Thompson advised. "He could be speaking the minds of several businessmen. There may be others worried about keeping their businesses viable who are just uncomfortable voicing their concerns."

"How do you feel, Pastor?" Lloyd asked.

Jane felt a twinge of admiration for Lloyd. No matter how strongly he felt about the matter, being mayor to all was still important to him. At least it was for the time being.

"I think this is a fine place just as it is. I've never heard complaints about its being too small or that it's too difficult to make a living here. It's idyllic, and Fairy Pond only adds to that feeling of tranquility. But…"

Ethel straightened like a little red hen, alarmed that there might be any doubt at all in the pastor's mind.

He continued. "But if it's true that the state is considering updating the road through here and rerouting traffic, we will have very little say in the matter. In that case, it's better that we be proactive and decide in advance how we want to handle such a situation rather than closing our eyes to it until it's upon us. Don't you agree?"

"Maybe it would be better to have development come slowly and on *our* terms rather than being bullied into making dramatic changes in the town," Fred said.

Lloyd pondered that. "Yes, I suppose that makes sense. It turns my stomach to think of diesel fumes, noise and pollution befouling our little town, but if we knew it was coming, maybe we could do some advance planning."

"But what if the road doesn't change and we're stuck with a gas station monstrosity and no Fairy Pond?" Viola asked. "Then what?"

Lloyd's shoulders sagged and Jane felt sorry for him. He was carrying quite a weight as mayor of their town.

He turned to Viola. "What do you think?"

"I think we should get a petition or something. Orlando Jones's son shouldn't be able to ruin our pond!"

"It may be *his* pond, Viola," Pastor Thompson said softly.

"Well, if his grandfather had known what was going to happen, he would have given all the land to Casper and written Orlando out of the will. I'm sure of it."

No one would touch that with a ten-foot pole, Jane noticed. What-ifs, if-onlys and looking backward instead of forward would get them nowhere.

"Fred?"

"You heard my two cents' worth at the meeting. My blood pressure goes up just thinking about it!"

"Vera?"

"I agree with what Fred said earlier. We've made a good living here. We have nothing to complain about. And it's always been worth it to us to live in such a beautiful, friendly, cozy place. I'd hate to lose all that now."

"Louise?"

"It's upsetting. I came back to Acorn Hill to find family, and I looked forward to coming to a place that seemed to have paused in time. I'm worried, and I'm not sure why. I have had many changes in my life, but for some reason, this seems particularly distressing."

"Alice?" Lloyd was meticulously making his way around the table.

"I love it just as it is," Alice said. She put her hand to her cheek. "You don't suppose our opening Grace Chapel Inn here gave anyone any ideas, do you? We only have a few rooms. I hope no one thinks that we sent out a signal that Acorn Hill needed changing."

"Nonsense!" Ethel blurted. "You did nothing of the kind, dear."

Jane did remember, however, how upset Lloyd had been at the idea of the inn's possibly bringing too many newcomers to town. Fortunately that had passed as he saw what a blessing the inn had been to travelers and locals alike. It also had not hurt that he loved Jane's cooking and managed to be a frequent guest at her dinner table. She would bet that now he would be the one petitioning if they threatened to close the inn.

"Craig, you're a relative newcomer to Acorn Hill. What do you think?"

Craig shifted in his chair and pondered the question

thoughtfully. "Part of what appeals to me about this place is the closeness to nature. Being a person who loves plants and flowers, I love the place just as it is. Of course, I also do a good business here. The citizens have been very loyal to my shop. The other thing that has been helpful to me is that every day I have deliveries in Potterston." Craig tried to look modest. "Word has gotten out that I do unique arrangements. My business is thriving without road changes, so naturally, I'd be happy if things stayed just as they are."

"Do you think that's true for everyone? What about Wilhelm Wood, for example?"

"Wilhelm cares more about traveling than making sure Time for Tea is profitable, yet I think he does well anyway. He has income from other sources, you know. I don't think either he or his mother care for change, but you'd have to ask him to make sure."

"What about Sylvia? She's not here to speak for herself either."

"She's in the same situation as Craig," Jane commented for her friend. "People are willing to travel to find a good fabric shop that offers a large selection and plenty of samples so they can see what they want to make. She's also been selling vintage clothing to interested parties, and her business has grown without her doing more than letting it be known what she has available. Customers go to her."

"I'm not sure if you'd get the same answer from everyone, however," Craig said. "The pharmacy might be strapped sometimes, and I know the restaurant can always use more business. And people like Justine Gilmore and Jose Morales could always use a little more work. There is a labor base here for anyone who might want to move in."

"The Colwins are doing just fine," Viola pointed out, referring to the young couple who ran Zachary's, a supper club in town.

"Are they?" Jane inquired. "Have we asked them?"

Viola looked surprised but remained silent.

"Jane, what about you?" Lloyd looked at her beseechingly, as if perhaps she could add some sense and order to what was going on around them.

She was sorry to disappoint. "Acorn Hill is exactly what I've needed in my life. Fairy Pond is my single most favorite spot in the entire area, and I feel panic rise in me at the thought of it being destroyed. And, frankly, I have no idea what to do about any of it."

A collective sigh filled the room. Jane had just put into her final words everything everyone else was feeling.

Vera dabbed at a tear that had rolled down her cheek. "It's just so sad. Fred and I got engaged at Fairy Pond."

"You did?" Ethel sat upright. "So did Bob and I." She turned to Alice and Louise.

With those revelations, the floodgates were opened and romantic stories flowed until Jane was sure every single couple in Acorn Hill and many who had moved away had all become engaged or had a romantic memory of the pond.

Even Wendell seemed to be affected by the mood in the room. He purred softly and wore an expression that could have been interpreted as sentimental as he sat watching from his place in a corner.

When the reminiscences began to dwindle and the room was again silent, Pastor Thompson spoke.

"Now, what do you think about all this, Lloyd?" he inquired—as if they didn't already know.

"Well, I think this intrusion is wrong and I'm going to challenge it," Lloyd said firmly. "I have long been in support of keeping Acorn Hill a pristine place." He squinted as if he were thinking hard. "An *historical* place, if you will. I've heard your stories, and I know there are many more. We can't let such a place go without a fight."

Jane blinked twice at that. Lloyd was already formulating his arguments. If he couldn't protect Acorn Hill from the future, he would at least fight to save its past. That, first and foremost, meant Fairy Pond.

"Besides, I knew the Jones boys pretty well at one time.

That Orlando had a heart of stone. We can't let the likes of him or his offspring ruin our town."

"What about Casper Jones?" Jane asked, knowing she was probably treading on sensitive territory. She kept her eyes averted from Louise. "Is he like his brother? Can't he do something about it?"

"Casper didn't like his brother much more than anyone else did," Louise said softly.

"It was as though he got all the sensitivity and emotional intelligence, and his brother got all the business acumen and shrewdness," Viola added.

"I doubt Orlando ever came back once he left town, and Casper certainly doesn't travel much." Fred looked grim as he spoke.

"Now that's an understatement, dear," Vera said. "Didn't he tell you that he hadn't been to Potterston in more than fifteen years?"

Jane nearly gasped at that.

"He did, but why should he? You know how he is."

Ethel nodded and Jane wanted to call out, "Tell me how he is! I don't know!" But she bit her lip and stayed silent.

"No, I don't think those two brothers had communicated in a long time."

"And Orlando's son?" Jane asked.

"If his father wouldn't come back here, why would the son?"

They were going in circles now, getting nowhere. Jane stood. "Maybe we should table this discussion. Everyone is upset. Things may look different in the light of day. Besides, if the council is going to poll the people in town to see how they feel about this, then we'd better wait awhile and not jump to any conclusions just yet."

Almost everyone nodded at the good sense of Jane's words. Only Lloyd seemed so lost in thought that he was a million miles away. Or at least somewhere in California, where Orlando Jones's son lived.

They sat around the table, no one wanting to be the first to leave. It was as if, Jane thought, there was comfort in numbers, and no one wanted to go home and think more about the ramifications of what they had heard. Things less serious than this had been known to divide friendships and create lasting hard feelings—and that would be worse than losing Fairy Pond.

Ethel jumped when someone knocked loudly on the door.

Alice's hand flew to her cheek. "I completely forgot! We have a new guest coming in tonight." She jumped up and hurried to the door. A few moments later, she escorted a nattily dressed man in his early sixties toward the reception area. Through the open dining room door, the friends could see that he was over six feet tall and that there were streaks of gray at his temples. His white shirt was stiffly starched, and the creases in his trousers were ruler straight. The suit coat he carried over his arm looked unwrinkled.

The man must not bend his arms or legs while he drives, Jane thought. *Who might he be?* Even she, who loved variety and adventure, was getting a little wary of who might show up at their door next.

Lloyd, who had left the dining room to stretch his legs, thrust out his hand to shake that of the stranger. "Lloyd Tynan here. Do you have luggage?"

"Just one suitcase."

"Let's go out and I'll carry it in for you. We didn't mean to be watching like a tree full of vultures to see you check in."

The man appeared grateful for Lloyd's offer. "Thank you. That's very nice of you. It's not necessary, however."

"Sure it is—for me. You don't know how stiff my legs are getting from sitting. Do *me* a favor and let me move around a bit."

Together they disappeared outside.

Everyone decided to take a break with Lloyd gone.

Viola and Ethel headed for the kitchen, and Louise poured coffee. They were all just settling down again when Lloyd returned, and Alice escorted the new guest to his room.

Fred, who wasn't used to the traffic through the inn, was curious. "Who is that fellow, anyway?"

Vera opened her mouth to remind Fred gently that it wasn't their place to ask, but Lloyd spoke first.

"Troy Landers, he said." Lloyd always enjoyed imparting new information. "Troy Landers of Golden Financial, Santa Monica, California. 'Bank with Us and You Bank with the Best,'" Lloyd read the slogan from a card that he had just been given. "He meant to be here earlier, but his flight was delayed."

"California, you say?" Fred's eyes narrowed and his color heightened. "And a banker?"

Not aware of the connection that Fred was making, Lloyd carried on. "Said he was here to look at some property for a client of his. Something his client is thinking of developing. He wanted a second opinion on the plan." Lloyd leaned back in his chair and crossed his arms over his chest. "He seemed pretty proud to be asked. He said he's worked with this client on several projects and likes to think he's able to discern what he's looking for in an investment. Sounds like an important job if you ask me."

"That 'client' wouldn't happen to have a name, now,

would he?" Fred's voice was deceptively disarming, as if it really didn't matter who this client might be.

"He didn't divulge that," Lloyd said importantly.

"What if he's someone to look at the Fairy Pond property?" Fred asked.

Suddenly jolted out of his relaxed discussion of the new guest, Lloyd burst out, "What! I sure hope he isn't. If those developers and this banker fellow gave him the green light, that young Jones could have people here knocking down trees and filling in the pond in little or no time."

That shocking observation hovered in the room for a moment, and Jane hurried to fill in the stunned silence and try to divert them from the direction their thinking seemed to be going. "What is this young Jones's first name, anyway?"

"I don't know but I'd venture a guess," Lloyd said scowling.

The others looked at him, puzzled.

"His father's name was Orlando Raymond Jones," Lloyd said. "With an ego like Orlando's, he was bound to name his son after him. And since a name like Orlando is out-of-date and old-fashioned, if I had to guess, his son goes by the name Raymond. Or maybe it's Ray."

Viola nodded. "It makes sense. Orlando had a big opinion of himself, and at times he used to be teased about his name."

"We'll just have to wait and see," Jane offered softly as she recalled that she had heard Philip Crane and Sam Horton talk about a man named Ray.

They didn't have to wait long. Within moments they heard footsteps on the stairs, and Mr. Landers appeared at the dining room entrance and addressed himself to Alice.

"It appears I've forgotten my toothbrush. Is there someplace nearby that I could buy a new one?"

If the new facility were here, you could, Jane thought, in spite of herself. Having nowhere to go at night for sundries was one of the things she'd missed most after moving back to Pennsylvania.

"I could open the drugstore for you," Ned offered.

Alice, however, saved the day. "I just bought a new supply of toothbrushes, toothpaste, dental floss, shampoo...all those things people seem to forget when they pack. Our guests appreciate our having some on hand." She hurried into the kitchen and reappeared with a brand-new toothbrush. "Here you are, Mr. Landers."

"Thank you," he said sounding surprised. "This is very nice—"

"Say, Landers," Lloyd said as casually as if he were about to discuss the weather. "That client of yours wouldn't be someone called Raymond Jones, now would he?"

"How did you kn—" Landers caught himself. "I'm unable to divulge that information at this time."

"I'll bet he goes by Ray," Lloyd mused. "Am I right?"

"Well, actually . . ." Landers looked uncomfortable. He turned to Alice. "Thanks very much for the toothbrush. I'd better go upstairs now." And before anyone could say anything else, he went up the steps, strode to his room and shut his door.

Craig Tracy shook his head. "Smooth move, Lloyd. I didn't know you were so good at getting information."

Lloyd harrumphed. "Common sense. Unfortunately, there's not much of that going around these days."

"What about Casper Jones?" The table fell silent and everyone looked at Vera. She hadn't spoken for a while, but now she certainly had everyone's attention. "He owns half the land too. Why can't he talk to his nephew and convince him that there are other places better suited to what he wants to build?"

"Casper doesn't like confrontation much, if I remember correctly," Ethel said. She shook her head back and forth. "No, no indeed, he does not like confrontation."

"Orlando relished confrontation—with classmates, teachers, his parents, even our own father," Alice said. "I wouldn't blame Casper for being sick and tired of it. I'm sure he got the worst of it. Orlando would make a scene with Casper quicker than with anyone else. Poor Casper, so intellectual and polite, simply hated that. He was embarrassed by his brother, but still, I know he loved him. It put him in an awful fix."

"It is part of why he disappeared right here in plain sight," Fred added. "The Casper I know is a thinker, not a fighter."

"Would it necessarily have to be a fight?" Vera asked.

"I don't see how it could be anything else, considering that the issue that estranged the brothers in the first place was the land we're talking about today," Alice said.

This was getting more and more complicated. Jane shifted in her chair. She felt as though she had walked into a theater and the play was already half over. Everyone present except her, Pastor Thompson and Craig had known something about Casper all along.

"After Casper and Orlando's father died, the property was divided, with each brother receiving half," Alice went on. "Casper, who was more like his father, wanted to respect his father's last wishes—to have the land be a natural habitat, a park, if you will. Orlando always thought his father had taken a tumble off his rocker about that one. What it came down to for him was selling the land and cashing in, or keeping it and leaving it as it was until the time was right to make the best deal for it."

"So Orlando would have gladly paved the land for a parking lot, and Casper wanted it to remain natural," concluded Vera.

"It was a nasty disagreement between them if I remember correctly," Fred said. "I was young, of course, but I remember that it created a horrible division between the brothers. I don't really blame Casper for not wanting to be out in public much after that. I think he got his fill of humanity back then."

"Like Cain and Abel," Jane reflected out loud. "Warring brothers. The older, Cain, intentionally chose to slight his Heavenly Father by offering a sacrifice of mediocre produce from his harvest. The younger, Abel, chose to do the best he could to honor God's wishes by willingly sacrificing his best animals. There are parallels, that's for sure. Hadn't Orlando wanted to sell the land even though he knew his father's desire would be that the sons keep it together? And Casper had been willing to do what it took to keep the land as his father had left it." She went on, "Hebrews 11:4 summed it up. 'By faith Abel offered God a better sacrifice than Cain did. By faith he was commended as a righteous man, when God spoke well of his offerings. And by faith he still speaks, even though he is dead.' Abel was willing to obey. Cain only grew more angry and jealous."

"You're right about those parallels, Jane, and the reference to Scripture makes that clear," Fred said.

"Was Casper a hermit back then?" Craig asked.

"No, he was quiet and very, very smart. But I wouldn't say he was a recluse, just something of a loner," Lloyd said.

"He never needed lots of people around him to get by. He'd go off hiking for days at a time," Fred added.

"He changed after that dreadful time with Orlando," Louise said softly.

Jane had almost forgotten that, of everyone in the room, her sister was most likely to know the answers to their questions. Silence hung in the room as everyone waited for her to continue. "It hurt him a great deal. I believe he became disillusioned with mankind. If his own brother could behave that way to his father and brother..." Louise shook her head. "He withdrew after that."

"And from you?" Jane asked softly.

"By then I was at the conservatory in Philadelphia to get my degree. I didn't return home very much after that. Later, when we were older . . . well, I had met Eliot by then . . ." Eliot Smith had been her music-theory teacher and later, her husband. "I didn't see Casper when I was home, but didn't think that much about it, I suppose." She was chagrined. "Youth is such a selfish time in life. Out of sight, out of mind where Casper was concerned."

"Out of everyone's sight and mind," Craig Tracy commented. "Amazing."

Out of the corner of her eye, Jane noticed Lloyd running his index finger around the inside of his collar, as if to allow himself some air. Unobtrusively she poured a glass of water from the pitcher and slid it in front of him. He picked it up and nodded his thanks.

"Are you all right?" she whispered.

"Hot, that's all." He tried to smile. "Hot under the collar."

He *was* very pink in the face. A flash of resentment ran through Jane. This situation was too much for a seventy-year-old man who loved this little place. Orlando Jones, with the help of his son, was managing to antagonize people even from his grave.

Jane realized how irate she felt toward this man whom—until recently—she'd never even heard of, and she regretted her angry spirit. She did, however, see how Orlando Jones could bring out the worst in people. It was happening right now, long after his death.

"Well, I suppose we really won't know more until we visit with the rest of Acorn Hill," Fred said. "If Joseph is right, and there are a lot of others who think new development would be okay, we might have to rethink this thing."

"Over my dead body," Lloyd growled. "While I'm mayor, I'll fight to keep things the same. I promised."

Viola, seeing Lloyd's distress, had the good sense to change the topic. "You will all be at Nine Lives tomorrow night, won't you?"

"What's going on?" Craig asked.

Viola glanced at him as if he had committed a felony by having to ask. "The reading, of course. A selection of Ben Franklin's essays and other writings. I decided to do it because Jane is always quoting Benjamin Franklin, and he certainly had a lot of clever things to say. I'm serving pie from the Coffee Shop, and Clarissa is making a cake in the shape of a kite in honor of Franklin's discovery of electricity. Won't that be nice?" She eyed Craig. "You will be there, won't you?"

"Wouldn't miss it," Craig hastened to say.

Viola looked around the table. "I'm sure none of you will want to miss it. It will be quite a social event."

"Who will be Benjamin Franklin?" Vera Humbert asked.

"Well, *I* will, of course." Viola looked as though she was puzzled by the question. "I've been told I have a wonderful stage voice and presence. Besides, other than Jane, I'm probably the most acquainted with the man."

"Of course," Vera said, hiding a smile. At least Viola wasn't trying to read Socrates or James Fenimore Cooper anymore. She had lost a lot of her crowd before she finished reading on those nights. She did, however, do a rather dramatic Edgar Allan Poe.

"Don't be late," she said as she stood and arranged one of her eye-catching scarves around her neck.

Soon all the guests had left except Lloyd and Ethel.

"Thanks, dears, for having this impromptu meeting," Ethel said. She had Lloyd by the arm and was steering him toward the door. He looked utterly exhausted by all that had transpired.

"Do you need a ride home, Lloyd?" Jane asked.

"No thanks. I have my car." He shook his head in amazement. "I just need some rest. Who'd have ever thought that this might happen?"

"Leave it alone for tonight, Lloyd," Ethel advised. "Don't let it keep you awake."

As Lloyd and Ethel walked out of the house, Jane heard him say, "Don't know how I can think of going to sleep at a time like this."

At first the sisters were silent in the kitchen as they cleaned up after the gathering.

"I'm worried about Lloyd," Jane said, finally breaking the silence.

"I'm worried about Aunt Ethel worrying about Lloyd," Alice added.

Louise was silent a long moment before saying, "And I'm worried about Casper Jones."

"Tell me more about him, Louise. I had no idea that he existed and certainly none that you'd seen him after you moved here."

Louise looked at Jane with a smile. "We ran into each other, that's all. And had a very nice visit for old times' sake. There isn't much more to tell. Casper was—and is—a very capable man. We had a good deal in common—music, literature, art. He was an artist at heart, I believe. It seemed he could do anything—paint, draw and sculpt. And it all came so naturally. He was a real Renaissance man."

"If he's so wonderful, why don't people seek him out? Why don't *you* seek him out?"

"Sometimes, I've discovered, that the more time one spends alone the less one desires to go out. It can seem unusual, even silly, what other people do. Casper isn't weird, but he is a solitary man. 'Live and let live,' he always said about his brother. 'Accept him as he is.' I think that's what Casper wants for himself also."

Chapter Ten

O n Thursday, the banker who had caused such a stir the night before did a disappearing act in the morning, Jane noticed. Some of the food that had been set out had been taken, but she had not even heard his footsteps across the dining room floor. The poor fellow had had no idea he would be walking into a firestorm the night before.

Jane didn't have much time to think about it, however, as her young friend Josie and Josie's mother, Justine, appeared at the door.

"Well, look who's here!" Jane opened her arms and Josie gave her a loving hug.

She put her hands on Jane's cheeks and asked, "Have you missed me?"

"Of course I have. Where were you yesterday?" Josie often stopped by to check the status of Jane's kitchen. She had an unerring nose for freshly baked cookies.

"We went shopping in Potterston yesterday and I got this new outfit."

Jane stood back so that she could study the new clothes. "Exercise clothing, I see." Josie wore a pale blue stretchy jacket and pants with a white stripe running down the outside of each leg and up the sides and arms of the jacket. "Very nice. Perfect for working out."

"You know I'm helping Mommy with her class," Josie reminded her.

Jane glanced at the cookie jar. "Would a few peanut butter cookies give you some energy for the class?"

Josie headed for the cookie jar. "I need *lots* of energy," she informed Jane as she managed to get four cookies into one hand.

"Josie..." her mother began.

"It's fine. Josie and I have a deal. I bake cookies, and she tells me if she likes them or not. Right, Josie?"

"I like these a lot," she mumbled, spitting cookie crumbs. "Where's Alice?"

Josie had taken a liking to all three Howard sisters. If Jane was busy, she often followed Alice or Louise around as they did chores around the inn.

"Cleaning upstairs. Why don't you go find her while your mom and I talk? Alice might even have a job for you."

Josie danced off happily. Already a hard worker like her mother, Josie felt proud to be given something to polish or dust.

"A cookie for you?" Jane moved the cookie jar to the table.

"I'd love to but I can't. Now that I'm teaching this class, I can't let my students see me with a tummy." Justine patted her flat stomach.

"I'll bet it's the only flat one in the room," Jane observed as she poured them each a cup of coffee.

Justine burst out laughing. "So far, but I have hope. I just love those people."

"It's really nice that you're doing this for the senior citizens. What motivated you to start?"

Justine poured cream into her coffee and stirred it thoughtfully. "I've been getting by since Josie and I moved to Acorn Hill—working for you, odd jobs around town, filling in for Sylvia when she wants to leave the store, even delivering flowers for Craig Tracy occasionally—but I don't have something that's *mine*. I saw an advertisement on a flyer that came from Potterston, saying I could get certified to teach classes like the one I'm leading. It wasn't terribly expensive, so I thought I'd give it a try." Justine's blue eyes began to twinkle. "And I loved it. What's more, it's perfect for me. I can teach classes as many nights a week as I can fill, or I can have three classes on one evening. It doesn't take away from anything I might do during the day, and it's at a place Josie can be with me. I don't need a babysitter, and I've discovered the older people love having her there. Right now, they aren't even charging me to use the room."

Justine shyly dropped her gaze as she continued. "I've always wanted something, some work, that's my own. This is it. My dream is that some day it could be a real business, with space for weights and exercise." She looked up again and her eyes were sparkling. "Wouldn't it be great to have a little gym and spa?"

"I'd be your first client," Jane said truthfully. "You have no idea how many nights after I'm done in the kitchen I could use a good massage and some stretching. It's a wonderful dream."

"I have lots to learn, but at least I can do it class by class."

"Is Acorn Hill big enough to hold your dream?"

Justine furrowed her brow as she considered the question. "Yes, and no. I'm already doing the senior aerobics class, and Vera Humbert has told me the teachers at school have expressed an interest in getting a class together. There are enough people in town to keep me busy, but, of course, not all of them are interested in 'hopping up and down and sweating' as a senior citizen told me at the Coffee Shop the other day."

"*Hmm.*"

"It turned out fine, though. Just as this woman was telling me that she didn't need me to help her lose weight, Hope Collins came along with a big piece of pie for her. Hope told her—pleasantly, of course—that maybe a small cookie might be a better choice if this woman wasn't

planning to take my exercise class. I didn't realize at first
that they were friends, but by the time they were done discussing the pie, the woman had enrolled in my new class."
Justine sighed. "I hope it's not going to be difficult. I wish
there were a few more people here in Acorn Hill. I love it
and would hate to be forced to leave it in order to establish
my business someplace where there are more potential
customers."

One point for the developers, Jane thought to herself.

Nine Lives was buzzing when Jane arrived. She sidled over
to the dessert table and eyed the delicacies.

Craig Tracy walked up beside her. "How nice that
you've come."

"I could hardly miss it. The way she's been talking,
Viola is doing this just for me. She knows how often I
quote Benjamin Franklin."

"For once I think one of these readings might be fun,"
Craig admitted. "Some of her other selected authors have
been less than . . . stimulating."

"You probably weren't here when she had a guest
reader, someone who'd written a book on the birds of
Pennsylvania. He spent the evening doing very bad imitations of many of those birds. It was quite exciting. We
thought maybe he'd pass out trying to do one bird call."

Craig laughed. "Well, let's see what Viola can do to poor old Ben."

But Benjamin Franklin was anything but poor old Ben, Jane mused, as Viola prepared to provide her tribute to his contributions to America. *Where would we be without him?*

In tough shape, that's for sure, she thought. *We wouldn't have bifocal glasses, for one thing. Louise has something to be grateful for right there. He's the one who invented the lightning rod and daylight savings time.* Jane frowned slightly at the thought of that last invention. She could have done just fine without daylight savings time. "Fall back" and "spring forward" usually kept her inner clock off for an entire month.

Franklin was the person who first organized a volunteer fire department, a subscription library and fire insurance. His paper printed the first American political cartoon—he really started something there—and the wood-burning stove that he invented is still named after him, the Franklin stove. What a man!

"'Certainty? In this world there is nothing certain but death and taxes.'" Viola's voice interrupted Jane's reverie. She had begun citing some of her favorite Franklin quotations. "'If you would know the value of money, go and try to borrow some.' 'Be always ashamed to catch thyself idle.' And one of Daniel Howard's favorites, 'A good example is the best sermon.'"

Jane remembered her father paraphrasing that. "Christ is in us," he would say. "He's living through us, and it should show, Jane. We might be the only sermon someone ever hears."

She had interrogated him on that point, she remembered. "What do you mean, Dad?"

"Have you ever met someone who simply seems to shine from the inside out, who stands out just because of his manner?"

"Sure." She had started listing people she knew from the church and family friends before adding, "And you."

That exchange had stayed with her all these years.

"'Tricks and treachery are the practice of fools, that don't have brains enough to be honest,'" Viola carried on, finding her stage voice in fine form. "'Early to bed and early to rise makes a man healthy, wealthy and wise.'"

She really built up steam during an essay on why Franklin thought that the rattlesnake would be a good symbol for America:

She has no eyelids. She may be therefore esteemed an emblem of vigilance. She never begins an attack, nor, when once engaged, ever surrenders . . . she never wounds 'till she has generously given notice, even to her enemy, and cautioned him against the danger of treading on her . . . I confess I was wholly at a loss what to make of the rattles, 'till I went back and counted them and found them just thirteen, exactly the number of the Colonies united in America; and I recollected too that this was the only part of the Snake which increased in numbers . . . She strongly resembles America in this, that she is beautiful in youth and her beauty increaseth with her age, 'her tongue also is blue and forked as the lightning, and her abode is among impenetrable rocks.

Jane was mesmerized. It wasn't until Craig Tracy whispered in her ear that she remembered where she was or whom she was with.

"Maybe Viola should take some of Ben's advice, 'Speak little, do much,'" he whispered.

After the reading, everyone gathered to have dessert and discuss the reading.

"One of your best readings ever, Viola. Right up there with Edgar Allan Poe," Fred Humbert said, patting her on the back encouragingly. "I never get tired of hearing about Ben Franklin."

"This was even more entertaining than the fellow with the bird imitations," Lloyd said enthusiastically. For the moment, at least, he had forgotten Acorn Hill's problems. "You've done yourself proud."

"Yes, I should say so," Wilhelm Wood said.

"Wilhelm, where have you been all week?" Alice asked. "We've missed you at Time for Tea." Alice purchased a good bit of tea for the inn from Wilhelm's store.

"I decided to take a few days to spend in New Mexico. Lovely place. Such rugged, impressive land. And the best food I've eaten, other than Jane's."

"I make a respectable burrito," Jane commented.

"Is that an invitation for dinner?" Wilhelm teased. He and Jane often spent time together to talk about his travels and his love of California, Jane's home before returning to Acorn Hill.

"Absolutely. We can set the date later."

"I'll count on it." Wilhelm looked around the room. "What else has happened since I left?"

Jane quickly summarized the situation with Orlando Jones's son, the developers, the bankers and the contentious town meeting.

"I just can't leave for a minute without something exciting happening, can I?" Wilhelm didn't seem terribly distressed by the news that Fairy Pond might be in danger.

"Aren't you concerned?"

He looked at Jane pensively, making an imposing figure with his graying blond hair and tall frame. He lifted one eyebrow. "Why should I be?"

"Because of the impact on Acorn Hill, of course."

He shrugged his shoulders. "I'm not here that much

anyway. Besides, it's probably time something breathed a little progress into this place. It's been the same forever."

And that's why we like it, Jane thought, but she didn't speak. She was surprised at how little Wilhelm seemed to mind what was going on.

Seeing the perplexity on her face, Wilhelm took Jane's hands in his own and looked into her eyes. "Don't get me wrong, Jane. I love this place. Frankly, though it wouldn't hurt for Time for Tea to have more traffic, it does just fine as it is." He glanced around the room. "But it might be nice to have enough people traveling through to support a couple more restaurants and a motel." He looked at her askance. "Not that I'd want to take any business away from you."

"The inn will be just fine either way, Wilhelm," Jane assured him, but she did have a sinking feeling in her stomach. "People just passing through don't always want the amenities of a bed-and-breakfast. They usually are in more of a hurry than that. It's about the pond itself that I'm concerned."

"I haven't been out to that pond in years. I always thought of it as a large puddle, frankly."

"Then you have no idea what we might lose, Wilhelm. It's beautiful out there. I paint there quite often, and the place has meant a lot to many people around town."

Wilhelm, still unconvinced, said, "I love history and I love progress, Jane. Why, I …" he paused and then began to chuckle. "Do you know, I believe my mother once told me that she and my father had their first date skating at that pond. I'd almost forgotten."

"See? Are you beginning to understand that Fairy Pond is a part of our history that we don't want destroyed?"

Again, Wilhelm pondered the question. "Frankly, I'll have to get back to you on that, Jane. We aren't residing in a living museum, you know. We'll just have to sit down and weigh the pros and cons."

Despite the pleasant mood the readings about Benjamin Franklin had created for her, Jane had a bad feeling about what was happening. As she walked home, she thought about Wilhelm's words. Just because she didn't agree with him, that didn't make him wrong. Obviously some *did* think that it was time that Acorn Hill open itself to the perils of progress. Jane remembered how Viola had come to the inn to tell them the news. "Speeding cars. Strangers everywhere. Burglars. Stoplights," she had said.

Suddenly Jane felt guilty for not having taken Viola more seriously that evening.

Chapter Eleven

I can't believe I have to play for this wedding tomorrow, right in the midst of everything else that is going on," Louise commented over breakfast the next morning. "Here it is, already Friday. I know Pastor Ken agreed out of the goodness of his heart, but—"

"Louise, playing for a wedding is—pardon the pun—a piece of cake, for you. You could do it with your eyes shut and…" Jane grinned. "Well, maybe you couldn't do it with one arm tied behind your back."

"That's not the least of it."

Jane glanced suspiciously at her sister. There was something in her tone.

"I have done something foolish. I agreed to something without consulting you."

Jane tilted her head to one side. "And?"

"Pastor Ken spoke to me yesterday. With all the commotion going on I had forgotten. He told me that the wedding on Saturday is *very* small and that they've mentioned a number of times how sorry they are that there are no rooms available at the inn for Saturday night."

"I thought we discussed this already," Jane said. "We have others here. We really don't have a place for more guests."

"But we do have room downstairs to host a small wedding reception. Correct?"

"Louie…"

"Something very small, Jane," Louise hurried on. "Just a cake and coffee would be fine. We can't send a young couple off on their honeymoon without some sort of celebration. Can we?"

Jane sighed. "Maybe I could, but obviously you can't. How many people are we talking here?"

Louise brightened immediately. "The couple, their parents, two bridesmaids, two groomsmen, an aunt and uncle and a few friends. Probably no more than twenty."

Jane smiled at Louise and patted her arm. "I can do *that* with one hand tied behind *my* back. We'll have cake, of course, and probably some minicroissants filled with chicken salad, a light pasta salad of some sort, fruit, nuts and punch. What color are the bridesmaids' dresses? Maybe Clarissa could make the cake, and I'll choose the punch accordingly."

Louise hugged her sister. "I knew you would come

through! Thanks so much. I know this is sudden, but it will mean so much to the family, and the extra income will be a blessing."

"What are chefs for?" Jane responded with resignation. "I suppose I'd better start a grocery list."

Their guests, the banker and two developers, had made themselves scarce. The sisters only knew they were in the house by the missing food and occasional footsteps on the stairs. Jane had given up trying to catch them in the dining room. The three must have had radar that told them when she was coming through. Once, she had seen them get into a car and drive toward Potterston. Although she would have loved to find out what was going on, they had given her no opportunity.

"It's none of my business anyway," she muttered.

In the grocery store earlier, Jane had overheard several conversations, speculations about what might be happening and how it would affect Acorn Hill. They ranged from the probable to the ludicrous. Remembering what Wilhelm had said about weighing the "pros and cons," she decided to start a list of each and see where she ended up. With a mug of tea and a pen and paper, she headed to the kitchen table.

She stared at the paper a long time before deciding that it might be best to start with the cons.

Cons:

1. Stoplights, burglars, strangers and dangerous traffic (Viola)
2. Destroy Fairy Pond
   A. The pond has historical significance
   B. Emotional significance
      1. Saves my sanity
      2. Saves Sylvia's sanity too
      3. Lots of people have wonderful memories of pond
      4. Uncle Bob and Aunt Ethel engaged there!
      5. What about Casper Jones's home?
   C. Environmental significance
      1. Can't be recreated
      2. Land is disappearing too rapidly as it is
      3. What about the *animals*?
   D. This will push us down the slippery slope toward becoming just like everyone else
   E. Wreck quality of life
   F. Increase dissension and hard feelings among citizens (or is it already too late?)

Jane chewed on her pencil. Or could it be that it would improve their quality of life? Who knew? Even she wasn't sure anymore.

G. Gas stations are ugly

H. It might devastate Lloyd Tynan

That, Jane realized, might be the worst of all—how upset Lloyd would be. She wasn't sure he could even wrap his mind around the possibility of Acorn Hill's changing dramatically. But that was exactly what would happen if the state decided to expand the road through Acorn Hill. Then a gas station with a convenience store would seem small in comparison.

She started, unenthusiastically, with the other list.

Pros:

1. Good for business (Joseph and Rachel Holzmann)

2. Wilhelm Wood, who is sensible, is in favor of it

3. Would ensure that Acorn Hill stays on the map a little longer

4. Good for inn guests who need gas or sundries

5. Would draw more guests

6. Might provide needed income for local economy

It was not as black-and-white as she had hoped it would be. Unless there was a deciding factor, something that radically tipped the scales one way or the other, the town was likely to be divided right down the middle on the issue.

"Poor Lloyd," Jane murmured. "Poor Fairy Pond."

⌒

"I'll be back soon," Jane said that evening as she picked up her purse.

"Where are you going?" Louise asked.

"Justine invited me to check out her exercise class again, the one Lloyd and Aunt Ethel attend. It's an opportunity I just can't miss."

"Does she want you to join?" Louise asked with feigned innocence.

"Oh, *I'm* much too young. Class members have to be seventy or older." She eyed her sisters. "But *you* are close to the right age."

"Don't bring that up!" Alice scolded. "I feel twenty-five and I plan to stay that way."

"A good reason for exercising. Want to come along— just to watch? You don't have to sign on the dotted line tonight."

Smiling, Alice and Louise followed Jane out the door, curiosity getting the best of them.

When they reached the church basement, they opened the door and were nearly blasted backward by the sound of recorded music accompanying the strenuous human activity.

"Lift your hands over your head, that's right. Clap, clap. Step, step. Other way, dear. Good job! Keep breathing, everyone. Don't hold it. You need to be able to follow the steps and breathe at the same time…"

Jane noticed that Justine had given that direction just in time. Ethel, in her efforts to execute the exercises properly, was holding her breath until her cheeks puffed up and a vein showed on her forehead.

Justine's class was growing. A couple whom Jane didn't recognize were intently trying to make their feet cooperate, and Martha Bevins, an older churchwoman at Grace Chapel, looked surprisingly limber as she bent at the waist. The exercises wouldn't even have stirred Jane's blood, but for people of this age and physical condition, Justine had created a perfect stretching workout.

The one who didn't seem to be enjoying himself was Lloyd. He was wearing his pumpkin orange sweatshirt and halfheartedly following Justine's directions, but his eyes were unfocused, and he didn't seem to be listening very well. Occasionally he realized that he wasn't keeping up with the rest and changed exercises, but for the most part, his thoughts seemed to be directed elsewhere.

"I know where Lloyd's at," Alice whispered. "His mind is miles away."

"Or not so many," Louise added. "His mind is at Fairy Pond and the Jones brothers' land."

"I think he's lost weight," Jane observed.

They all stared at Lloyd's generous stomach. The orange sweatshirt didn't stretch quite as tightly as usual over the bulge of his belly.

"I believe you are right," Louise remarked. "I noticed that at Viola's reading at Nine Lives, he didn't even go to the dessert table."

"Nerves," Alice deduced. "That will do it every time."

"I hope this isn't too much for him," Jane said.

"I'm glad he's trying to take better care of himself," Louise said. "Maybe the reason he didn't eat any desserts is that he's dieting."

"I think I would have heard about that," Jane commented. Then Justine asked the class to pull chairs into the middle of the room to support them while they did leg lifts, and the sisters' attention was diverted.

Louise and Alice left immediately after the class ended, but Jane stayed around to talk to Justine.

"You have an enthusiastic class," she commented.

"They're the best. So cute and so eager to get this right. I have such admiration for their spirit. I hope I'm that way when I reach seventy."

"And they like you too. I can tell."

Justine slipped on a hooded jacket. "I'm going to the Coffee Shop with Josie. I promised her a piece of pie. Would you like to come?"

"I'd love it."

Since none of them—Jane, Justine or Josie—needed to watch their figures, the pie turned into an entire meal with burgers, fries and an order of onion rings.

"I hope none of my class comes in to see this," Justine said. "I've been encouraging them to watch their fat intake."

"I *like* fat," Josie announced as she patted her stomach. "And I don't have any."

"Just keep it that way, my little lady. We can't eat like this all the time."

When Josie wandered off to chat with a young friend, Justine spoke. "I'm glad we're doing this. I've wanted to talk to you."

"About what?"

"I'm a little concerned about Lloyd in my class. Your Aunt Ethel is doing well, but Lloyd is very distracted. He just doesn't seem to have the enthusiasm that the others have."

"He's got a lot on his mind."

"I know. I hope that's it. I love those people and don't want things to go wrong for them."

"You are a true gift from God, Justine." Jane took the younger woman's hand and squeezed it tightly. "Thank you for caring so much."

Saturday morning, Troy Landers, Sam Horton and Philip Crane checked out of the inn a day early. Jane was busy preparing food for the wedding, Louise was at Grace Chapel working on her music and Alice had decided to do some decorating and was stringing white lights wrapped in white netting over the tops of the windows in the dining room.

"By the way," she said, when Jane walked into the room, "since our other guests left a day early, I told the bride and groom that the rooms would be available for the convenience of all at the reception. They were so pleased."

"That's wonderful, and I can't say I miss those fellows who were here. I didn't like the way they behaved. It was…" Jane searched for a word. "…sneaky."

"They didn't like all the questions people were asking them. I'm sure they weren't very popular with a lot of people in town."

"It's not really their fault," Jane pointed out. "They were just the closest target. I wish Orlando Jones's son Raymond would come. He's the one we need to talk to."

Alice shook her head sadly. "I doubt we'll see him. He doesn't care about the people of Acorn Hill. He doesn't even come to see his Uncle Casper."

"I think Casper should try to do something about this."

"That's asking a lot, Jane, from a man who doesn't want to be around people and dislikes confrontation."

"Is he . . ." Jane didn't want to sound harsh but she needed to know. ". . . a coward?"

Louise chose that moment to return from the church. "Casper? A coward? Hardly. He served in the military and was awarded several honors. But he is a sensitive man. I believe that the troubles with his family drove him underground."

"Then isn't it time for him to come out?"

"His nephew is still causing trouble, even from a distance, Jane. You see that. Besides, Casper was always very independent. He's quite brilliant. He told me once that he never minded being alone because he was always too busy to notice. He was always happiest reading, building something or inventing something."

"So his life is just the way he wants it?" Jane could hardly imagine.

"Apparently."

"I still think someone needs to talk to him."

"Lloyd has said he will do it."

"Lloyd has taken on everything."

"Not quite," Alice corrected. "I could use a little help stringing these lights."

Jane wished she could have been at Grace Chapel with Louise and Alice for the wedding, especially when she saw the lovely bride with long dark hair and a slender silk column of a dress climb out of the limousine.

The groom had arrived earlier with some of the family members. He looked handsome and nervous pacing outside the church as Jane put the final touches on the food and table, mostly fragile flowers and a few extra satin ribbons. She observed him peeking at his watch and looking down the road for his bride-to-be. She smiled when he saw the limo on the horizon and ducked into the church to be sure he didn't see her before the ceremony.

That was the trouble with Jane's being a behind-the-scenes person at special events—"behind the scenes" usually meant being too far from the action.

The wedding, according to Louise when she returned

to the inn, was lovely. "They'll be here soon. Is everything ready?"

It certainly was. The house was decked out in festive lights, white bows and netting, the equivalent of diamond jewelry on an already lovely lady's neck. Clarissa's cake, decorated in pink and yellow, was another of her masterpieces. Jane had matched the color of the punch to the pink roses and an ice ring of strawberries and edible flowers floated in the center of the bowl. The effect was stunning, and as the wedding party arrived, the sisters enjoyed their expressions of gratitude and amazement.

One by one, introductions were made.

"I'm Nino Angelo, the groom's father, and this is my wife Maria." Nino then introduced them to the other new in-laws, while the bride and groom and their friends were off admiring the inn.

As usual, the sisters made sure the party was running smoothly and then faded discreetly into the background.

The festivities lasted far beyond the departure of the bride and groom on their honeymoon. It was late when Mr. Angelo came to find Louise, Jane and Alice in the kitchen. There were tears in his eyes as he pumped their hands. "You not only saved us a lot of confusion by allowing us to be here on such short notice, but you also made this a perfect wedding for our kids." He paused. "I feel God in this place. What a fine way to start out in married life. If there is ever anything, and I mean *anything*, I can do to return this favor, let me know."

"It's our pleasure," Louise assured him. "And God *is* here. I'm glad you sensed Him." To Louise's surprise, Mr. Angelo suddenly gathered her into his arms and gave her a hug.

Jane nearly giggled at the pop-eyed surprise and pleasure on Louise's face.

"*Anything*," Nino said. "Now you remember that."

Later, as they sat around the kitchen table doing a cheerful postmortem of the party, Alice gave a gusty sigh. "Amazing, isn't it? How different our guests are from each other? Mr. Angelo was so appreciative and enthusiastic over every little thing. Jane, he thought your food was out of this world."

"And then there is Genevieve Thrumble," Louise said, wincing. "She left a mark on the inn in quite a different way."

"And I'm grateful for every single one of them," Jane said. "Even the Thrumbles. God has given us the opportunity to see quite a spectrum of humanity, hasn't He?"

"That is one way to look at it," Louise said doubtfully.

"And best of all, today the wedding was a rousing success," Alice proclaimed.

"No wonder I'm so tired," Jane groaned. "I don't know about the rest of you, but for me it's time for bed."

Chapter Twelve

*J*ane," Louise said as she breezed by the kitchen door early Monday morning. "Pastor Ken is bringing me a thank-you letter from the people in the wedding party. Apparently Mr. and Mrs. Angelo wanted us to get it as soon as possible. I told him it would be fine if he came for supper."

Then she came back to ask, "It is all right, isn't it?"

"If he likes macaroni and cheese. It's a simple meal tonight, but I made a lot."

"Your macaroni and cheese is hardly *simple*. How many types of cheese do you use in it?"

"Four."

"And those exotic pasta shapes? And pure cream? Not simple at all."

"If you say so. I just hope that—"

"Oh, Jane, dear. Aunt Ethel called last night. She sounded so forlorn that I asked her and Lloyd to join us for dinner too. He hasn't had much time to spend with her, and I believe she's getting lonely. Now, what was that you were saying?"

"I was saying that I hoped Lloyd and Aunt Ethel wouldn't drop by. It's a terrible meal for people on diets."

"Portion control," Louise said firmly. "That's all there is to it."

Easier said than done, Jane thought after her sister had gone. Louise was a highly disciplined woman, professional and meticulous about all the parts of her life. *She* could manage portion control. Jane wasn't so sure about Ethel and Lloyd.

She sat down on a stool by the counter to frost a German chocolate cake that she had made from scratch. Coconut, pecans and chocolate were a heady combination, and she would ordinarily cut a piece for herself immediately, but now the cake had to be intact for dinner.

Louise was puzzling her a good deal these days. This thing with Casper Jones had Jane stumped. There had obviously been some strong feeling between the two of them at one time. Louise was still protective of him, not letting anyone say anything derogatory about him or his dealings with his brother Orlando.

She had acknowledged seeing him since she moved back to Acorn Hill. Did she still love him? That thought struck Jane like a slap. In some ways, she supposed her sister did. Might she have any influence over him? Could she get him to do something about his nephew? Jane drew herself up short. Now she was considering manipulation to settle this Fairy Pond issue. For Louise to approach Casper after all these years would be out-and-out exploitation of their once-close relationship.

Jane sighed as she swirled the delectably rich frosting over the cake. Perhaps, with any luck at all, Raymond Jones would decide this little place was not worth troubling himself over, and he would lose interest and leave them all alone.

That was a pipe dream if there ever was one, Jane was to think later.

Pastor Thompson was first to arrive for dinner, and, since Louise and Alice were busy upstairs, Jane put him to work setting the table.

While he was busy, she opened the envelope that he had been kind enough to deliver. She read out loud:

Dear Ladies of Grace Chapel Inn,

We want to express our sincere gratitude for welcoming our friends and family with open arms. Your faith is lived out in action, and we feel blessed to have had the chance to meet you and enjoy your lovely inn.

All the members of our wedding party are grateful for your many kindnesses. You will long remain in our prayers.

With warm regards,
The Angelos

Jane looked up. "How sweet!"

"People do see your faith shining through," Pastor Thompson commented. "And it is obvious that people love you for it. You have people dropping in on a regular basis. I'm amazed that you and your sisters aren't exhausted."

"Do you think it's our witty conversation and charming personalities, or do you think it has something to do with the food?" Jane teased.

"A little of each. There's so much gossip flying around town that even Hope Collins at the Coffee Shop told me she couldn't keep it straight. I think the conversations here at the inn are much more appreciated. You and your sisters don't spread wild rumors."

"Wow! Then the gossip is getting to be a real problem."

Pastor Thompson paused in his work with a bunch of spoons in his hand. "It may be, but *this* place remains a haven where people can talk and not hear themselves quoted all over town. I see people every day who are upset because a neighbor or friend doesn't agree with them about what should or shouldn't happen to Acorn Hill."

"It doesn't seem there's much we *can* do about it either way."

"That doesn't matter as much as that, for once, there's genuine animosity building among the residents. I hate to see it, Jane."

"Me too. Maybe tonight will be a break from all that."

That turned out to be a serious miscalculation.

❦

There was a commotion on the front porch, and Jane heard Alice and Louise running down the stairs to see what was going on. She and Pastor Thompson exchanged a concerned glance and dropped what they were doing to hurry toward the hall.

Jane, who had never been quite sure what the word *apoplectic* meant, knew a moment later.

Lloyd and Ethel had arrived and were standing outside on the porch. Lloyd was definitely apoplectic—seething and spitting mad. His face was almost as red as Ethel's hair.

"Look at this—ganging up on us, that's what they're doing!" Lloyd sputtered.

Ethel held her hands to her cheeks as she observed Lloyd and muttered, "Oh my, oh dear, oh dear. Now, calm down, Lloyd. You don't want to pop a vessel."

"I'll pop something, that's for sure. Why, I'd like to pop that young Jones in the nose. And the mayor of Potterston while I'm at it."

"What's going on?" Jane asked.

"Lloyd just got around to looking at his mail before we were to come here, and . . ." Ethel looked dismayed. "It doesn't seem to be very good news."

"Another understatement," Jane heard Pastor Thompson say beneath his breath.

"Let's just sit down and gather our wits about us," Alice suggested. "And then you can tell us all about it."

Lloyd made his way to the dining room table, his anger unabated. He waved two envelopes and sheets of paper in the air. "Look at this, just look at this!"

"It's hard to read a moving target, Lloyd," Jane said. "Why don't you just tell us what they say?"

"One is from the mayor of Potterston reminding me of the Chamber of Commerce's consideration of a proposal to join Potterston in a campaign to draw more tourists to the area. Even if we don't go in with them—and I don't think we should—it's going to change everything. Their letter says they've hired someone to lead the campaign and will go at it 'with all the funds at our disposal.' Traffic snarls, too little parking, it will create a need for more law enforcement and cause an uproar when people find tourists taking up parking spaces so they can look around. We pride ourselves on being a peaceful town. We don't want a bunch of tourists disturbing us."

"That's really not *such* an unreasonable letter, Lloyd," Pastor Thompson said gently. "You already knew what they were up to."

"I suppose." Lloyd's shoulders relaxed a little. "But I

still don't like it. They're planning to go ahead with the campaign whether we join them or not. People and traffic will likely drift over here anyway."

"If you can't lick them, join them," Alice said practically. "Maybe we could promote our fine churches."

Lloyd scowled, not yet ready to listen to a positive approach to the situation.

It occurred to Jane that Lloyd hadn't been himself for some days now. She missed his jolly mood and even the size of his appetite. Now he was forgetting to eat meals; the old Lloyd often managed to sneak in a couple of extras.

"What about the other letter?" Louise asked.

They were all surprised to see Lloyd sneer before he answered. "It's a letter from a lawyer out in California, telling us that we are 'fortunate' enough to have someone planning to develop property in our town. He says his client is proceeding with due diligence and plans to follow 'the letter of the law' moving ahead. He wants information on how to proceed. He hopes that the town of Acorn Hill and his client will have a 'long and equitable' relationship and that—this is the killer—he, as the attorney, hopes he will not be required to use any legal action in getting the client's project up and running."

Lloyd crumpled the letter in his fist.

"Was that a veiled threat?" Louise gasped.

"It certainly sounded like one."

"Raymond Jones *is* just like his father. He doesn't miss a trick."

"So what this letter is really saying," Jane attempted to clarify, "is that everything will be dandy as long as Acorn Hill agrees with everything this client wants."

"And they'll make trouble if we don't?" Louise asked.

"How dare they!" Ethel sputtered.

"They dare because they have the right," Pastor Thompson said gently. "If Raymond Jones owns land around Fairy Pond free and clear and the zoning is appropriate, he can do what he wants on that land."

Jane glanced at Lloyd and was shocked. It was as if he had shrunk before her eyes. He looked all of his seventy-plus years and then some. Her heart went out to him. The poor fellow was just doing something he believed in—protecting this town from too many outside influences—and he had come face to face with what seemed to be a very large business machine. And, by the look of him, Lloyd was beginning to see the scope of what was ahead.

Jane was putting away the last of the serving pieces and straightening the chairs around the table when she heard a tiny knock at the door. It was Ethel, a long coat thrown over her bathrobe.

"What are you doing here so late?" Jane asked as she

opened the door. "Alice and Louise are already in bed—and it looks like you were too."

"I couldn't sleep, dear. I need someone to talk to."

"I'm available. Come in." Jane led her aunt into the study. Surrounded by books and other memories of Daniel Howard, it seemed the place to be. Ethel obviously needed calming, and this was the most comforting place in the house.

"What's going on, Aunt Ethel?"

Ethel's hands fluttered to her face in agitation. "It's Lloyd."

Jane waited quietly.

"Something has happened to him ever since this development issue over Fairy Pond came up. He's not the same man. He's short-tempered, impatient, intolerant. And he's lost his sense of humor completely. He used to be such an..." Ethel blushed. "...affectionate man. And now he's like an old lion with a thorn in his paw." She crossed her arms over her chest and announced. "He's gotten so *annoying*."

Then her head drooped. "And I'm worried about him."

Jane's heart went out to her aunt. Lloyd had been "escorting" her around for some time now. "Lloyd and Ethel" had become as common a phrase around town as "cream and sugar" or "pie and ice cream." Lloyd made Aunt Ethel's life far less lonely and vice versa. She, in her own way, was suffering as much as her friend.

"Maybe Pastor Ken would spend some time with him."

"He's tried. Lloyd keeps shooing him out of the mayor's office, saying he's too busy to think about himself."

"Then Pastor Ken should go to Lloyd's house...or yours. Lloyd might be more receptive to what Pastor Ken is saying if he realizes how much it affects you as well."

Ethel looked doubtful. "Lloyd has a very thick head for a sweet man. Stubborn as a mule, that man."

"And you care a great deal for him and don't want to see him like this."

Ethel's eyes welled with tears. "Exactly."

"We'll pray about it."

"I've been praying. And praying, and praying and—"

Jane reached for Ethel's hands. "Let's do it right now."

They both quieted, and then Jane began to speak. "Dear Lord, our friend Lloyd is miserable right now. He's so loyal to the citizens of this place and wants to do what is best. I believe he's getting overwhelmed, Lord. Help him through this. Give him the insight to know what to do and the wisdom to realize that he can't take all this so personally. And help Aunt Ethel to be strong for him, Lord. Thank You that we can come to You in our time of need. Amen."

Ethel sniffled and wiped a tear from her eye. "Thank you, dear."

"We'll both keep praying. Maybe we should be praying

that Lloyd learns to control his emotions so that they don't get so far out of hand."

"Amen to that." Ethel got to her feet and opened her arms to Jane. Hugging her niece as if there were no tomorrow, Ethel said, "I'm so glad you came back to Acorn Hill. I don't know what I'd do without you."

Jane watched Ethel make the short trip to her own house. "I'm glad I came back to Acorn Hill too, Auntie," she whispered. "I'm not sure what I would have done without all of you either."

Chapter Thirteen

"Do you need anything from the hardware store? Time for Tea? Anywhere? I'm going to town." Jane called up the stairs to Louise. It was Tuesday, and some of her errands were long overdue.

Louise appeared at the top of the stairs.

"I'm going to see Viola at Nine Lives when I'm done with these chores," Louise added. "If I think of anything, I can pick it up myself."

"I'm going to stop at Sylvia's Buttons and a few other places, so I'll be gone awhile," Jane called back as she left the house.

She waved to Jose Morales, who was trimming the shrubbery around Grace Chapel, and said hello to Clara Horn, who was walking her potbellied pig Daisy. Daisy was thriving under Clara's care, and, if pigs could smile, Jane was sure she would be doing it right now. Her little hooves clipped along the sidewalk and . . . could it be? Had Daisy had a *manicure*? No, Clara seemed to have put stickers of flowers on those little black hooves, but Daisy was definitely more dressed up than usual.

Jane glanced at her own hands and realized she had forgotten to put on hand lotion. She sighed. Daisy's feet looked in better shape than her hands, which were roughened from chopping ingredients and too much hot dishwater.

She couldn't do anything about her overworked hands at the moment, but she could take a few minutes for herself before she began her errands. Instead of going directly to Fred's Hardware and the General Store, she turned left to the Coffee Shop and went inside.

Hope Collins was working, expertly "slinging hash," as she called it, carrying a big tray of food in one hand and pouring coffee to patrons along the way.

"Hey, Jane. I'll be right with you. We still have a piece of blackberry pie. Ice cream on that?"

Although she wasn't terribly hungry, Jane enjoyed eating food she hadn't had to cook—especially the Coffee Shop's pie. "Sure."

Hope brought the pie and then returned with two cups and a coffee pot. "Mind if I join you? It's my break time and my feet are killing me."

"I'd love it."

Hope sank down into the seat across from Jane with a sigh. "I can't remember the last time my feet were so sore. It's been crazy in here the past couple days."

"What's the occasion?" Jane took the coffee mug in both hands, closed her eyes and inhaled the delicious aroma. The only coffee she had ever found that she liked as well as this was her own. It had taken years of combining beans and experimenting with brewing before she came up with her own private blend.

"Where have you been? On a ship at sea? Everyone is in here because of the flap over Raymond Jones and the land at Fairy Pond. Nobody wants to talk about anything else."

"Oh, that."

"Aren't you interested?"

"Very, but I hate to see our community bickering." Jane stared at Hope. "What do you think about the whole thing?"

"If it happens, it happens. I'd rather it didn't. I could live with another gas station. The Dairyland gas station isn't that big. Of course, I've never seen more than two or three cars in line at a time, which tells me it's serving us just fine. And I'd hate to see it run out of business. They can fix anything that's wrong with a vehicle, and you can trust them to do it economically and well. That's worth a lot to me. Seems to me the fellows wanting to build this thing— the 'white elephant,' as Mayor Tynan calls it—must be pretty sure that the state is going to enlarge that road that leads to Acorn Hill and so more traffic comes this way."

"And Potterston is already drawing up an advertising campaign to bring more tourists into the area."

"We're probably the only town in Pennsylvania trying to *stop* progress," Hope said. "Does that mean that we've got things all wrong...or all right?"

"I don't know. I'm not so afraid for the town itself as I am for Fairy Pond. It's such a beautiful place, and the ecology is so delicate. I think we'd be losing something wonderful if bulldozers went in there and did their worst. The wildlife and the birds, what would happen to all that?"

"I'm sorry to say it, but I don't think many people have really considered that," Hope said. "You know how it is. Everyone is asking the question 'What's in it for me?' You either find a way you'll benefit or not. If you see a big advantage from having Acorn Hill grow, then that's what you want." Hope leaned forward and whispered, "I think June is kind of excited about the prospect."

June Carter owned the Coffee Shop and was Hope's employer.

"It makes sense," Jane admitted. "You'd have a lot more customers here if we had more traffic."

"Good for June, bad for my feet," Hope said pragmatically. "My friend Betsy Long thinks it would be exciting. I don't know exactly what she's expecting, but I'm afraid she might be disappointed." Hope leaned back in the booth and rolled the coffee mug between the palms of her hands.

"I do understand why Zack and Nancy Colwin like the idea. They've got a nice supper club that would definitely attract people."

Jane sighed. "It's so complicated. How can we stay as we are and still move forward?"

Hope shrugged helplessly. "You've got me there."

Jane put some money on the table. "Thanks for the visit. I should probably be on my way."

"And I ought to polish up the coffee machine. June likes it sparkling." Hope looked at Jane with sympathetic eyes. "Don't worry, Jane. You better than anyone should know that God can take care of it. He knows what's best. All of us will just have to ask Him to help us out."

"Thanks, Hope. I needed to hear that."

As she walked out into the sunshine, she thought about what Hope had said. Prayer was the clear way to go here. And, Jane thought guiltily, here was a test of her faith that she had not expected. When one asks God to do something, one has to know that He will do what's best—whether we always like what that is or not.

Jane stopped at the Acorn Antique Shop next. Joseph Holzmann was nowhere to be seen, but his wife Rachel was sitting at the back of the store reading a magazine. As usual, Rachel looked lovely, her dark hair held up with Victorian hatpins. She always dressed well for her customers. Jane knew that the antique shop wasn't always bustling but that they had some very wealthy customers who purchased items regularly.

"Hi. Quiet today?"

Rachel looked up and smiled. "Hello, Jane. Good to see you. Can I help you with something special today?"

"No, I'm just taking a few minutes for myself. I had coffee with Hope and I wanted to say hello to you."

"How nice. Joseph is gone, and it's very boring here today. I'm glad for a visitor."

"How's business?" Jane asked with concern.

"Okay. At least it's all right on one end. The shop has built a reputation for fine things and outstanding service. Thanks to Joseph, we do a lot of business with people in Philadelphia and even out of state. If a customer wants something special, he knows that if we don't have it, we will look until we find it."

"So the store isn't your only moneymaker?"

"No, but I wish it could be. I love having people come in and discover something they love. We've talked about moving the store to someplace bigger, but we just can't leave Acorn Hill."

Jane glanced around the lovely space and could appreciate what Rachel was saying. This was a store that could rival those in a large city. She understood why the Holzmanns were eager to have more walk-in traffic.

When she said good-bye and walked again into the

sunlight, Jane's head was spinning. She was "getting it," the differing reasons behind the dissension. But understanding the conflict more fully only made her more concerned that whatever happened, there would be an element in Acorn Hill left unhappy.

She stopped at the bakery to order goods for the inn and then wandered into Sylvia's Buttons around the corner. Sylvia was in the back, standing over her cutting table where a quilt was taking shape—a huge quilt, from the look of the stacks of cut fabric lined up on the table. Sylvia was frowning.

"Hi. Troubles?" Jane admired the piece of the quilt that was completed. "It looks great."

"There's a fabric in there I don't like. The color seems ... off." Sylvia pointed at a marigold yellow floral. "Too ... too something."

"Looks too much like mustard?" Jane asked.

"That's it! I don't want any mustard in this quilt." Sylvia put her hands on her hips. "I'm afraid I'll have to change it. What a job."

"Better now than when the whole thing is done," Jane said.

"Thanks for not trying to talk me out of changing it. You're the only one who really understands color and how it can bug you if it's not right."

Jane chuckled. "I won't tell you how many times I've

painted over a canvas just because I wasn't satisfied with a color. Changing a quilt is just a little more obvious to the outside observer."

"Other than helping me, what are you up to?" Sylvia picked up a bolt of fabric in a soft, golden yellow and held it up to the other fabrics. "Now that's more like it."

"I'm taking the long way to Fred's Hardware to pick up some scissors I ordered. Among other errands, I'm going to post a letter to the courthouse in Potterston to see if they have a copy of the property taxes paid on the inn. We're working on our budget and trying to gather copies of all our payments and expenses. Alice couldn't find the originals, so I thought I'd help her out."

Sylvia put down the fabric she was holding. "May I walk with you? I've been staring at these little bits of fabric so long my eyes are about to cross."

After Sylvia had put up her "Closed" sign and locked up, they walked down Acorn Avenue, passing by Wild Things. "I hear that Wilhelm Wood and Craig Tracy had heated words in Nine Lives yesterday," Sylvia said.

"Heated?"

"Well, not that heated, but with more spark than usual. They got into it over the Joneses and their land. Wilhelm said Raymond Jones has a right to do whatever he wants with his land no matter what his Uncle Casper or the rest of the town thinks. Craig believes that everyone has the responsibility to be a good citizen of the community he's in. Of course, Raymond isn't in Acorn Hill and has probably never been here."

"I don't like it, Sylvia. Craig and Wilhelm arguing? Doesn't that seem out of character for them?"

"Not anymore."

Jane pondered that. Maybe Sylvia was right. Maybe this was the new state of affairs, and this was how things would be from now on. Then she shook off that thought. No, Mayor Lloyd Tynan was on the job. No matter how much he made them chuckle with his boisterous ways, he was determined and tenacious. When he sank his teeth into something—other than food—he was like a terrier. Lloyd didn't give up easily.

"Wow!" Sylvia commented. "Fancy car. Who do you think that belongs to?"

Jane glanced down Berry Lane and saw a silver Jaguar parked between the town hall and Nine Lives Bookstore. It looked as though it had just been driven off a dealer's lot.

"Nice. I suppose it belongs to someone visiting. I can't imagine anyone in town owning something like that."

At that moment, Viola came out the front door of her shop. She waved Jane and Sylvia toward her. "You'll never believe it! Do you know to whom that"—she pointed a finger—"car belongs?"

"Don't have a clue," Jane said.

"Raymond Jones."

It took a minute for that bit of news to sink in.

"Raymond? As in the nephew of Casper? The one who's never been here before?"

"The very same. Clara Horn saw him with her own eyes."

"How could she know it was him if he's never been here before?" Jane asked, trying to process this new turn of events.

"Because he looks exactly like his Uncle Casper. Same strong square jaw, brown hair with a hint of curl, brilliant blue eyes. Built the same too, Clara said. She remembers Casper from when he was young. He was the most handsome man in Acorn Hill at that time. Louise had herself quite a catch there. Too bad it didn't work out. Well, anyway, he's a picture of the young Casper."

"Sounds very good-looking," Sylvia said.

"Pretty is as pretty does," Viola intoned. "We'll just see."

Just then, a customer entered Nine Lives, and Viola bid them a quick good-bye. "And if you find out what he's up to let me know."

"I'd like to get a look at this guy myself if we ever come across him. He sounds like he's easy on the eyes," Sylvia said, an impish look on her face.

"Someday I'd like to get another look at his uncle," Jane

admitted. "It's hard to imagine that Louise fell in love with someone when she was a girl. Now, she's so ..."

"Socially correct? Uptight?" Sylvia teased.

"You could say that. Although she is softening. She's much more fun to be around than when I first came home and she and Alice were trying to be my mothers instead of my sisters. Louise has always had a strict sense of propriety. It's hard to imagine her having a teenage romance."

"Knowing Louise, I'm sure it was very proper and discreet."

"But in love? With someone other than Eliot? I hate to admit it, but my curiosity is killing me. Nobody else seems to think it's weird, but I'd like to visit with the man who lives in the woods behind Fairy Pond."

Since they were now in front of town hall, they decided to go in to check out the new brochure stand in the lobby. When they entered the building, they heard loud voices coming from the offices designated for the mayor.

One was low and masculine. It was impossible to make out any words that were said. The other voice, however, was louder and very familiar.

Lloyd Tynan, Mayor Lloyd Tynan of Acorn Hill, was yelling at the top of his lungs.

Chapter Fourteen

You can't do this! You'll destroy the ambience of this entire town and you'll ruin one of the most beautiful, pristine spots within two hundred miles. Think how your grandparents would have hated to see this happen. Think of your Uncle Casper."

The door to the mayor's offices opened, and a good-looking man with broad shoulders and a solid, well-proportioned build walked out.

He *did* look like Casper Jones—at least the little bit of Casper that Jane had seen.

"This isn't about my grandparents or my uncle, sir. This is about the fact that I own that land, and it's mine to do with as I wish. And I wish to put a twenty-four-hour gas station and convenience store on that property."

"But the land..."

"Granted, it's pretty, but there's a lot of beautiful land in Pennsylvania that's *not* mine. Someone can save that." The younger man, who looked upset—but not wicked, as some of the townspeople had drawn him out to be—gazed sternly at Lloyd as Lloyd walked with him to the door.

"Once everything is in place, we'll start construction. A lot of work will have to be done to take down the trees. I'm inclined to just fill in that swampy area you call a pond, but that decision will be made within the next week. My banker and the developers I'm working with were all a little leery about their reception in this town, Mr. Tynan. Please don't try to bully any more of my people. There's nothing you can do to change my mind or stop this project. *Nothing*. Do you understand?"

Lloyd stared at Raymond Jones, dumbstruck, having just been chastised as though he were a child. Jane felt like crying. For a proud man like Lloyd, nothing more humiliating could have taken place.

"It's settled then," Ray Jones said. "You are welcome to come to the grand opening we'll be having. It should be quite festive. Maybe I can get that old hermit uncle of mine out of his shack for once." He shook his head. "From what my father told me, there are other odd people in Acorn Hill, but I doubt any are odder than Casper. Good day, Mr. Mayor."

And with that, Ray Jones swept out the door, going who knows where, not even noticing Jane and Sylvia standing agog in the lobby.

Immediately Jane turned her attention to Lloyd.

He stood, his fingers twitching helplessly at his side, his mouth working but with nothing coming out. His color drained away, leaving him pale and sickly looking. Bella, his secretary, stormed out of the office, stood by Lloyd and addressed Jane and Sylvia. "There was no talking to that man. He had his mind made up. He assumed in advance that everyone would hate his idea, and he let it be known he didn't care. He wouldn't even allow Mayor Tynan to carry on a conversation with him." She hovered around Lloyd like a hummingbird around a flower. "And he said he wasn't even stopping to say hello to his Uncle Casper. Orlando certainly raised a chip off the old block."

"Lloyd, are you okay?" Jane ventured. "You look so pale..."

"Water," he croaked, "just some water."

Bella raced back into the office and came out with a bottle of mineral water, which Lloyd swallowed eagerly. Then, as if for the first time, he actually noticed Jane and Sylvia standing there and the office doors in the building all open, staff peering into the hallway. This seemed to bring him out of his daze.

"I'm fine," he tried to assure them, "just fine. No use letting a miserable, misguided fellow like him ruin my day. We'll find a way around this, just you wait and see."

Jane wished he sounded like he believed it.

"Everybody back to work!" he called out, and the heads in all the open doorways disappeared. "And you two, what do you girls think this is, the circus?"

Jane suppressed a grin. Even at fifty she was still a girl to Lloyd.

"Are you sure you'll be okay? He seemed to really upset you—"

"Just like acid indigestion, and I'm not going to pay any more attention. We'll sort this out, yes we will!" And Lloyd disappeared into his office.

"He seemed to recover rather well after his confrontation," Sylvia commented.

"I hope you're right. He still seems to think we can stop Raymond Jones, and, for the life of me, I can't imagine how."

"You think he's in denial?"

"I don't know what to think anymore. The only thing I know for sure is that Casper Jones was smart to go into seclusion if that's what his family is like."

They were partway back to Sylvia's store when Sylvia said, "Casper Jones! Maybe he can stop all this. Maybe there's something in the deed for the land, or—"

"Don't you think Lloyd would have thought about that by now?"

"Oh!" Sylvia's shoulders sagged. "I suppose so."

"Still, I'm not ready to give up. There's got to be something."

Sylvia went back to her store, and Jane, after completing her errand at the hardware store, made a beeline for Ethel's house. As she lifted her fist to knock, she realized that there was lively music playing in her aunt's living room. Jane leaned over and peeked through the lace-covered window.

Ethel lay on the floor in her leotard, sans pumpkin orange sweatshirt, a headband keeping her Titian red hair out of her eyes as she did a series of leg lifts.

Jane knocked and waited.

It took a minute before Ethel arrived at the door, her bathrobe modestly in place.

"It's just me, Aunt Ethel," Jane assured her. "You look fine."

"Come in, dear. I was just doing an extra workout." She pulled the headband out of her hair. Ethel's eyes narrowed. "I know for sure that some of the other ladies are doing extra exercises on their own."

"Are you in a race?" Jane asked, amused. She sat down on the couch.

"We have a little er…contest going." Ethel blushed. She was not the betting kind. "The first one to lose five pounds will be taken to lunch by the others. I had no idea how competitive I was until the challenge was made. Maybe I shouldn't have taken part."

"It's for your own good," Jane said pragmatically. "It's motivation to exercise."

Ethel's expression lightened. "Exactly right. It's good for me." Then she studied Jane. "What are you doing here, my dear? Just come for a visit?"

"No. I thought I should tell you what happened in town today." And Jane explained the scene at the town hall,

Raymond Jones's words and Lloyd's reaction. "He handled it pretty well eventually, but I'm concerned that he'll think back on it tonight and become more upset. At one point today he seemed almost in shock."

Ethel was suddenly a whirling dervish. She hurried to the bedroom, pulling at her clothes, and returned in no time wearing a skirt and blouse. "I have to go to him. He's been beside himself over this. And now they're almost ready to start tearing into Fairy Pond. He needs my company."

"I think you're right. And he probably needs to have more friends on hand. Bring him over to the inn for dinner tomorrow. I'll call Sylvia, Craig and Pastor Ken. It might help Lloyd to discuss his situation with those who care deeply about him."

"I'll do that, dear. Now I'd better go." Then Ethel trotted out of the house, leaving Jane to close up.

⤳

"I can't believe it. I just can't *believe* it." Alice whacked at the carrots for dinner on Wednesday evening. Jane was tempted to ask her why she was cutting them as if they had been attacking her. "Now what?"

"Now we deal with it," Louise said grimly. "Oh, that awful Orlando. Look what he has done." Louise was thinking of the day before when Lloyd had become so upset.

"Raymond has to take responsibility for this, Louise.

He's the one who is so callous about the community. And," Jane chose her words carefully, "perhaps Casper has something to do with this too. He should have spoken up."

Louise opened her mouth as if she were about to defend Casper and then closed it. "He got so fed up with everything and everyone that he quit trying years ago. I don't suppose he even cares anymore. Still..."

"You can lead a horse to water, but you can't make him drink," Alice intoned.

"Whatever that means."

"I hear footsteps coming up the walk," Louise said. "I'll see if it's our company."

Soon a small group of invited friends was gathered around the dining room table. All were grimly silent. Ethel and Lloyd had not yet arrived.

"They're very late." Alice glanced at her watch. "You don't suppose—"

At that moment, the doorbell rang. Without waiting for anyone to answer, Lloyd and Ethel entered.

The usually well-groomed Ethel had not combed her hair and it looked especially unruly. Lloyd wore a similar "do"—he had been running his hands through his gray hair in frustration, no doubt. The effect was that they both looked as though they'd been struggling through gale-force winds.

The rest stood and then settled back into their chairs after Lloyd and Ethel were seated, not knowing quite what to say or do. Pastor Thompson took charge. "Sorry you had to clash with Raymond Jones, Lloyd. We heard that he was in your office yesterday."

Lloyd looked at him as if he hadn't heard a word he said. He rubbed his arm as he spoke. "It wasn't a bad day, Pastor. Just business as usual."

Uh-huh. Jane wondered what that was about.

"We'll get it all worked out. No doubt about it. I'll figure it out . . ." his voice trailed away. When he spoke again, he said, "Is that stroganoff, Jane? What are we waiting for? Let's eat."

It was a bizarre meal, with everyone but Lloyd wanting to talk about Ray Jones's visit. Lloyd behaved as though it hadn't even happened. If anything, his appetite was heartier than usual. He ate with gusto. Occasionally he reached up to massage his left shoulder as if it was bothering him.

They were done with their meal and sipping coffee around the table when Craig Tracy said, "I heard that Jones has decided not to try to save any of the woods around the pond, at least nothing that would interfere with his plans." He grimaced. "It's going to be a mess."

Jane felt sick to her stomach. Alice closed her eyes and gave a little groan.

Lloyd, without warning, pounded his fist on the table. Ethel, who was seated beside him, patted to no avail at his arm. "Now, Lloyd—"

"No! No, no, no! It's not going to happen. It can't happen! He's going to change his mind. I wrote Casper a letter asking him to talk to his nephew. The man can't be so callous that he won't even listen to ..."

Lloyd seemed to lose his breath for a moment. "I ... ah ..." He rubbed his arm vigorously, as if it was hurting him. "What was I saying?" He sounded as though he was having trouble breathing. "Can't let someone like Ray ..." Lloyd leaned back in his chair. "Got to catch my breath ... shouldn't get so excited ..." Then he slumped in the chair like a portly rag doll.

Ethel let out a moan. Jane, Sylvia, Louise and Craig jumped to their feet, Craig's chair tipping backward and crashing into the wall, and stood as if frozen. It was Alice and Pastor Thompson who spun into action.

"Jane, call 911," directed Alice. "Tell them we have a possible heart attack. Then call Potterston Hospital and tell them I'm coming in with someone. Ask that a cardio-ogist be there when we arrive. Open a window, Sylvia—give us some air!"

Ethel stood with her hands over her mouth and her eyes big as saucers staring at Lloyd, who had slid to the floor holding his arm as if in great pain. His face was gray, and his breath came in quick gasps.

"Just stay calm, Lloyd," Pastor Thompson said, kneeling on the floor next to Lloyd. "Help is on the way, and we have Acorn Hill's finest nurse right here. Try to relax."

Louise, who had hurried out of the room, came back with a thin blanket and a glass of water. She handed the blanket to Alice, who spread it over Lloyd's lower body. The water she handed to Craig Tracy. "Aunt Ethel, Craig has a glass of water for you."

Craig quickly made his way to Ethel, who had to be helped with the glass.

For Jane, time seemed to slow down dramatically. It was as if they were all moving through a dream sequence, slowly, slowly . . . and where was that ambulance?

Sylvia grabbed her arm. "I'll get my car and we'll follow the ambulance to the hospital. I imagine Alice will be going with Lloyd. Ethel can come with us."

Pastor Thompson looked up. "Perhaps your Aunt Ethel would like to ride with me. I might be of some spiritual help . . ."

He exchanged a meaningful look with Jane, who immediately interpreted its significance. *Just in case he doesn't make it.*

"I'm sure that would be a comfort," Jane said. "Thank you."

"Then I'll drive you, Pastor, and you can sit with Ethel in the back," Craig offered. "I'll have room in front for Louise, if she's coming, and Jane and Sylvia can follow. That way we'll have more cars in Potterston if they're needed."

"I hear a siren," Sylvia said.

Louise was waiting at the door when three paramedics —a woman and two men—arrived. She held open the door for their gurney and the equipment they carried. As they surrounded Lloyd, Louise turned to Jane. "Stay as long as you need to, all night if necessary. I will stay and hold down the fort here. If Aunt Ethel wants to stay at the hospital, I can pack a bag for her and send it over tomorrow." Something flickered in Louise's eyes and she mouthed a single word. "Pray."

Jane couldn't hear what one of the paramedics was saying to Lloyd, but she saw relief in the mayor's eyes. His mouth was working but no sound was coming out. Jane's own heart felt as if it were being crushed inside her chest.

It seemed to take forever before the trio made the decision that Lloyd was stable enough to be moved to the gurney, which had been lowered next to him. After they eased him gently onto it, they raised it until Lloyd was lying at table height. As the two men were working with Lloyd, the woman was on the telephone to the hospital, relaying readings and the condition of their patient.

Ethel stood as near to the gurney as she dared, wringing her hands.

It occurred to Jane that Ethel would lose a part of herself if Lloyd died. Granted, they weren't married—although Jane had always secretly entertained the idea that someday Lloyd would pop the question—but they were steadfast companions and dear friends. It had become so common to see them together that Josie and others had begun to say their names as if they were one. "I saw LloydandEthel uptown." "Are LloydandEthel at church yet?" "When are LloydandEthel coming?"

Jane watched her aunt as the paramedics made sure that Lloyd was stabilized for the ride. Ethel had stopped wringing her hands but was now clutching them over her own chest instead. Jane was relieved to see Pastor Thompson's hand on her shoulder to steady her.

Just when they had all almost given up hope that the crew would ever move him, the man who seemed to be in charge said, "Let's go." They were out of the house in a flurry. Alice followed them and stepped into the ambulance behind the patient. As the doors closed on them, Jane could see Alice bending to whisper something in Lloyd's ear.

Dear God, keep him safe! Jane prayed silently.

Chapter Fifteen

ednesday night was never-ending.

Whatever was wrong with Lloyd, it had to be bad, Jane decided. Wouldn't someone have come out to tell them something if the news were positive? With every minute that passed, Ethel seemed to deteriorate a little further until finally she was sitting in an uncomfortable, formed-plastic chair weeping into a soggy handkerchief. Pastor Thompson had stayed as close to her as her own shadow, sensing her needs without her having to ask. Jane had already sent up more than one prayer of thanks for his assistance.

"Coffee, Aunt Ethel?" Jane held out a steaming cup that she had purchased from a machine next to the closed cafeteria.

Ethel shook her head.

"Tea then." Jane held out the cup that she held in her other hand. "With lots of sugar."

"You're such a dear, but I just don't feel like a thing." Ethel's eyes darted to the doorway as an aide passed. "Don't you think we should hear something soon?"

"Alice has been by to say that he's not in crisis."

"'Not in crisis'? That doesn't seem quite enough for me."

Jane handed the coffee to Craig and took the tea for herself. Sylvia was dozing in one of the miserable chairs. Pastor Thompson decided to head to the hospital chapel for a while to pray. All of them except Ethel had been in and out of the tiny sanctuary during the night. It was soothing and calm there. Lined with wood, housing a tiny table with a cross, and behind that, a piece of backlit stained-glass art, the chapel offered a fitting place for prayer and contemplation. There were six miniature pews, three on each side facing the front, each big enough to hold three people. Jane had hoped Aunt Ethel would find comfort there, but she preferred instead to be out in the brightly lit, uncomfortable waiting room, waiting for news of Lloyd.

"You've been a trouper, Craig," Jane said to her friend. "Thanks for sticking this out with us."

"What are friends for?"

"That's an interesting question."

"What do you mean?"

"I've been thinking about friendship and what it can, or cannot, withstand. This issue over Ray Jones and Fairy Pond, for example. I see people I think are true friends so polarized over this topic that their friendship is being threatened. Then I begin to wonder—is that possible if a friend is really true?"

"Love me, love my opinion, you mean? And if you don't love my opinion, you aren't my friend?"

"Something like that. It's beginning to appear that that's how people feel. Whatever happened to 'love me, *respect* my opinion'? We seem to be having a difficult time separating others' beliefs from who they are as human beings."

"If you think Fairy Pond should be sacrificed for the sake of progress you are a bad person? And if you think it should be saved, you are good?"

"And vice versa. Our thinking is being clouded by our emotion over an issue." Jane frowned. "I believe friendships should be determined by more than that." She was quiet for a moment. "Frankly, I like having friends who are willing to disagree with me, who know I'll love them no matter what."

"Really?"

Jane grinned at him. "I'm not always right, I've discovered. But sometimes I am. It's good to debate and discuss, but what I see in the current conflict is something else."

"Dismissing people because they don't agree with one's viewpoint?"

"Exactly."

"What do you think should be done about it, Jane?"

"I've been praying about it. I believe God wants us to struggle with issues, He wants us to be alive to what is around us, and He doesn't want us to throw the baby out with the bathwater, so to speak."

"Or, in this case, the friend out with the pond water?"

Jane laughed out loud. "That's it, Craig. Respect, agreeing to disagree, avoiding stomping all over each other's feelings and values—that's the lesson here."

"So, before we're done, we may be thanking Ray Jones for giving us this opportunity to deepen our friendships?"

Jane drew a deep breath and smiled at Craig. "That may be tough, but that's how I'm going to try to look at it from now on."

Just then, Dr. Bentley, a physician who lived in Acorn Hill, entered the waiting room. Everyone stood at once. He gestured that all should sit down.

"I just got here for my rounds and heard that Lloyd had been brought in a few hours ago."

Is that how long it's been? Jane marveled. *It seems like forever.*

"I checked with the doctor in the emergency room. Mr. Tynan has, of course, had a heart attack. It was necessary to put in a stent, but he is doing well. The doctor said to tell you that Mr. Tynan is going to be moved to intensive care shortly, and that he preferred that the patient have no visitors for the rest of tonight unless there is close family present."

"He's going to live?" Ethel asked.

"We have no reason to believe otherwise."

"Praise God!"

"Alice said I should tell you that she would stay with Lloyd tonight since he has no immediate relatives nearby and that she'll keep you all informed about Lloyd's condition. And," Dr. Bentley looked directly at Ethel, "she said that you were supposed to sleep at the inn tonight and not to worry."

"Thank you, Dr. Bentley," Pastor Thompson said.

"No problem. I'll be here all night and tomorrow, and if you have any questions, leave them with the nurse, and I will answer them promptly." He smiled kindly at the little group of Lloyd's friends. "He's in good hands. You go home and get some sleep."

"Sleep? I'll never sleep again the way I'm feeling." Ethel moaned.

Yet, by the time they were three miles from the hospital, she was already nodding off, exhausted from fear and relieved to know that Lloyd had done as well as he had.

Sylvia and Jane talked as they followed Craig Tracy's tail-lights down the road toward Acorn Hill.

"I thought he was going to die right there on the dining

room floor," Sylvia admitted. "His face was so contorted and he fell to the floor like a—"

"Stone," Jane finished. "I hadn't really thought about how much weight Lloyd has been carrying around. I'm feeling guilty that I let him eat so much at the inn. I should have been feeding him salads and fruit plates."

"What Lloyd puts in his mouth is not your fault," Sylvia said bluntly. "We all have to take responsibility for our own bodies and how we treat them. I never saw anyone throw him to the ground and force food down his throat."

"Still…"

"Quit it, Jane. Your Aunt Ethel is trying to take the blame for his being ill by saying she should have done more about how agitated he's been. Now you think you should have fed him differently. If anyone is to blame, it should be that young Raymond Jones. He's the one who got Lloyd so upset in the first place."

"And he's just doing what he has a perfect right to do," Jane pointed out. "There's no one to blame, exactly, but I do wish I could think of some way to stop the destruction of Fairy Pond."

"Now that Lloyd is ill, who will be its prime defender?" Sylvia wondered.

Jane groaned. "Who's been the next most involved with this? Me. But I don't know what I can do except keep saying that it shouldn't be touched." She recalled the words she had uttered not long ago. *I'm spending the next few months tending to my own business . . . Ever since I moved to this quiet, sleepy little town I've run myself ragged . . . I came here to slow down after the pace of my life in California.*

"What if we got a petition going?" Sylvia suggested. "Would that help?"

"I have no idea, but it's worth a try. If we can't stop Raymond Jones legally, he's not likely to pay attention to a petition unless . . ."

"Jane, what are you thinking? You've got a very odd tone in your voice."

"I'm not sure yet, but there are some ideas brewing in my head." She straightened in her seat and there was a hint of steel in her voice when she spoke again. "And the first thing I have to do is make a little visit to the mysterious Casper Jones."

"You are going *where*?" Louise's voice edged upward a notch when Jane revealed her plan on Thursday morning.

"We know perfectly well that Lloyd can't have any more worries or concerns. Alice told us that Lloyd had to concentrate on getting better. Period."

"You might find that a most interesting experience.

Casper does not view things the way that most others do," Louise said.

"Obviously. I'm very curious to find out how that mind of his works. What would make a man into a recluse like that, Louise?"

Louise sat down at the kitchen table. Absently she crumbled a scone into bits. "If I were to guess, I don't think that Casper would think of himself as a recluse."

"No? What do you call a man who disappears and never comes out until he needs ten-penny nails or twenty-five pounds of sugar?"

"Casper never needed people the way others often do. I've said that before. He's independent and self-sufficient. He's also a studious man who's interested in so many things —nature, philosophy, history . . . why, I believe if Casper found his way into the Smithsonian in Washington, DC, he would never come out of there."

"If he's so independent, how did the two of you become friends?"

Louise smiled and Jane noticed softness in her features that often appeared when his name was mentioned. "We had a lot in common. Casper enjoyed music. He's a self-taught musician."

"Is the fact that he's so self-sufficient one of the reasons that no one seems terribly concerned that there's a hermit living on the outskirts of town?" Jane still couldn't comprehend that.

"No. I think that people *forget* he's there, and he likes it that way."

"Is he ..." Jane searched for the right word and could only come up with one. "...weird?"

"The Casper I knew was very charming. Just not very interested in the complications of the outside world."

"Why didn't the two of you stay together, Louise? Eliot was wonderful, but I hear in your voice that you were once in love with Casper too."

"We were very young. We both had educations to pursue. Even then, Casper was given to reading for hours on end or inventing things. It just wasn't meant to be." Louise looked pensive. "But I've never regretted knowing him either."

"Do you think he'll let me speak with him?"

"I don't see why not. Casper may be idiosyncratic, but he's never been rude."

He's never been rude, never been rude, Jane kept repeating to herself as she walked the path toward the home of Casper Jones. It was no wonder that so few knew he lived here. The trees were so close together and the underbrush so thick that she could hardly find her way, even after Fred Humbert had given her directions.

Suddenly a thought struck her. Did Casper have a gun? Was he the kind who would use it to chase off interlopers? *He's never been rude, never been rude.* The clearing came upon her like a surprise, a jewel glinting in a dark forest. She heard someone gasp and realized that it was *she.*

The trees opened slightly on a lovely rough-hewn log cabin home surrounded by gardens. A pasture and open fields could be seen further in the distance past the trees. It was like a photo one might see on a calendar or postcard—pristine, beautiful, perfect.

The log house was topped with a roof of bright green shingles. Green shutters flanked the windows and hand-hewn window boxes erupted with red, yellow, purple and blue flowers and green hanging vines. A couple of rocking chairs sat on the porch. On the cushion of one slept a huge, golden tabby.

Jane almost laughed out loud when she noticed two pygmy goats doing their share of the lawn care, nibbling delicately, almost as if they had been trained to mow in rows. As she neared the house, she heard voices—no, one voice. It was animated and clear.

She found that though the voice was unfamiliar, the words were not.

I find it wholesome to be alone the greater part of the time. To be in company, even with the best, is soon wearisome and dissipating. I love to be alone. I never found the companion that was so companionable as solitude. We are for the most part more lonely when we go abroad among men than when we stay in our chambers. A man thinking or working is always alone, let him be where he will. Solitude is not measured by the miles of space that intervene between a man and his fellows . . . The farmer can work alone in the field or the woods all day, hoeing or chopping, and not feel lonesome, because he is employed . . .

Curiosity piqued, she followed the sound to the back of the house. There the man she had seen before, today wearing tan cotton pants and a red, green and navy plaid shirt, hoed a row of carrots. On the ground beside him was a boom box, and issuing from its speakers were the familiar sounds of a book on tape.

I have a great deal of company in my house, especially in the morning, when nobody calls. Let me suggest a few comparisons, that someone may convey an idea of my situation. I am no more lonely than the loon in the pond that laughs so loud, or than Walden Pond itself . . .

Of course, she thought. *Thoreau. Who else?*

Jane cleared her throat, but the gentleman didn't seem to hear her. He was humming under his breath as he worked. She stared at his profile. He was as she remembered him, about Louise's age, with silvery gray hair and a small, neatly trimmed mustache. He held himself with a dignified bearing. Even in work clothes he looked imposing, as if he had only recently been walking the halls of the state capitol. A gentleman farmer. She cleared her throat again.

This time he heard her, but he didn't seem startled or even surprised to see Jane, tall, slender and striking in her jeans, denim jacket and the painted T-shirt she had slashed with orange, red and yellow.

"Hello," he said pleasantly. "To what do I owe the honor of this visit?"

"I...uh..." Jane felt blindsided. She hadn't known what to expect of Casper Jones. An odd, skittish fellow? Someone to be made angry by an intruder? Anything but a charming, well-groomed gentleman whose eyes were sparkling like blue diamonds. She thrust out a hand. "I'm Jane Howard from Acorn Hill. You knew my family."

"Ah, you've grown up a lot since I last saw you. Louise used to talk about you constantly."

Jane felt the urge to sit down—here, on the grass—anywhere. "You remember?"

"I'd never forget." He peered at her. "You look a little pale. Would you like a glass of water? Iced tea? An Arnold Palmer?"

Jane stared at him and burst out laughing. "You make those?"

"It's just a mix of iced tea and lemonade, my dear. Very refreshing, don't you think?"

Jane stumbled after him to the house, mesmerized by his straight back and steady gait. A boom box? Arnold Palmers? What other surprises were in store for her?

Plenty.

There were soft cushions on the rocking chairs, more window boxes and pots of flowers, a rough but lovely table with these words etched into the top:

"If a man does not keep pace with his companions, perhaps it is because he hears a different drummer."

Henry David Thoreau

The *Wall Street Journal* lay discarded on the other rocker. The fat tabby eyed Jane with disdain when his owner picked him up on the way to the kitchen and gently put him on a cushion on the porch floor. The cat turned around three times and crumpled into the softness. A couple of licks of his fur and he fell asleep again.

The little goats had made their way to that side of the house and were meticulously nibbling at the grass. Then Jane noticed a basset hound looking at her with sad, droopy eyes. He was at the far end of the porch and not inclined to get up or bark. Instead his tail flopped twice against the porch floor before he rested his head between his paws again.

At that moment, Casper came through the screen door carrying two Arnold Palmers and a plate of delectable-looking cookies.

"You baked these?" Jane blurted as he set them down on the table between them.

"Not these. I do enjoy working in the kitchen, but sometimes I'm just too busy." His eyes twinkled again. "But that's what mail order and the Internet are for, aren't they? Order it and it arrives at the door via a deliveryman. It's a wonderful world."

"So you aren't as isolated as everyone thinks," Jane blurted again, immediately wanting to kick herself.

He chuckled. "Not at all." He pointed to a huge woven basket full of what looked like magazines and catalogs. "The outside world is right there for me whenever I need it."

He leaned back in his chair, took a sip of the beverage and studied Jane. "But you aren't here to talk about my close association with mail-order catalogs and the Internet, are you?"

Charmed and completely disconcerted, Jane stammered, "Well ... no."

"I didn't think so." He smiled at her and settled back in his chair as if he had all day and all night for her. "Then tell me, Ms. Howard, what brings you here?"

Not knowing where to start, Jane just opened her mouth and let it all pour out—how she loved Fairy Pond, Lloyd's promise to keep Acorn Hill unchanged, the developers, the town meeting, the bickering that had begun, Lloyd's heart attack and the imminent destruction of Fairy Pond.

Casper listened patiently without comment, but he straightened in his chair at the news of Lloyd's heart attack.

"Will he be all right?"

"I certainly hope so. I have no idea how he will handle seeing the land leveled for new construction."

Casper did not comment. He sat there with a weighty sadness in his countenance. If Jane had had to pick a single word to describe Casper at that moment, it would have been *grieving*.

"This breaks my heart," he said finally. "And I'm afraid there is little I can do. My nephew Raymond is absolutely correct about which of us owns that land. That area is fully in his control."

"Couldn't you *talk* to him? Convince him that he's making a mistake?"

"Talk? To Raymond? I don't even know where he is. I'd talk to him if he wanted to talk to me. I'm afraid my brother Orlando tainted every portion of that boy's life. I know Orlando never said a kind word about his family or this place. He was a bitter man."

"How sad!" Jane said.

Casper looked mildly amused. "Orlando wanted his own way and usually got it. He took my mother and father on a roller-coaster ride. He was in trouble from the day he learned to walk." Casper tented his fingers and rested his chin on them. "He was too strong-willed for my parents to tame. They were both mild people, honest, hardworking, but no match for Orlando. He was in desperate need of discipline and yet—"

"But *you* didn't turn out that way." Jane clapped a hand over her mouth. "Oh, sorry, maybe I shouldn't have said that."

"That's quite all right. The fact is that I went in the opposite direction from my brother—avoiding him taught me that solitude has its virtues. 'There can be no very black melancholy to him who lives in the midst of Nature and has his senses still,' Thoreau said. I've found that to be true. The richness and beauty of nature, the multitude of books there are to be read, music to be heard, paintings to be painted . . . why, I am busy all the time, and I've only scratched the surface."

Jane smiled at his enthusiasm. Casper Jones was right. He was too busy to be bothered with society. "But what about church?" Once again Jane hoped that she hadn't asked an inappropriate question.

Casper bent to pick something out of a basket on the floor beside him. It was a well-worn Bible. "Here is my instruction manual, Jane. I've never had a question that I couldn't find the answer for in here. Besides, with Sunday's radio filled with sermons and theological discussions, I listen to some very fine preachers every week." He smiled a little sadly. "So far I've found none as insightful as your father."

The two chatted quite a bit more, and Jane found Casper an intriguing gentleman. She would have liked to continue their conversation, but she realized that she might be keeping him from his work schedule, and she didn't want to be a burden. They parted company with Casper bowing toward her, his face bearing a kindly smile.

One couldn't help liking Casper Jones, Jane decided as she walked back to Grace Chapel Inn. They had talked for nearly three hours and those hours had flown by like minutes. What a remarkable man he was. She could see now why no one seemed particularly worried or concerned about the reclusive Mr. Jones. Anyone as self-sufficient and independent as he was didn't need others worrying about him. What's more, he was not "alone." His contact with the outside world through books, radio and the Internet probably rivaled that of most of the citizens of the town.

But, although she had met the mystifying recluse and found him to be quite normal after all, she still didn't have a plan for saving Fairy Pond.

Chapter Sixteen

On Saturday, Jane ran into Patsy Ley in the downstairs waiting room at Potterston Hospital. "Hi, Patsy. What are you doing over here today? Sick friend?"

Patsy smiled warmly. "You could say that. Henry and I came to visit Mayor Tynan. I thought I'd leave them alone for a while."

"May I join you? I don't really want to intrude either. Since Alice isn't working today I thought I'd come to see Lloyd. I rode over with Sylvia—she had some errands to run. How is he doing?"

Patsy had a girlish giggle that seemed slightly out of place for someone her age, but it was always endearing to Jane. "I think he's doing remarkably well. If he doesn't get out of the hospital soon, however, some of the nurses will be taking early retirement."

"Alice said that Lloyd's a little frustrated that the doctor won't let him do Acorn Hill business from his hospital bed."

"A *little* frustrated? I'm afraid he'll give himself another heart attack if he doesn't settle down." A frown flitted over

Patsy's smooth forehead. "Henry and Pastor Ken are worried about him."

"We are too. And Aunt Ethel is beside herself. If he's this upset now, I don't know what will happen when they start to break ground." Jane put her hand to her own chest. "I'm not sure what I'll do either. I feel so helpless. I've made several calls to state officials to see if there's any way to stop this, and everyone says that it's Ray Jones's land, so he has the right to do what he wants. He's gone through all the proper channels."

"It seems such a waste of a beautiful area. Maybe his Uncle Casper could..."

"That's what I thought too. So I went to visit Casper Jones myself."

Patsy's eyebrows arched and she looked shocked. "So you saw him then? With your own eyes?"

"I take it you haven't?"

"No. Of course, we aren't lifelong residents of Acorn Hill either." She looked curious. "What is he like?"

"He's charming, well-read, content and very much at ease with his own thoughts and with silence," Jane said. "I went not knowing exactly what to expect. What I found was someone who loves nature, who loves to read, to write and even to compose music. He tends a beautiful garden, makes his own furniture and can get around the Internet with ease. As far as I can tell, he lives the way he does by choice.

"Once I heard this man existed," Jane admitted, "I wondered why no one who knew him seemed to think it odd that he so rarely came to town or that he had little to do with anyone. Now I understand why. They *knew* him. They realized that he liked being alone, that it wasn't a hardship for him. He's perfectly friendly and cordial, and not the least bit dependent on others to keep him entertained and happy."

Patsy considered what Jane had said. Then she started to recite:

"We live thick and are in each other's way, and stumble over one another, and I think thus lose some respect for one another. Certainly less frequency would suffice for all-important and hearty communications…It would be better if there were but one inhabitant to a square mile, as where I live. The value of a man is not in his skin, that we should touch him."

When she had finished, Patsy added, "My father loved Thoreau. He quoted him so often that I still remember some of the passages. Papa thought that the idea of a man's going off to live alone at a place like Walden Pond, to be alone with his thoughts and to appreciate nature as it is meant to be appreciated was a wonderful thing. As a little girl, I, of course, thought that sounded horrible. To be alone?

Without playmates? 'But what about the birds?' he'd say. 'Would you like to know if you could tame a deer or have a hummingbird drink from a flower you hold in your hand?'" Patsy laughed. "I wasn't really interested, but I did try to imagine how still and patient I would have to be to entice that hummingbird to me."

And, Jane thought to herself, *It wouldn't surprise me one bit if Casper could do just that*.

"Is he a Christian?" Patsy asked.

"There is every indication that he is. He has books on faith and theology, Bible commentaries and the like mixed in with books on architecture, history, art, and how-to books on canning vegetables and sketching. We discussed everything He loves God's creation."

Patsy nodded. "Maybe my husband could visit with him sometime." She looked slightly shy. "I think he would enjoy visiting with someone like Casper Jones. Henry appreciates people who aren't afraid of silence."

Jane understood immediately. Pastor Ley had a stutter that grew worse when he was under stress or when he was expected to speak in public. Casper would give him plenty of time and space in which to speak. Nothing was hurried in Casper's life.

"I suppose I should go see the patient," Jane said, suddenly dreading the idea of facing Lloyd. What could she say to him that could make him feel any better? Nothing. Lloyd was the kind of man who kept his word. Losing Fairy Pond and not keeping his promise that Acorn Hill would remain just the way it had always been were enough to devastate a man like him. "Good-bye, Patsy. Lovely to chat with you."

Lloyd looked considerably smaller and older in a hospital bed than he did enjoying himself at the inn. His gray hair was sticking up, and he hadn't shaved since his attack. His fighting spirit, however, did not seem to be damaged.

"There you are! I'm glad you came. I have a few things to ask you after Pastor Ley and I get through talking about the hereafter."

"Good morning, gentlemen. Now Lloyd, you aren't planning to go there soon, I hope," Jane said gently, a teasing note in her voice.

"Only on God's time, not mine. I was just assuring Pastor Ley that when I leave this earth, I'll already know my destination." Lloyd pointed at a hard-backed plastic chair. "Help yourself.

"Yes sir, I was thirty-five years old when the Lord and I had a little discussion. He told me that I could continue in the way I was going and make a mess of my life, or I could repent of my sins, confess them and try His way for a while. I took His option and have never regretted it."

"Sounds like He was very clear," Pastor Ley commented.

"He spoke loudly enough, I guess, but I didn't listen

the first few times. I grew up thinking God was corralled into Sundays and not to be let out during the week. Took me a while to figure out I got it wrong, that God is an everyday sort of fellow."

An everyday sort of fellow. That's one way to put it, Jane mused.

"Now He and I discuss His plans for my day and I go about doing them." Lloyd shook his head in bewilderment. "I wonder where I went wrong here. I was sure I was doing the right things and ... now this."

"Maybe now isn't the best time to be pondering that question, Lloyd. Your business right now is to recover." Pastor Ley exchanged a meaningful glance with Jane as he stood to go. "I'll be praying for you."

"And me for you, Pastor. And both of us about what's happening to Acorn Hill."

Jane and Lloyd sat quietly after Henry Ley had left, both lost in their own thoughts. Finally, she spoke. "I hear you've been a bit hard to handle, Lloyd."

"Those nurses insist I can't do paperwork, can't talk on the telephone, can't get excited. Why, not being able to do those things is what's making me sick. If I could get my secretary here for half a day so I could dictate some letters and discuss a few matters, I could—"

"Don't hold your breath for that. Even when you get

home, you'll have Aunt Ethel hovering over you like mist over a meadow. And she's better at giving orders than any nurse."

"You've got that right," Lloyd said fondly. "She's already said that we're taking walks every night after supper and giving up red meat." Lloyd suddenly looked worried. "That's not going to be a problem for you, is it, Jane? At the inn, I mean. I don't want to cramp your style at dinnertime."

She swallowed a smile. Apparently Lloyd assumed that he'd be eating at the inn a great deal after he was released from the hospital. "I'll make sure I have something on hand for you."

"No need to make something special for me. Ethel said she'd talk to you about cooking more fish and chicken."

So she and her sisters were to be intimately involved in Lloyd's recovery. Ethel had obviously already decided that. Jane supposed she could have been annoyed that Lloyd and her aunt so easily assumed that they were expected at the dinner table more than occasionally, but she liked the idea of "family" and of a full table of conversation and laughter.

"We'll do all we can to get you well as soon as possible. I'm sure everyone in town will."

"Everyone but Raymond Jones."

"You can't think about that right now, Lloyd. That's what got you here in the first place." Jane gestured at the hospital walls.

"Did you make those calls I asked you to make?"

"I did. Ray Jones has followed the letter of the law. There's no stopping him."

"There's *got* to be a way!" Lloyd chewed on his upper lip. "He's got to have overlooked something—something small, something that he thinks is unimportant."

Something small, something unimportant. Jane's mind whirled and settled on nothing.

"Please don't get your hopes up," Jane pleaded. "Can't we talk about something else?"

"Not much else I'm interested in."

"I have good news for you . . . about something other than Fairy Pond."

"Can't think of anything that would cheer me up."

"Justine has agreed to cook and keep house for you until you're feeling better, and the price is right."

Lloyd's eyes brightened. "She has? Why, that's mighty nice of her. I'm not much of a laundry man, and even I am getting a little tired of my *usual* lunch."

"What's that?"

"I usually fry up some meat, put it on a bun, have some chips and a bowl of ice cream."

"Those days have now ended, Lloyd."

"That's what Ethel says." He looked hopeful. "But maybe Justine can think of something."

"She was pleased to get the job. I think she and Josie are getting by, but extra money helps."

"Then I'll give her a raise before she starts."

Jane laughed out loud. "It sounds as though you will be a wonderful employer, Lloyd." She paused. "If you behave yourself, that is. Otherwise you'll terrify Justine, and she'll feel guilty that you're trying to work and she can't stop you."

"I know, I know. Everyone from Ethel and the doctors to the janitor tells me the same thing. I can't believe the number of people sticking their heads into my room and telling me to be more careful from now on."

He leaned back against the pillows with a contented look on his face. "The one good thing that's come out of this mess is that, until now, I never realized how many friends I really had in Acorn Hill. The nurses say they've never seen a patient with so much company. Why, the first day or two, they just had to turn people away."

Jane watched emotion play on Lloyd's features.

He continued. "All this trouble over Ray Jones and the pond, the people who hadn't spoken up until now saying that they'd like more business in Acorn Hill . . . I thought maybe I'd been doing it all wrong . . ."

Insecurity and self-doubt have no age limits, Jane realized. A rush of gratitude ran through her. *You are our only hope and*

strength, Lord. Without You we are nothing. Lloyd wants only to do Your
will. Help him find that path—and keep him healthy, while You're at it.
All good things come from You. Amen.

At that moment, Ethel tottered into the room under a
load of books she was carrying. Her hair was even redder
than usual—a sure sign that the color job was fresh. She was
dressed in a pink suit with a white ruffled blouse and
she looked as if she could have been plucked from one of the
bouquets that lined Lloyd's room. She plopped the books
down on the bedside table next to a pitcher of water and a
glass and straightened her jacket before greeting them.

"Hello, Lloyd. I think you have a little more color in
your face today. Jane, how nice to see you."

"You came just in time," Jane said. "Lloyd's been having
visitors one after the other. I came as the Leys were about
to leave, and now you're here."

"I hope it isn't too much," Ethel worried.

"I never get tired with any of the Howard family
around." Lloyd seemed to have a catch in his voice.
"Especially you, Ethel."

Jane watched her aunt flush with pleasure and smiled
inwardly.

"I brought Lloyd some books to look at while he's rest-
ing." Ethel spread the books out so that they could see the
titles.

They were a selection of not-quite-best-sellers: *Cooking for the Heart Patient, Cholesterol and You, Walking: The Key to Fitness and Heart Health, Maximizing Your Relaxation Skills* and *Retirement: The Fun Is About to Begin.*

Lloyd snorted so loudly that Jane thought he might scare the nurses in the hall. "What's this about, Ethel? Why didn't you bring me a good mystery instead of wasting a bunch of money on this?"

"I did bring you a mystery. To read after you're finished with these." Ethel patted her purse.

"I think I'll be leaving now," Jane said as she backed toward the door. This scene was a little too domestic for her taste. Lloyd looked about to hyperventilate as he stared at the relaxation book. Besides, Ethel could handle it. She looked to be in charge.

"Bye, dear," Ethel said.

Lloyd raised his hand in farewell, and Jane escaped into the hall.

Sylvia found her there, still laughing.

"Lloyd must be doing well."

"I'm not sure. Aunt Ethel just dumped a bunch of diet, exercise and relaxation books on him. And even a book on retirement. You might not want to visit him for a while yet. Let him get over that retirement hint. Want some coffee?"

"Love some."

"Hospital cafeteria or the coffee shop down the road?"

"Need you ask?"

Once they were ensconced on chairs beneath the awning outside the little coffee shop, Sylvia leaned back, crossed her arms and asked, "So what do you think about all of this?"

"I really don't know. I feel helpless. And, although Lloyd is doing well right now, I'm afraid of how he'll do once the project starts."

Sylvia frowned. "I'm worried about more than that."

"What do you mean?"

"I was in the Coffee Shop yesterday afternoon and was amazed to discover how polarized some of the people are becoming over this issue. The majority of the town's people are in Lloyd's camp, but there are a few who are welcoming change."

"Lloyd's 'camp'? We aren't setting up war zones here, are we?"

"Not many are talking like that, just a handful. Most people, even if they think a little more business wouldn't hurt, like Acorn Hill just the way it is. There are a few, however, who are even talking of putting up a candidate in the next election who can 'speak for them.'"

"Who would that be?"

"No one says who. I think it is just braggadocio, but this

Ray Jones business seems to have brought out the worst in some people."

Jane picked at her cream-cheese brownie. The town she had come to love again, her friends, the wooded haven in which she sketched—all were on perilous ground. How had it happened so quickly?

"We can't be complacent, even for a moment, can we?"

"It doesn't seem like it." Sylvia stirred her coffee. "Do you think Lloyd needs to know about any of this?"

"Eventually. But he's certainly not up to it now."

Chapter Seventeen

The following Saturday Lloyd was ready to come home from the hospital. He, it seemed, was the only one who was ready for the event.

Ethel had been worrying about it ever since she realized that he wasn't going to get worse. It seemed to Jane that worrying somehow gave her aunt strange comfort. Unable to do anything else while Lloyd was in the hospital, Ethel busied herself thinking about "what ifs."

"What if Lloyd isn't strong enough yet and he falls?" she stewed.

"He's been getting his strength back. He's walking every day at the hospital," Jane said calmly. She and her sisters had been doing this "what if" exercise with their aunt for what seemed like forever.

"What if they didn't keep him long enough and something else should happen?"

"He's been there longer already than many other heart patients. They've watched him very carefully. And he's received excellent treatment," Alice said.

"But what if he gets mixed up about his medication? Lloyd's not much for taking pills, you know."

"What if," Louise turned the tables on her aunt, "you went to the drugstore and got one of those pill dispensers they sell? Then you can fill each little compartment with the day's pills and check up on Lloyd. If there's a pill left at the end of the day, you'll know he has to be more diligent."

"But what if he calls while I'm out?"

Louise, Jane and Alice exchanged looks. They were all exhausted from the upheaval, not only in their family, but also in Acorn Hill. Still, they couldn't blame their aunt for worrying.

Ethel was deeply concerned about Lloyd with good reason. The length of his hospital stay had been extended by two days, not because of physical problems but emotional ones. Despite their efforts to keep him cheerful and directions not to have any mail that looked like it might contain city business, Lloyd had fallen into a depression. Even in the hospital, word had gotten to him that the good citizens of Acorn Hill were not of one mind about the changes threatening Fairy Pond. The Howard sisters, always known to be level-headed and thoughtful, had become sounding boards for both sides of the issue even though they were nieces of Ethel Buckley and, hence, close to the mayor.

"I must go to the drugstore," Ethel announced. "I think

that pillbox is a wonderful idea. You know how Lloyd is. He hates to be nagged, so maybe the pillbox, sitting in plain sight, will remind him to take care of himself." She looked at her nieces. "Do you need anything from the store?"

"I'm running low on tea again. Pick out something you think would be good. Maybe Wilhelm will even brew you a sample," Alice suggested.

"Today is the day the Good Apple makes those exquisite French doughnuts," Jane added. "I much prefer buying theirs to working so hard for the same result. Could you get a half dozen?"

"And stop at Sylvia's Buttons, would you, Aunt Ethel?" Louise asked. She pulled a loose button out of her pocket. "And see if she can match that with anything she might have in stock. Otherwise I'll have to change all the buttons on that jacket."

Happy to feel useful, Ethel tallied her errands and started out.

When she was gone, Alice slid into a chair with a sigh. "You know, Lloyd had better come home and prove to Aunt Ethel that's he's feeling better, and he'd better do it soon."

Louise and Jane nodded grimly. They were running out of ideas for errands and projects to keep Ethel busy.

⌒

Jane had invited Sylvia to join her at Fairy Pond that afternoon. Sylvia brought hand-stitching—doll clothes made from quilt scraps. Jane brought her box full of paints and brushes and a stack of tiny three-by-four-inch canvases on which she painted tiny pictures of the creatures at the pond—frogs, toads, salamanders, a variety of bugs and birds, and even one of a deer that crept out of the woods to nibble on a particularly tasty-looking patch of grass at the edge of the clearing. She was also working on a series of the resident wildflowers and plants around the pond.

"Are you doing that so we can have memories of this place?" Sylvia asked softly. "I think we could sell those at my shop. There are a lot of people who would like to have some tangible memories of this pond."

"I can't seem to get enough of this place now that I know it will soon be gone."

"It's sad, isn't it?"

"Terribly." Jane felt her eyes fill with tears. "Destroying this place is a travesty, Sylvia. And for what? A gas station? Speculation that a more active roadway will create more business? Buildings can go up any time. Replacing Fairy Pond would take decades even if it could be done."

"Is it sure to happen?" Sylvia asked.

"Even Fred Humbert believes that it will. He's finally admitted that there seems to be no stopping it. If it hasn't already been made official, it soon will be."

"Then it seems to be out of our hands," Sylvia commented sadly.

"Yes. Even Casper Jones's hands." Jane studied the beetle she was painting before it scurried away. "He was very unhappy with his nephew, but, as he said, legally it is not something that he can change."

"And what about Casper's peace of mind?"

"He's terribly concerned. First and foremost, he doesn't like his nephew's callous behavior. Second, it carves away at the buffer between his land and the road. He told me he would try to contact his nephew, but that I shouldn't get my hopes up."

"Did he say anything else?"

"Just that while Ray probably didn't have exactly the same personality as his father, he had been raised by him, and attitudes sometimes rub off."

"Sounds to me like that's a gentle way of saying Ray isn't any better than his father."

"I don't know, Sylvia. I wish I did. Then I might be able to figure out some way to get to him and convince Ray to leave Fairy Pond as it is."

Jane gave a frustrated little grunt. "Hold still, you little fugitive!"

"What are you doing?" Sylvia asked.

"Trying to do miniportraits of all these tiny creatures. It's obvious that beetles don't like posing for portraits."

"Then paint the snails," Sylvia said pragmatically. "Even if they keep moving, you'll be done with your picture before they get away."

"You're right." Jane looked around until she found a likely candidate and began to recreate the gracefully rounded shell of a pale gray snail.

As she painted, the fragments of an idea began to form in her head.

"What's the prognosis for Lloyd?" Fred Humbert asked Jane as she shopped for paring knives and steel wool.

"Good. It's amazing what the medical community can do these days. He'll have to eat right, take walks, rest and do the things he should have been doing all along—that we all should be doing."

"Makes me think, that's for sure." Fred scratched the back of his head purposefully. "Of course, unless there's a hardware crisis somewhere in the world and hammer plants or thumbtack trees all go bad, I won't have the kind of stress poor Lloyd's been under."

Jane had to smile at Fred's sense of humor. "Maybe you'll be mayor of Acorn Hill someday. You'd do a good job."

Fred shook his head emphatically "I won't run. Unless they ask me. Then I'll run for sure—the other way."

"You're not a political animal then?"

"Nope. Besides that, Vera would have my hide. She says I don't get enough done around the house as it is." He grinned. "Got to keep the wife happy, you know."

"Then she's a very lucky woman."

Fred preened a bit. "I like to think so."

What should have been a happy homecoming for Lloyd seemed rather glum, Jane observed. Although Ethel had made sure the house was spotless and there were fresh flowers from Wild Things on the table, Lloyd barely seemed to notice his surroundings. In fact, he even passed the large stack of mail on the table in the foyer and went directly to his easy chair and sank into it as if he were a hundred years old. Justine and Josie were there to greet them, and even Josie's dancing around him like a hyper pixie didn't bring much of a smile to his face.

His lack of interest in his surroundings was a bit disappointing for them all. Ethel and Justine had scrubbed the house from top to bottom. Jane had made a colorful "Welcome Home" sign, and Clarissa from the Good Apple had even sent over loaves of fresh bread.

But none of it held any appeal for Lloyd.

"Depression," Alice whispered in Jane's ear.

"From being ill?"

"Maybe, but I think it's also the combination of that

and what's happening in town and with Fairy Pond. He had visitors who discussed it with him even though the rest of us didn't. He still feels like he's failed somehow."

"But that's ridiculous. This was completely out of Lloyd's hands."

"Of course it was, but it's not me you need to convince of that. It's him. He knows too that if Ray Jones builds this place and the highway doesn't get improved or bring through that much new business, the pond will have been lost for nothing."

"Hasn't Ray Jones thought of that?"

"I'm sure he has. I don't think he cares. He has enough money to build a dozen places like this. He's a speculator. He already owns the land. It makes sense to him."

Jane believed that. She just wished it all made sense to *her*.

Impulsively, she turned to go home.

Jane was glad that her sisters weren't home to ask her what she was doing. Casper, who, remarkably, had his nephew's cell phone number, "just in case," had given it to her during her visit. Jane had almost turned Casper down, unable to imagine any circumstances under which she might call Raymond Jones. Now she found herself dialing the number and holding her breath.

"Ray here," a brusque voice came across the line from wherever Raymond Jones was located.

Jane winced; he certainly didn't sound very friendly.

"Uh . . . hi . . . my name is Jane Howard and I live in Acorn Hill—"

"Oh, man, don't you people ever give up?"

"What do you mean?"

"I suppose you're calling for that . . . what's his name? Floyd?"

"Lloyd? Lloyd Tynan?"

"Yeah. The guy who keeps pestering me to rethink this development thing. Come to think about it, he hasn't called in a while. Is he on vacation?"

"Lloyd had a heart attack. He's been in the hospital."

There was silence on the other end of the line. When Ray spoke, there was a new tone in his voice. "Listen, I'm sorry about that. But if the guy took everything as seriously as he did a miserable gas station, it's no wonder . . ."

"He's really hurting," Jane said honestly.

Ray Jones sighed a put-upon sigh. "Listen, I'm sorry that I'm causing your mayor such a problem, but look at it my way. We did the numbers. There's potential for growth any way you look at it. With or without more traffic, it will promote cash flow. I own the land. You're in an area with huge tourist potential. It's a win-win as far as I can tell."

"But Fairy Pond—"

"That slough? My dad always called it a mosquito-breeding puddle."

"It's lovely there!"

"And it's *mine*. Listen, Ms. Howard, I don't mean to be difficult. I know that my father and uncle had a falling out. I know that I'm a stranger here. I also know it is *my land*. What I do with it is my business."

"If we could somehow raise the money—"

"Frankly, I don't need the money."

"Then why?"

"The wheels are already in motion, Ms. Howard. Now if you will excuse me, I have people to consult with. Good-bye."

Jane listened to the dial tone for a moment before hanging up the phone. Jones was honest. He didn't care. There was potential for moneymaking—even though he didn't need the money. The land was his and he had decided to do something with it. Period. No emotion, no remorse and certainly no interest in changing his mind.

The discouragement Lloyd must have felt clutched at her chest. It appeared that all that was left to do was to say good-bye to Fairy Pond.

Rather than mope around, Jane did what she always did when she was frustrated. She baked. Another German chocolate cake. Macaroons. Coffee cakes with cinnamon streusel. Pie.

When Louise and Alice returned several hours later, the entire inn smelled like a bakery.

Following her nose, Alice entered the kitchen. "What's going on here?"

"I just felt like baking."

"For whom? The Pittsburgh Steelers?"

"Just working off a little frustration."

"Would this have anything to do with Lloyd and the parcel of land that has been under constant discussion lately?" Alice poured a cup of tea, picked up a cookie and sat down at the table.

Jane was halfway through her story about calling Ray Jones when Louise entered. She sat down quietly and listened.

"So you have exhausted the options?" Louise asked.

"It seems so. I still feel like there has to be something... something small that I've missed, and I have no idea what it is." Jane shook herself out of her reverie. "When I was out at Fairy Pond, I felt like I was close to something, but..." She raked her hand through her hair. "I don't know. I just don't know."

Louise put her hand on Jane's as it rested on the table. "Please don't blame yourself. Lloyd tried, you tried and Casper tried. Now it's time to move on."

"How's Lloyd going to handle that?"

Louise sighed. "I don't know, but he will have to."

Chapter Eighteen

"Has anyone stopped to see Lloyd lately?" Jane asked on Wednesday as she put the morning's dishes into the dishwasher. He had been home four days and she hadn't seen as much of him as she had planned. Grace Chapel Inn had been busy. Ned Arnold had returned to the inn for a few nights while he filled in once again as pharmacist at the drugstore. The rest of the inn's rooms had been taken by traveling businessmen who came late and left early. The inn felt a little empty with no one lingering over coffee in the morning or asking directions to the nearest shops or sights.

"Not for a couple of days," Alice admitted. "I've talked to Aunt Ethel, however. She says that Justine is doing a beautiful job cooking and cleaning for him. She's even washed windows, cleaned carpets and offered to repaint the kitchen. Aunt Ethel says that Lloyd's home hasn't looked so nice in years."

"She is a definite blessing," Louise concurred. "But perhaps we have relied too much on her. I didn't see Lloyd yesterday either, knowing that Justine has everything under control."

"I'll stop by today." Jane closed the dishwasher and punched a button. "I've been experimenting with low-fat casseroles for Lloyd's freezer. Justine can't work for him forever."

"She'd probably like to," Alice responded. "She needs the money and he needs the help. It also takes a big load off Aunt Ethel's shoulders. You know how she would worry if someone weren't looking after him."

"She would try to do it herself," Louise added. "And she is not as young as she thinks she is."

After her sisters left the kitchen, Jane rubbed her lower back with her hands. She wasn't feeling very peppy herself. This upset over Fairy Pond had taken more out of her than she cared to admit. She had tossed and turned the night before. Sleep hadn't come until after three o'clock. Every time she dozed off, her dreams went back to Fairy Pond. Sometimes it was serene and beautiful; at other times there were bulldozers running over it, and every tree and blade of grass was gone.

She looked around the kitchen for something to take to Lloyd and settled on an apple, an orange and a fresh pear. Not his favorite snacks, she knew, but ones he should get accustomed to eating.

The day was beautiful. Jose Morales was working on the grounds of Grace Chapel as she passed. Jose lifted a hand in greeting and smiled his wide, bright smile. A workman was washing the windows at the Coffee Shop and Joseph was sweeping the sidewalk in front of his antique store. The air was crystal clear and the sun so bright that Jane found herself squinting toward the sky.

Lord, You've created such beauty that it takes my breath away. I feel so sad today because I know that there's nothing I can do to stop the construction at Fairy Pond. But I've just realized that although I've done plenty of worrying and fussing about it, I don't think I've ever really turned the situation over to You completely. What it comes down to, really, is that it is all Yours anyway. I ask that Your will be done. I'm letting this whole issue go, Lord, and giving it to You. Lloyd's heart attack probably came from trying to handle the impossible. Only You are equipped to do that. And Lord, we're all worried about Lloyd. I ask that You help him in the ways he needs it most. Amen.

Justine answered Jane's gentle rap on the door. Her face was creased in a frown. Jane stepped into the house and breathed deeply of the smells of lemon cleanser and floor polish blended with fresh air. White curtains were blowing gently at the open windows, and she could see a quart jar filled with daisies on the dining room table. There were even strains of a praise tape playing somewhere in the background.

"It's wonderful in here!" Jane blurted. "What happened

to all those musty old magazines and books Lloyd kept around his recliner? And those heavy, old-fashioned drapes—gone! I love it."

"Lloyd gave me permission to do what I wanted. I think he believed he wasn't long for this world, and it wouldn't matter anyway," Justine said with a wry smile. "So I took all the magazines to the library. Nia said she'd put an orange sticker on the corner of every one of them so that when Lloyd came in, he'd know which were his if he wanted to read them." Justine lowered her voice. "Frankly, I'm already trying to think of ways to get him out of the house. The library would be a perfect outing. I may ask him if we can take some of the books next. They're in the attic."

"And those ugly curtains?"

"Your Aunt Ethel and I put them with the trash. We also tossed in the grocery sacks Lloyd has been saving forever, socks without mates and all the junk mail he never got around to sorting."

"Well, it looks wonderful. Lloyd must be delighted."

Justine's shoulders sagged. "I wish he were."

"What do you mean?"

"I'm not sure he's even noticed. He doesn't want to stay downstairs and read or talk with me. He constantly insists that he's tired and needs to lie down. I open the curtains and pull up the shades in his bedroom, and before I know it, he's got them closed again, tight as a drum. I've told him he'll turn into a mole and want to live underground if he's not careful."

"What does he say to that?"

Justine's face twisted in pain. "Not much of anything. He rarely reacts to my teasing. In fact, last time I said it, he said, 'I probably belong underground anyway.'"

Jane gave a low whistle. That was as unlike Lloyd as anything she had ever heard.

"Sounds like his depression isn't lifting."

"I'm glad you came by today. I was going to call you anyway if you didn't. I didn't want to tell your Aunt Ethel about this because I thought it might scare her."

Jane nodded. "It would—and she probably suspects it already."

"Is there anything we can do?"

"I'll talk to Pastor Ken. He has chatted with Lloyd, but perhaps he could do more. He has a lot of training in counseling. When does Lloyd have to go in for his next doctor's appointment?"

"Friday. I'm going to drive him and your aunt."

"Good. The doctor needs to know this too. I have a hunch it's not uncommon for people who've been through something like this to be down, but it's a matter for professionals."

Justine looked supremely relieved. "Thank you."

"No, thank you. You've been an answer to prayer," Jane said with heartfelt gratitude. "Lloyd and Aunt Ethel both love you. Without you I'm not sure what we would have done."

Jane didn't say that they had even contemplated moving Lloyd into one of the rooms at the inn so that he wouldn't be alone. But being here, in his own house, probably would make his healing progress go much more rapidly.

Justine flushed. "They've been so generous to me, paying me more than I asked. I'm going to be able to pay off some bills and buy Josie some new clothes. She's grown like a weed, and I've had a hard time keeping up."

Jane reached out and gave the young mother a hug. "And don't forget you have me and my sisters to turn to if things get tough. Anytime. For anything."

The young woman gave a sigh, tears welling in her eyes. "God really does shine through you. I can see Him."

At that moment, they both heard a thump coming from upstairs. It sounded like something hitting a wall.

They turned and dashed upstairs together.

Jane and Justine burst into Lloyd's room as he was winding up to throw another book against the wall beyond the foot of his bed. His arm dropped to his side when he saw them.

Without speaking, Jane walked over and picked up the first book. *Mayoral Duties: The Story of a Small-Town Mayor* was the title. Then she looked toward the bed and saw the volume he had been about to throw. *Building Community Step By Step*. Beside him on the bed was another book, *The Demise of the Small Town in America*.

"No wonder you're throwing those," Jane commented calmly. "I would too. Can't you find anything more upbeat to read?"

"And hide my head in the sand a little longer?" Lloyd said gruffly. "This stuff is nonfiction, and I'm facing reality, that's all. Nothing wrong with that."

"No?" Jane walked over and tugged on the curtains until they were wide open. Lloyd put his hand over his eyes to shade them. "Remember that this is reality too. Have you noticed how breathtaking the weather is today?"

Lloyd, who had often come into the inn spouting a promising weather report, looked glumly at the pristine sky.

"Would you like to go for a little walk? Aunt Ethel told me that you had doctor's orders for mild exercise."

"What good will it do?"

"Plenty. It will make a new man of you." Jane held out a hand to Lloyd.

He stared at that too but didn't take it.

"Lloyd?"

"It's no use, Jane. What if I think it's pointless to become a new man? I'm disappointed with the old one."

"Lloyd Tynan, don't you *dare* blame yourself for what Ray Jones is doing! You've done all you could short of trying to buy the property yourself." Jane noticed a sudden change in Lloyd's expression. "Lloyd, you didn't! Did you?"

"He laughed at me," Lloyd mumbled. "Laughed out loud. Said nobody had enough money to buy it. Said he wanted to make his mark on Acorn Hill just like his old uncle and his father had. He laughed at me, he laughed at Casper, he laughed at all of us."

"Have you told anyone this before now?"

Lloyd shook his head.

"No wonder you've had such a hard time, keeping things like that inside." Jane moved toward him and kissed him on the forehead. Then she stepped back and put her hands on her hips. "Shame on you, Lloyd, for not letting us help you!" Then she tucked her arm around Lloyd's elbow and helped him to his feet. "And right now, I'm going to help you get out of this room and into the sunlight."

On the way home from Lloyd's house, Jane saw Sylvia outside her store.

"Do you have time for coffee?" Sylvia's lapels sprouted pins and needles and she had a tape measure draped around her neck. "I'm closing for an hour—I need a break."

"Sure. I wouldn't mind bending your ear either."

Together they walked toward the Coffee Shop. Sylvia put the tape measure in her pocket but left the pins in place. Inside, there was only one booth left, and the noise of chattering voices reminded Jane of walking into a henhouse— cackling and crowing everywhere.

Hope headed toward them with two cups and a carafe. When she got to them she plopped the cups onto the table. "I tell you, I don't know what's wrong with everybody these days."

"What do you mean?" Jane asked as Hope poured her coffee.

"Fuss and stew, speculate and argue, taking sides . . . all of Acorn Hill seems to have an opinion on Fairy Pond, and they suddenly all want to talk about it."

"What do you mean, 'argue'?" Sylvia asked.

"Progress, no progress, progress, no progress—like that. Best I can figure, nobody really wants Fairy Pond to go, but some are thinking that a couple more jobs in town would be a good thing. I do think it's finally starting to set in that soon we'll be seeing bulldozers instead of bullfrogs out there."

"Are people getting nasty?" Jane was thinking about poor Lloyd, who would be devastated if he thought the citizens of his town were at odds about something he felt he should have done something about.

"No, not really. I just think that everyone only wants to go back to the way we were—happy. Why, there wouldn't have been any trouble at all if that Raymond Jones wanted to put his gas station and convenience store on the road going toward Potterston. It wouldn't change Acorn Hill a whit, and there'd be a few new jobs to boot. But it seems that the decision has been made. Now, would you two ladies like pie?"

Chapter Nineteen

The next morning, Jane related her story about Lloyd to her sisters, and also what Hope had told her and Sylvia at the Coffee Shop.

"Frankly, I'm worried," Louise said. "I just don't see how any of this can have a happy ending for everyone. Someone is bound to be hurt."

"I'm trying not to be pessimistic," Alice said. She put her chin in her hands and sighed. "But it's getting harder and harder."

"It seems to me that all we can do now is figure out how to pick up the pieces after Ray Jones storms through here causing chaos."

"I wonder what his Uncle Casper thinks of all this," Alice mused.

Louise looked up as she felt her two sisters staring at her.

"Well, I don't know! Jane is the last one who talked to him."

"He's a very sweet man. So smart. He's really made a lovely home for himself out there. With the Internet, pets, a huge garden and a cozy house, I can see how he could be content." Jane eyed Louise. "It's still odd for me to think of you and Casper as high school sweethearts."

Louise blushed. "I know Casper would do something if he could to stop this fiasco. I have been praying that something will happen to solve all this, but so far—"

"So far it doesn't *seem* like God is working. That doesn't mean He isn't, however," Alice concluded.

"You are right, of course." Louise sighed.

Alice turned to Jane. "What are your plans for this morning?"

"I made a batch of low-fat oat bran muffins. I thought I'd take them to Lloyd. I must admit that I miss having him come over to snack with us."

"Well, my prayer is that he'll be back here soon, doing that very thing," said Alice.

"If I have to be ready for Lloyd every minute, the rest of us will lose a few pounds too," Jane commented with a smile. "Low-fat diets have that effect."

"It might be good for all of us."

On her walk across town, Jane chatted briefly with Fred, whom she met in front of the Coffee Shop; waved at Clarissa Cottrell as she swept the sidewalk in front of the bakery; and poked her head into Craig Tracy's store to say hello. It was a warm, sunny, bustling, happy day around

Acorn Hill. Everyone went about his business as if nothing were going to change. Jane believed that some of the townsfolk had no idea how big a change might be coming.

She was pondering this when Florence Simpson accosted her on Acorn Avenue. Florence's already remarkable, highly plucked eyebrows were arched to dangerous heights, a sure sign that she was appalled-amazed-alarmed about something. Her stout body was swathed in something that appeared to be a cross between a housedress and a muumuu, and her slight swagger told Jane that Florence thought she looked mighty fine.

Jane was accustomed to Florence because Florence and Ethel were friends, not always the *best* of friends, but friends nonetheless. There was often friction between them, yet they never seemed to give up on each other either. Florence persisted in telling Ethel what to do, and Ethel persisted in returning the favor. Sometimes it was a rocky friendship, but it endured.

"Jane Howard, I need to talk to you." Florence announced imperially.

"Here I am."

"You have got to do something about your Aunt Ethel."

"What do you suggest?" Jane steeled herself.

"She needs help, treatment."

"Aunt Ethel hasn't mentioned not feeling well."

Florence tapped her temple with the forefinger of her right hand. "She needs it up here."

"Aunt Ethel needs *psychological* help?" This was a new twist on an old theme. Florence often thought Ethel needed "straightening out," but this was the first time she had suggested that sanity was an issue.

"I'm not saying she's crazy, dear. I'm saying that she is emotionally distraught over Lloyd's illness and not handling it well at all. Why, she turned down an invitation to my annual summer coffee party so she could go sit with Lloyd. Imagine!"

I can imagine—I would. Jane resisted the urge to give expression to her reaction.

"She's not taking care of herself, Jane. Justine is on hand. Let *her* sit with Lloyd." Florence lowered her voice conspiratorially. "And what does he need 'sitting with' for anyway? He isn't breathing his last breath, is he?"

Jane chose not to make a comment about Florence's compassion and heartfelt concern for Lloyd's welfare.

"He's had a difficult time, Florence. Aunt Ethel is worried about him."

"And I'm worried about *her*. No one misses my annual summer coffee party unless something dire is happening." She skewered Jane with her eyes. "I think your aunt is going off the deep end worrying about Lloyd."

Jane sighed. She wasn't going to get out of this conversation easily.

"Actually, she has been worried. We all have. Lloyd doesn't have a lot of family, and the Howards are as close to family as he has in this area. He and Aunt Ethel are dear friends. It's difficult to see someone you care about suffer."

"He's not still worrying about the pond, is he? I know he thought he could use his mayoral clout and make that Ray Jones just go away, but I think he forgot just how little influence a small-town mayor has against a big-city developer. He should just," and she snapped her fingers together smartly, "snap out of it."

"Easier said than done," Jane said. "He has had a heart attack, after all."

"Ethel hasn't. You tell her that she can come over and get a box of cookies and sweets that I saved for her from my party. She loves my snickerdoodles, ginger snaps and butterscotch fudge. I also made her a few little casseroles to pop in the microwave. The woman needs to be taking care of herself, or she'll begin looking gaunt, and women of her age . . ."

Jane noticed that Florence hadn't said "women of *our* age."

". . . don't look good emaciated. Sunken cheeks and neck wattles do not appeal."

In her own indiscreet, bossy way, Florence was trying to help, Jane knew.

Jane flung her arms around the startled Florence and gave her a hug. "That's so sweet of you. I appreciate your concern for my aunt, and I want to assure you that we're taking good care of her. And I'm sure she'll be delighted to get those treats and casseroles from you—your reputation as a cook is well established."

It really is.

That took the wind out of Florence's critical sails.

"Well, I ... How nice of you to say so."

As Jane watched, Florence walked away mumbling something about "at least Ethel has nieces with common sense . . ."

"Kill 'em with kindness" was Jane's motto. She loved these funny, well-intentioned characters around Acorn Hill, and she was certain of the goodness—perhaps obscured at times—that made them so dear to her.

Lloyd had pulled his drapes again, and Justine was distraught.

"All he wants to do is sleep," she complained as Jane came in the front door.

"Maybe he's tired?" Jane asked, but she doubted it.

"Sometimes I can hear him stirring in his room, but when I go to check on him, he's sawing logs like a lumber mill. He's pretending, Jane. I know he is, just so I won't pester him to get up and take care of himself." Justine started to wring her hands. "He leaves food on his plate and says he's not hungry, and once..." Justine's voice caught. "I saw tears on his cheeks."

"Has Pastor Ken been here?"

"Yesterday. But Lloyd told him he was tired."

"So he left?"

"Yes, but right in front of our patient he asked me when Lloyd was most rested. I told him about three in the afternoon when he woke up from a nap." Justine smiled a little. "And Pastor Ken said 'I'll be here at three, then, when Lloyd can't chase me out.' I know he said that so that Lloyd would know he meant business."

"Good." Jane was thinking hard and fast. "When is his doctor's appointment?"

"Tomorrow, late in the afternoon. Pastor Ken also told him he'd drive him to his appointment and go in with him. Lloyd didn't like it much, but he finally agreed. Pastor Ken convinced him by saying that if he drove, your Aunt Ethel could rest." Justine was silent for a moment. "I don't know of any other argument that would have convinced Lloyd to let the pastor take him."

"That's wonderful. Pastor Ken can let the doctor know what's going on because Lloyd certainly won't."

"I hope it helps because I don't think Lloyd is getting any better," Justine whispered.

"Let me go check on him." Jane mounted the stairs and stood in the open doorway of Lloyd's room.

He was snoring loudly.

Jane backed away from the door and returned to the first floor knowing full well that Lloyd could never be an actor. He did the worst job of pretending he was sleeping of anyone she had ever known.

Chapter Twenty

*J*ane couldn't sleep that night. No matter how hard she tried, she couldn't get either her aunt or Lloyd out of her mind. Finally, knowing that when loved ones were placed in her mind and heart like this, her concern wasn't going to ease until she prayed for them, she scooted out of bed, dropped to her knees, put her head in her hands and began to pray silently.

Dear Heavenly Father, Lloyd and Aunt Ethel are both in such a state right now. I ask that You will ease their fears, lift them from sadness and set them on a path to joy and healing. It's odd how quickly we can go from happy to sad, from believing everything is fine to believing that nothing is fine. I thank You that You are the constancy in our lives. Help Aunt Ethel and Lloyd to experience the comfort of You. I don't even know what to ask for, Lord, but You know what we all need—so we'll have that—whatever is Your will. Amen.

It was almost ten o'clock on Friday morning by the time Jane had collected the last of the breakfast dishes, cleared the buffet of food, put out brownies, coffee cake, biscotti and trail mix for any guests who might have a delayed food craving, and handed off the rest of the cleanup to Alice.

"What are you doing, packing a lunch?" Alice asked Jane as she put foil-wrapped items into a paper bag.

"Sort of. I made some low-fat bars for Lloyd and am bringing brownies and coffee cake to Justine and Josie. Justine doesn't have an ounce of fat to spare. If she eats what Lloyd's eating, she'll fade away."

"Do you think that Lloyd is really fading away? Losing weight, I mean?"

"Yes. Haven't you noticed that he's been looking gaunt?"

"I've probably been wanting to believe it isn't so. It's so hard to think of our dear friend that way." Alice scrubbed at a nonexistent spot on the counter. "I hope he gets back to his old self soon."

"I can make the same wish for our aunt. She's been looking strained as well."

"What about her exercise? Isn't that helping?" Alice asked.

"Josie told me that Aunt Ethel hasn't been going since Lloyd got sick."

"Really? Aunt Ethel never mentioned to me that she'd stopped going."

"I don't think she wanted us to know. She probably thinks we'd make a fuss and make her go back to class."

"Which we would." Alice pointed out.

"Exactly," Jane agreed. "It's not going to help to have two sick loved ones on our hands."

"Louise and I have invited Aunt Ethel to have lunch with us in Potterston today. We all have errands and decided that perhaps it would be a good idea to get Aunt Ethel away from Acorn Hill before we tried to talk to her about how she's handling the Lloyd situation. Can you come too?"

"Thanks, but if you two are going to be with Aunt Ethel, I think I'll go back and spend some time with Lloyd. Justine is a trouper about cleaning and meals, but she really doesn't know what to do when Lloyd's feeling so down." Jane gave her sister a steady gaze. "I hope you make some headway with our aunt. She needs to take care of herself— and she needs to feel happy again."

"Same with Lloyd."

Both sisters almost imperceptibly squared their shoulders as if girding themselves for the battle of the day.

Josie was sitting on the front steps of Lloyd's house holding a doll and singing to it softly. When she saw Jane, her smile grew bright.

"Hi. I'm putting my baby to sleep. She's been fussy today."

"She has?" Jane sat down by the little girl and put an arm around her. "Why has she been fussy? Tummy ache? Wet diaper?"

"No. Just fussy."

"Now what caused that?" Jane drew back the blanket Josie had wrapped around her doll.

"Her life has been unhappy lately," Josie explained enigmatically. "Sometimes that happens, you know. Then the rest of us have to take very good care of her until she's feeling better about everything."

"I see." Jane had a hunch that Josie wasn't simply talking about her doll's problems.

"Who explained all this to you?"

"My mom," Josie said. "She says Mr. Tynan is feeling the same way lately." Her brow furrowed. "He's had lots of naps, but he's not better yet. I hope my doll gets better soon." Josie turned her gaze to Jane in alarm. "But what if she doesn't get better?"

The innocent question sent a zing of alarm through Jane as she realized that that was exactly the same question she had been asking herself about Lloyd. *What then? What if he really did give up? What if he continued to feel he'd failed Acorn Hill?*

"I'm not sure, honey, but I believe that we can keep on

loving people until they love themselves ... until they feel better."

Josie hugged her doll in such a stranglehold that it nearly popped the doll's head off. "I'm gonna love my baby just like that."

Then, in the next heartbeat, she flung the blanket off the doll and shook it "awake." "Look, Jane, she's feeling better!" The doll, whose eyes had been closed in repose, looked fully alert now because when Josie lifted her to a vertical position, her eyes automatically popped open.

"I did it, Jane. I loved her till she felt better." Then Josie disregarded the miraculous healing of her doll, grabbed her by one leg and announced, "I'm going to ride my bike."

On the way into the house, Jane wished Lloyd's recovery could only be as easy.

Justine was in the kitchen arranging cherry tomatoes on a bed of lettuce, bean sprouts and spinach.

"Lunchtime already?" Jane asked.

"I thought I'd try it a little early. He didn't want any breakfast. I found a recipe for fat-free dressing that I wanted to try, so ..." Josie stood back and looked at her colorful creation. Then she sighed. "I'll bet that he won't eat this either, I'm sure."

"What does he eat?"

"Sometimes he'll agree to a little cereal and skim milk. He liked my homemade soup. Other than that, he's pretty much turned everything down after a bite or two." Justine smiled wryly. "But Josie and I have been eating well. There are always plenty of leftovers."

Reminded of why she'd come, Jane handed the paper bag to Justine. "Treats for you and Josie. The healthy stuff is for Lloyd—if he'll have it."

"Thanks, Jane, from Josie and me . . . and from our patient. I even had to nag him into drinking some tea today. After much talking, he promised me he'd take a shower later so I could change the bed." Justine's eyes looked sad. "He's just not himself, Jane."

Then who is he? He's a shell of himself, someone emptied of purpose and filled with disappointment, Jane thought. Lloyd's situation was beginning to scare her.

He had pulled the shades again, Jane observed as she rapped on the open door of Lloyd's room. He was sitting in a large recliner watching television. The sound was turned off and several people were obviously making fools of themselves on a game show. The light from the television flickered, casting moving shadows across his face.

"Come in." Lloyd's voice sounded hollow, uninterested.

"It's me, Jane."

To her surprise, Lloyd straightened and sat up. "Oh, it's you. Good."

Heartened by the welcome, she walked into the room and took the straight-backed chair in front of him. "You must be feeling better today."

"*Hmmm.* Yeah, better. I hoped you'd come."

"I'm sure the others will be along before the day is out. Louise and Alice took Aunt Ethel to Potterston with them for lunch, so I wouldn't expect anyone until later."

"Good, good. Ethel is getting out. I'm glad to hear that. She's been around here fussing at Justine and me till we're both crazy." He shook his head fondly. "That woman."

To Jane's surprise, she saw tears in his eyes.

He grabbed her hand. "Ethel is a wonderful woman, Jane. She's been good for me. I hope she knows that. I've tried to tell her."

Jane didn't know what to say.

Then Lloyd switched gears. He pushed himself out of his chair and walked to the dresser where he started moving things around.

His movements were decisive, and a flicker of hope lit in Jane. Maybe this was a turning point.

He found what he was looking for, a long, unaddressed white envelope. He picked it up and brought it to Jane before sitting down again in his chair.

"I have a big favor to ask of you, Jane," he began. "I've always respected you. You left Acorn Hill, made your way in the big world and were able to come back and appreciate what we have here. You're smart, Jane. And I trust you. That's why I want you to read this before I send it. I want every word to express what I feel ... and I don't want to be discounted as a rambling old man."

Mystified, Jane reached for the envelope he handed her. It was unsealed, and inside was a single page, a letter, typed on an old manual typewriter, likely the one that sat on a table in the corner of the room. She unfolded it gently and began to read.

Chapter Twenty-One

*J*ane's fingers tightened around the paper as she read.

To the Members of the City Council and Citizens of Acorn Hill:

This letter is to tender my resignation as Mayor of Acorn Hill. I feel that I have not served you as fully as I would have liked and that I have failed to carry out my campaign promises; therefore, I am stepping down from my position as mayor.

I ran—in large part—because of my belief that Acorn Hill has a life of its own away from the outside world, and that that life should be preserved. My promise to keep our town from becoming just another tourist trap is one I have obviously been unable to honor.

I have also grown to realize that my vision for Acorn Hill is not everyone's vision. In my enthusiasm to keep Acorn Hill pristine, I have not fully considered the community's need for new jobs and for more business.

In light of these oversights and because of my declining health, I am resigning my position as Mayor of Acorn Hill.

Respectfully yours,
Lloyd Tynan

Jane looked at Lloyd with dismay. "You can't do this!"

"I can and I have. I just want you to check it over in case I missed something or made a spelling error. I couldn't let Ethel look at it because she'd probably blow a gasket, so I'm asking you. It's decided, Jane. Do me a favor and don't argue with me about it. I'm not one to stay where I'm not wanted or when I see the handwriting on the wall."

"Just because you haven't been able to stop a piece of property from being developed doesn't mean you haven't been a good mayor. That's like saying that because the bread I was baking didn't rise correctly I'm a bad cook."

"Hardly the same." Lloyd got a stubborn look on his face and hunkered down in his chair.

"What if Louise said that because some of our guests didn't like the firmness of the bedding at our place, she was leaving the inn, that she didn't want any part of a place that was less than perfect?"

"Nonsense! Everyone likes everything about the inn."

"Really?" And Jane began a litany of Gen Thrumble's complaints and threw in a few of the others they had received since opening the inn: "Coffee too cold, coffee too hot, water too hot and too cold, need early check-in, need late check-out, too many starches for breakfast, too few starches for breakfast."

Lloyd looked surprised, as if he had believed that the inn ran on greased wheels, without a hitch.

"We're just a cozy bed-and-breakfast, Lloyd, yet people find plenty to complain about. You've been the mayor of our town for years, and this is the first major issue that's caused you to waver. You've done a wonderful job. Give yourself some credit! Besides," and Jane felt grateful that she had run into Joseph Holzmann on the way over, "I saw Joseph this morning and asked him specifically if the town was really divided over this."

Lloyd looked just a wee bit interested.

"He said no."

"Then why was there talk of replacing me?"

So, Lloyd had heard that.

"According to Joseph, that and everything else was pure frustration speaking, not the truth. Everyone is confused. We all love Acorn Hill just the way it is and yet, when confronted with the possibility of a little growth and expansion and more, better-paying jobs, well, you can hardly blame some people for getting excited. But that talk died down very quickly, especially when Craig Tracy mentioned the fact that whether Acorn Hill got more jobs or not, Potterston was going after them, and there would be plenty of places to work there."

She saw a tiny flicker of hope in Lloyd's eyes, but it quickly dimmed.

"And all that business about our town breaking into two camps?"

"Nonsense, according to everyone I've talked to."

"Doesn't matter," he said stubbornly. "It's just not the same."

"Lloyd, will you promise me that you will not resign for the next two weeks? Will you think about this more clearly? Talk to Pastor Ken. If, after two weeks, you still think you can't serve the community as mayor, then—and only then— consider resigning."

"I knew I shouldn't have shown it to you." He reached futilely to grab it away from her.

"I'm so thankful you did. Lloyd, you aren't feeling well. You're emotionally upset. Would you advise anyone else in your shoes to do something so drastic if he were in the state you are in?"

"Of course not, but—"

"Then take your own advice. Will you wait two weeks and then reconsider?"

His shoulders sagged, and Jane knew she had gotten her point across.

He did not look happy with her. "I don't know what difference it makes. In two weeks Fairy Pond will probably be gone, and there will be preparations for the new construction in its place. It will be an easy decision then."

It struck Jane that he was probably right. Still, handing in his resignation right now didn't seem prudent. It wouldn't be good, either for Lloyd or for Acorn Hill. She was relieved that he had agreed to hold off for now. It gave her a chance to think. There was something . . . there *had* to be something.

She knelt beside Lloyd and took his hands. "Can we pray?"

Lloyd smiled. "I suppose we'd better start. There's not much else that can save me or Acorn Hill."

Taking his dour answer as a yes, she began. "Dear Heavenly Father, we've got a dilemma here. You know all the parts of the puzzle—Lloyd, Ray and Casper Jones, the appreciation so many of us have for the natural beauty of Fairy Pond, the citizens of Acorn Hill. We ask that You step into the middle of this problem so that Your will may be done. We ask for Your healing grace for Lloyd and the community. We turn it all over to You and ask that You make something sweet and good from all this turmoil. And thanks for always being here for us when we need it most. Amen."

She felt Lloyd's hands tremble in hers. "Amen," he whispered.

She stood and held out his resignation. "Do you want to keep this or should I?"

"You can. But only for two weeks. Then I want it back in my hands. You hear me?"

"Loud and clear, Mr. Mayor."

Lloyd scowled at her, but Jane sensed a tiny hint of relief in his face.

Jane didn't feel like going back to the inn. Instead, she stopped by Sylvia's Buttons. Sylvia was just closing the shop.

"Why are you closing up in the middle of the day?"

Sylvia sighed and set her shoulders. "It might sound funny, but I've decided that this is just too beautiful a day to be trapped inside and..."

"And what?"

"And I wanted to enjoy it at Fairy Pond because this might be one of the last times I can." She held up her bag. It contained one of her pieces to be hand quilted. "And who knows when I'll get any hand quilting done after it's gone?"

"May I go with you?"

"Of course. I see you have the right shoes for the walk, but do you need any art supplies?"

"No. I just want to go there and think."

"About what?"

"About the pond. There's something niggling in the back of my mind that I just can't come to terms with. A solution, maybe. Some connection I should be able to make between Fairy Pond and all that's going on ..." Jane shook her head. "And I have no idea what it is."

"This doesn't sound like you, Jane. Come on. You need Fairy Pond even more than I do."

It was, it seemed, more beautiful there than ever. It was as though nature had dressed the hideaway for its going away party. Flowers bloomed and fat frogs lazed in the sun.

"Will you think I'm awful if I just sit down and cry?" Jane asked. "I can't bear to think of earthmovers and bulldozers in here wreaking havoc."

Sylvia pulled a wad of tissue from her bottomless bag. "Here. Have some. I had a hunch I might do the same thing."

They sat in their favorite spots, so silent that buzzing bees sounded like low-flying airplanes and the occasional *ribbit* of a frog seemed remarkably loud. The canopy of green overhead embraced them. The peacefulness of the place gently absorbed Jane's distress.

Finally stirring, Jane sat up and looked at Sylvia. "Why couldn't Raymond Jones be here today? Why can't he appreciate this place?"

Sylvia didn't answer, but another voice did.

"My brother never taught him about the finer things in life. Orlando only taught Ray about money—how to get it, how to keep it, how to make more of it."

Jane and Sylvia both straightened abruptly. Their heads turned toward Casper Jones.

Casper stood in an opening in the thicket, leaning on his gnarled walking stick. He looked much as he had on the day Jane had first met him, except that today he wasn't wearing a hat, and his neatly parted gray hair added to the distinguished quality of his appearance. It struck her again what a good-looking—contented-looking—man he was. Casper was a most unlikely hermit.

"We didn't hear you coming," Jane said inanely.

"I'm sorry if I startled you." Casper bowed toward Sylvia, and she smiled. "I was just coming to sit here awhile myself and ponder the ways my brother has managed to make things miserable for people even from the grave."

"From what I gather, he did it legally and apparently within his rights," Jane said. She moved to one side of the long split log on which she was sitting. "Care to join us?"

After introductions were made, the threesome made idle small talk. Jane could tell Sylvia was just as charmed by Casper as she herself had been the first time they had met.

"I rarely ran into anyone over here until you started to come," he said to Jane. "Now there are many times I come by to check on things and someone is here. You rediscovered this spot for folks."

"I didn't mean to intrude—"

"You didn't. As we well know, this land is not my property. I suppose you could say we're all trespassers of a sort on my nephew's land." He teased a toad with the tip of his cane to make it jump. "Pretty soon even these little guys may be regarded as trespassers."

Casper put his walking stick on the ground beside him. "It's a shame too. This spot is a hotbed of odd little creatures." He reached out and picked up a fat green caterpillar and allowed it to crawl across the palm of his hand.

Jane stared at the little creature, mesmerized. So small, so complex... She reached out to touch its fuzzy body. "And some people can still say there is no God," she marveled. "How can such creatures be mere accidents? Have they ever *really* looked at a caterpillar or a bird or a fish?"

"Tennyson..." Casper said, looking as though he was trying to recall something. "Alfred, Lord Tennyson expressed much the same sentiment." He reflected another moment and then recited:

> Flower in the crannied wall,
> I pluck you out of the crannies.
> I hold you here, root and all, in my hand,
> Little flower—but *if* I could understand

What you are, root and all, and all in all,
I should know what God and man is.

"How lovely!" said Sylvia. "He would have loved Fairy Pond."

"Thank you, Casper. If only I could express myself with Tennyson's gift for language." Jane spotted a small flower with purple petals and moved off to examine it.

Sylvia and Casper chatted as Jane foraged around on the forest floor. She poked at the ground with a stick, lifting leaves and moving rocks until she found a snail. She held it in the palm of her hand as it drew itself inside its shell. It would peek out eventually, she knew, when it thought the danger was past. As she sat there, something Lloyd had said began to echo in her ears, something he had said about stopping Ray Jones.

"There's got to be a way!" Lloyd had said. "He's got to have overlooked something—something small, something that he thinks is unimportant..."

Jane gasped so loudly that Sylvia and Casper turned to stare at her.

"There *is* a way!" she blurted. "I think I know a way!"

"To do what?" Sylvia asked.

"To try to save Fairy Pond."

And before either Sylvia or Casper could respond, Jane took off running.

Chapter Twenty-Two

*J*ane was out of breath when she reached the inn. Hurrying as she was, she nearly bumped into Louise as she stood on the porch watering flowers.

When Louise caught up with her, Jane was inside the house pawing madly through Alice's bookkeeping records and registries.

"What on earth are you doing? You are not an Olympian, you know. Running through the street like a teenager."

Jane ignored her and pulled open a drawer. "Where is the card file that Alice keeps?"

"Card file? Whatever do you—"

"You know. If we have guests they often give us their business cards. Where does she put them?"

"Usually they are in that drawer."

"Then why aren't they here now?"

"I have no idea." Louise shook her head in bewilderment.

"They have to be somewhere."

"Maybe that's what she was working on in the study the other day. She had a little file box—"

Jane bolted out of the room so quickly that Louise could not even finish her sentence. Then Jane was back, carrying a small tin box filled with business cards. She dumped them on the table and began spreading them about.

"You have just mixed them all up again," Louise scolded. "What on earth has gotten into you?"

"I just figured out what has been bothering me all this time about Fairy Pond. It was something Casper said."

"Casper? Is he coming?" Louise got a little pink in the cheeks. "I would love to chat with him, you know."

"No, he's not coming. He doesn't even know what he's done. It was what he said when he was holding that caterpillar —"

"You have lost me entirely, Jane. Have you lost your mind as well?"

"I think I've just begun to find it again." Jane pounced on a small white business card. "Aha! Here it is!" She glanced around. "I'll use the phone in the kitchen."

"Whom are you planning to call?"

But Jane was already in the kitchen, punching numbers.

Louise followed her, pantomiming her previous question.

Jane giggled at the sight. "Peter Gowdy," she mouthed.

"Who?"

"One of our guests. The man who works for the government."

"Oh, the snail and slug fellow? Why on earth do you want to talk to him?"

Peter Gowdy picked up before Jane could respond to Louise.

"Hello. Gowdy here. How may I help you?"

"Peter, this is Jane Howard. I'm from Acorn Hill. We met when you stayed at our inn—"

"The fabulous breakfasts! How could I forget?" His voice was warm and pleasant. "What can I do for you?"

"I was wondering about the snails."

"Really? I'm just wrapping up that study. In fact, you're lucky you caught me. I've been gone from the office until today."

Jane felt her heart pounding in her chest and willed herself to calm down. If she didn't, she felt that she might end up like Lloyd.

"I wanted to ask you if it is possible that there are any unusual creatures around Fairy Pond, I believe I mentioned the place to you."

"Unusual? How do you mean?"

"Something that you might find that would stop construction of a bridge or highway. A little plant or bug—"

"A threatened or endangered species, you mean?"

"Exactly!"

"Well, I don't know," Peter said hesitantly. "I was primarily interested in the snails, and I'm not sure if I visited near the place you mentioned."

"I know it's asking a lot, but could you possibly come and look again? Just in case, I mean."

"Just in case of what?" He sounded puzzled.

"A developer is planning to level the property around Fairy Pond to put up a convenience store and gas station. There seems to be no legal way to stop him, but I was wondering if . . . just on the off chance—"

"There might be a legitimate way to prevent him from going ahead with the project?"

"Yes. I know it's a lot to ask, but I'd be happy to pay you for your time, and you did say that sometimes people have had to build around threatened or endangered populations."

"I'd like to help . . . as a friend, so no more talk about pay. Actually, I'll be driving out that way in a couple of days. I have some new funding for a project I'm working on. We're making an attempt to protect wetland habitats from encroachment or destruction. Sounds like your Fairy Pond might be right up my alley."

"Come and stay at the inn. As long as you like—on the house."

"Deal. I'll see you soon."

Jane put down the phone and sank into a chair. It was then she noticed that Louise's eyebrows were arching.

"On the house?" Louise said.

"We can't pinch pennies now, Louie. This is my last, best—only—hope for stopping Raymond Jones. I can't think of another thing. Peter told me there were several threatened species in Pennsylvania. If we could find one of those—"

"Or the pot of gold at the end of the rainbow."

Jane looked at her sister with exasperation. "Don't go negative on me now. So much depends on this."

Louise softened. "Including Lloyd?"

"He's a mess." Jane didn't mention his written resignation to her sister. "I think it will damage his physical health—even his psyche—if things go wrong."

Louise sighed. "I'm afraid you might be right. Whoever would have thought that Orlando Jones could wreak this much havoc?"

By Monday, Jane thought she might burst, thinking about what she had done and about not telling anyone but her sisters. She had sworn them to absolute secrecy. If word got out, it would only make matters worse if people got their hopes up, and then had them dashed.

She had been so nervous for so long that every bit of freezer space in the inn was full. She needed Lloyd back here in fine form and with an appetite to get rid of some of the low-fat concoctions she had made in her agitated state.

When she couldn't cook anymore, she pursued an alternative activity—she painted. And sometimes she painted big.

"What are you going to do with that roll of canvas, Jane, make a tent?" Alice asked as she watched her sister tote it down from the attic.

"Stretch it and paint on it. I've wanted to do something bigger than bugs and frogs at Fairy Pond, so I thought this was the time to do it." Jane eyed the stack of stretcher frames she had on a table in the hallway.

"Excess energy?" Alice asked mildly.

"Enough to fuel Philadelphia," Jane admitted. "I have to expend it some way."

"Then instead of working on a canvas, why don't you go to Nine Lives and tell Viola you'll paint a mural for her? She's asked for that, you know, and she is a dear friend."

Jane groaned. "That's supposed to calm me down? You know Viola. She'll be giving me 'hints' until I go completely mad."

"It will be fun," Alice said. "And good for you. Try it—you might like it."

Liking it was probably out of the question, Jane decided on Tuesday, but she had to admit that it was interesting. Viola had already primed the five-by-seven-foot portion of the wall she wanted painted and had made a list of the "historic" events and scenes she wanted depicted. They were not historic in the usual sense, but, Jane supposed, they were important to Acorn Hill.

"I can't tell you how glad I am to hear that you're willing to paint for me, dear. I know you're so busy, but this will be such a joy for my customers, don't you think? And educational! Where do you think you'd like to start?"

By having my head examined, Jane thought. *That would be the best place.* Still, Viola had purchased paints and even a drop cloth. All Jane had to do was begin.

"I only have a day or so to work on this, Viola, so it can't be as complicated as you've indicated here on your drawing." She held up a piece of paper with almost every square inch covered in sketches. "If you trust me, I'll do something that I think will be appropriate for your store."

"Oh, dear. I had plans . . ." Viola thought hard about it. "But beggars can't be choosers, now can we? You go ahead, dear, and I'll keep customers away from your work. I'll leave it in your hands. And there will be books in this for you. Count on it."

Some hours later, Jane wondered about that promise to leave matters in her hands. Viola had come to "consult" with her every fifteen minutes about her choices of colors and about what the finished work was going to look like.

"It really doesn't look like anything yet," Viola observed.

"I'm just putting the background in," Jane assured her, making broad strokes with a brush. "And I've made a few sketches so that I'll have an idea of what goes where."

"I can't see them." Viola nearly put her nose on the wall to look.

"You will." Jane leaned on the ladder. "I'll tell you what. If you'll give me a few more hours alone with this wall, I promise you'll be pleasantly surprised."

"You will come and get me if you have any questions, won't you?"

"I won't have any. I know just what I'll do. Trust me."

"Yes . . . well . . . if you insist . . . Nothing wild and crazy now, like that mermaid painting in your bathroom at the inn."

Finally alone, Jane squinted, surveying what she had accomplished so far. Then, with Viola out of sight, she took a paintbrush and dipped it into a bucket of yellow and began.

Jane checked her watch sometime later as she stepped back to view her work. Not bad. She had chosen to do an impressionistic interpretation of Viola's list, starting with a suggestion of the streets of Acorn Hill running across the center of the wall. She had used broad strokes to give the appearance of buildings, and then a finer brush to paint in just the most necessary details. She had drawn in all the business signs, of course. There was Nine Lives proudly displayed as well as the sign for Grace Chapel Inn. She had used bright colors—reds, yellows, greens—and she had worked fast. What might have taken her days—had she painted in great detail—she had managed to bring together quickly and successfully in a few hours.

"You did that?" Viola spoke from behind her.

Jane spun around. "Yes. Isn't it all right?"

Viola had her hands over her mouth and her eyes were wide.

"It's lovely! Remarkable!"

Jane held up the brush in her hand. "I think I've discovered something new. I can paint very quickly with a very big brush."

"I'd been thinking of having lots of detail, of course, but this … this … it's art!"

Jane hadn't expected praise. She still wasn't sure she was hearing that Viola actually liked the bold strokes of the impressionist-style mural. Jane, almost to her own surprise, liked it very much too.

"Van Gogh, Monet … and you!"

"Well I wouldn't go *quite* that far," Jane said, holding back a chuckle. She was surprised when Viola ran to the door of the shop, slammed it shut, locked it and flipped the sign in the window to "Closed."

"Is it already that time?" Jane looked at her watch. "It's too early to close yet, Viola."

"Of course it isn't. I want to have a special showing of our new piece of art. We can't have people wandering in here and seeing it before we're ready."

"I'm not done yet. I'll drop in once more to finish some last details."

"More details? Why, it will be so lovely! I'll call Clarissa right away. I'll have her make a cake in the shape of a painter's palette. It will be so charming…" And Viola was off and running, planning the big unveiling of Jane's work.

"Had I known how pleased she'd be and how little time it would take me," Jane said to her sisters at the dinner table on Thursday, two nights later, "I'd have done the mural much sooner. Now Viola doesn't want to open her shop until after the unveiling tomorrow."

"Have you heard from Peter yet?"

"No. He didn't say exactly when he'd be through Acorn

Hill. I called his office again but got his voice mail saying he'd be out of town for a while. I guess we'll just have to wait patiently."

"Aunt Ethel came home angry from Lloyd's today," Alice commented as she passed the potatoes to Louise.

"No kidding? Why?"

"She said, and I quote, 'He's being a big, difficult, spoiled baby about this.'"

Jane thought back to the resignation letter she had in the top drawer of her dresser. "Maybe it's not so much that he's being a baby, but that he cares so deeply and feels he's failed the community."

"But he hasn't! No one thinks like that," Alice protested.

"He does."

And that, Jane mused, was the dilemma. And if Peter Gowdy couldn't help her, their next big problem would be Lloyd himself.

Chapter Twenty-Three

*J*ane, if you don't settle down, we will find you sound asleep on the kitchen floor one morning, a spoon still in your hand!"

"Relax, Louie, this is my last batch of sticky buns. After all, it's Friday, the show is tonight." Jane opened another package of nuts and began whacking them into bits.

"It wasn't necessary for you to agree to bring food for Viola's art show, even if she offered to pay for your services," Alice pointed out.

"Viola is paying for all the ingredients. I'm just preparing them."

"By the way, she's even had a few calls from Potterston about people coming to see your work," Alice added.

"That's just silly. I spent very little time on it. If they want to see my work, then they should look at some of the things I have upstairs."

"Oh, that reminds me," Louise said. "Viola asked me if you would bring some of your other work. She has apparently decided to promote you as her new marketing project. Books *and* art."

"Say it isn't so," Jane groaned. With Viola's brand of enthusiasm, who knew what she had gotten herself into now?

"Humor her," Louise advised. "It is just for one night. She is being very generous."

Under other circumstances, Jane would have said no immediately, but she needed to keep busy. She still hadn't heard from Peter Gowdy, and when she went to Fairy Pond the day before, she had seen stakes in the ground. Someone had been out there measuring, preparing for what was to come. Her stomach turned over each time she thought of it. She needed something to distract her. It might as well be Viola's latest enthusiasm for her work.

At noon, Jane began toting canvases to Nine Lives. Viola instructed her to bring them in through the back door and to "be sure to keep the fronts concealed. We don't want any passersby to get an early peek at the show."

Jane tactfully didn't remind her that several of the pieces had been floating around Grace Chapel Inn for some time now.

"I have a few easels we can use," Jane offered. "Otherwise I don't know how you'll display them all."

But Viola had thought of everything. She had taken down the posters depicting her favorite authors, leaving space for Jane's work. She had put plastic hooks on some of the bookcases to hold canvases and even roped off sections of the room so that the viewing public wouldn't get too close to the pictures and do them harm. She had a buffet table set with white linen and a bouquet from Wild Things.

"Why, it's really lovely in here!" Jane exclaimed, pleased and warmed by the woman's effort.

"It is, isn't it?" Viola clapped. Then she eyed Jane. "But you haven't looked very happy about it."

"Me? I'm delighted with your work, Viola. I think it's terribly sweet of you and I'm happy to help. I just can't get my mind off Fairy Pond and Lloyd."

Viola frowned. "Oh dear. I had hoped that planning this showing would help. Louise told me how upset you've been."

"And so you were doing this for me when you did all this?" Jane was deeply touched.

"And for me. And for Acorn Hill. Your work is wonderful —both your painting and your cooking—and this is a chance to show you off. But I did hope that it would take your mind off those troubles too."

Jane hugged the older woman. "You sweetie, you. Thank you. And it has helped. I just thought I had one more thing up my sleeve to try and time is running out."

She helped Viola arrange the pictures, move chairs, adjust bookshelves and tidy the floor. And with every sweep of the broom, she prayed silently. *Help us through all this, Lord, one way or another. Your will be done, and give us the strength to accept whatever turn this takes. Help Lloyd and revive his spirit. I know that lots of people have been praying about this and we will accept Your will. But if there's any chance . . . Never mind, Lord. You knew what I was going to say. Amen.*

Jane stopped at Sylvia's before going home. The quilt Sylvia had been working on was done now and displayed in the shop. Two ladies were clucking and fussing over it, and one wanted to buy all the material to make one "just like it."

Jane sat down on a stool behind the cutting table and watched Sylvia expertly pull bolts of fabric, measure them and cut fat quarters with a rotary cutter. In no time the woman was leaving the shop with fabric, thread, a pattern and various and sundry quilting tools.

"You make that look easy," Jane commented when they were alone. "It would have taken me all day to measure and cut that stuff. And you looked so sure of yourself. Aren't you afraid of making a mistake?"

"This is lots easier than you think, but it would take *me* a year to paint the mural you did in Viola's store."

"You peeked?"

Sylvia laughed. "She let me in because she couldn't stand it any longer. She said she wanted to show someone the mural, and she knew that even if I'd seen it, I'd come again tonight. It's fabulous, Jane. How you could depict Acorn Hill in such broad brush strokes and make it seem so real...Wow!"

"So you *are* coming tonight?"

"Wouldn't miss it. Viola's not kept it a secret that you've been preparing most of the food. She will probably have her biggest crowd ever."

"Quite a marketer, that Viola. She's got a display of art books and how-to-draw books right next to the cash register, just in case someone gets the bug to do her own thing."

"I could take lessons from her," Sylvia said with a laugh. "Want a cup of coffee?"

"No, but I do want to ask you a favor."

"Sure. What is it?"

"Aunt Ethel thinks that it would be good for Lloyd to get out of the house. She wants him to come to Nine Lives tonight to see some friendly faces."

"Great idea."

"Of course, Lloyd has been protesting, but I think he's softened to the idea. Normally I'd help Justine and Aunt Ethel to take him over, but because I'll have to provide food, I won't be free to do it. Would you mind driving to Lloyd's and picking them up? He's a handful for Justine, fussing as he does, and Aunt Ethel gets rattled and just flutters around saying 'Oh, Lloyd. Now, Lloyd.'"

Sylvia grinned widely. "I can just see it. Sure, I'll pick them up. Maybe I'll go early and take them for a drive as well."

"Just don't go by Fairy Pond, even if Lloyd asks."

"Something new in that regard?"

"It's been staked out. I imagine there will be bulldozers pulling in there any day now."

"Oh, how sad!"

Jane bit her lip. *Oh, Peter, where are you?*

Jane stood in front of her closet studying the kaleidoscope of color inside.

Alice knocked on the door and came in. "Trying to decide what to wear?"

"Something artsy, I think." Jane whipped a vivid-blue jumpsuit off the rod. "What about this?"

"Very blue."

Jane tossed it on the bed and dove for something else. "This?"

"Very, very orange."

"Well, then, what would you suggest?"

Alice studied the interior of the closet and pulled out a cream-colored set with narrow legged pants and a long, almost toga-like top. It was one Jane had hand-painted for herself for the opening of a new art gallery in San Francisco. "This is lovely."

"Not too dressy?"

"Not a bit. This is your debut in Acorn Hill."

Jane laughed out loud. "I've been debuting over and over ever since I got here with one thing or another. Don't you think people will get tired of me soon?"

"Highly doubtful," Louise said from the doorway. "I'm your sister, and you have always kept *me* wondering what you will do next."

"Louise is right," Alice agreed. "Even though I know better, I still somehow keep expecting you to pull a rabbit out of your hat where Fairy Pond is concerned."

"I wish I could, Alice, but even I am losing hope." Jane felt disappointment coursing through her. It appeared that Peter Gowdy was not coming after all. She had been so *sure* he would. Maybe something had come up. Otherwise he surely would have called—wouldn't he? It would be horrible if he arrived after the trees had been taken out and the pond filled in. She shuddered just thinking about it.

"Well, for tonight at least, no thinking about Fairy Pond and no talking about it either. Aunt Ethel called and said that Lloyd has 'grudgingly' agreed to go to Nine Lives tonight. She says she actually thinks he's looking forward to it, but he's become so curmudgeonly of late that he won't let it show."

Jane picked up the garment Alice had chosen. "Okay. No Fairy Pond tonight. Only fun and good cheer."

"That's my girl," Alice encouraged. "Now get ready. It's almost time to go."

⁓

Nine Lives had never looked better. Viola had polished the front window and put up a huge sign, "Art Show Tonight." On a second sign she had written, "Artist Has Done Her Own Baking for the Occasion."

Jane hid a smile. That was something she had never seen at an opening in San Francisco. Maybe she had started something new.

What amazed her even more was that there was a line waiting to get in.

Wilhelm Wood was one of those patiently waiting.

"You, my dear, have fans, groupies. What can I say?"

"Wilhelm, you silly, have you been waiting long?"

"I would wait for hours if necessary. And we've attracted several more curious souls who now want to know what's happening inside Viola's store."

"Well, thank you. It feels good. And I can use anything right now that will make me feel good."

He looked at her with a compassionate expression. "Things will work out as they should, Jane."

"I know." She patted him on the cheek. "Now I suppose I'd better sneak inside and get ready for my fans."

"You do that." Wilhelm smiled at her fondly.

Feeling uplifted, Jane entered the store and Viola's whirl of last-minute activity.

Viola looked like one of Jane's paintings—one of her especially vibrant ones. She wore a caftan, the fabric of which exhibited orange giraffes, blue elephants and other bizarrely colored creatures of the Serengeti. On her ears she wore huge, purple disks that hung almost to her shoulders. In addition to her signature scarf, she wore earthen beads around her neck. She twirled for Jane when Jane entered.

"Do I look like the hostess of an art gallery?" she wanted to know. "This is how I imagine one to be. Am I close?"

Jane studied her and thought of the sleek, black-garbed curators she was accustomed to working with.

"Viola," she finally said, "you are a piece of beautiful art yourself."

Viola flushed with pleasure. "You are such a dear. How does everything look? Are we ready?"

"As ready as we'll ever be."

"Then let's throw the doors open and begin."

To Jane's surprise, the crowd outside Nine Lives had grown even larger. There was a commotion toward the back of the line, and Jane recognized Ethel and Lloyd in the midst of it. People were pushing toward Lloyd and reaching to shake his hand and wish him well. Everyone looked delighted to see him, and Lloyd was looking pretty pleased himself.

"Yes," Jane murmured. "This is working out beautifully." Tonight Lloyd could see for himself how much he was cared about and valued. Then he could put to rest whatever fears and negativity he was feeling and return to the business of getting well and being mayor again. Then she noticed Sylvia and Justine entering the store. Justine looked impressed.

"I'd heard you were an artist, but I had no idea..."

"I love your use of color," Sylvia chimed in.

"Are these for sale?" A gentleman whom she did not recognize addressed Jane. "My wife has fallen in love with that seascape over there. We honeymooned on the Pacific Ocean, and we'd love to buy a reminder of it."

Jane was blushing and saying "Thank you" as fast as she could.

"The food is outstanding. I may check in at the inn just to eat there."

"Do you give out your recipes?"

"I can't reach the cookies."

Jane looked down to see Josie standing with a frown on her face.

"All these big people are eating all the food, and I can't reach the cookies." Josie looked positively irate.

"Come on, honey. There are plenty of cookies. Why

don't I get some for you? We can wrap them up, and you can eat them whenever you want."

That brought a smile to the cloudy little face. They made their way to the buffet table and Jane realized just how right Josie was. It looked as though a wave of locusts had been through, leaving nary a crumb.

Fortunately, Jane had reserves stashed under the table in plastic containers. First she filled a napkin with goodies for Josie and then she began to set out more food.

Craig Tracy meandered over to pay her a compliment. "Great time, Jane. Thanks for making it possible. This town needed a little pick-me-up. I'm so glad Lloyd is here. I think he's having a wonderful experience, and it's good to see him out and about."

"Thanks, Craig, but I must admit, I didn't think of it—Viola did. She's Acorn Hill's social coordinator these days. And you're right, we all needed a pick-me-up. After tonight, I don't think Lloyd's going to want to hide out in his room any longer."

"I agree. He's talking about organizing a cleanup day for the city and then having a town picnic afterward with games and music. That doesn't sound like a mayor who has given up."

Jane imagined the joy that she would have in tearing up that resignation letter of Lloyd's, and her heart lifted. At last something was working out.

It took her a moment to realize that the room had quieted somewhat. She turned from the table and what she was doing to see what was going on.

What she saw was Peter Gowdy making his way through the crowd, eyes searching for his friend from the inn. When he found her, a smile spread across his features. "Jane! There you are! I'm sorry I didn't come right away. I got held up in Lancaster, but I'm here now. I should have called. Am I too late?"

Chapter Twenty-Four

Curiosity filled the room but Jane, unwilling to admit what she was trying to do or give any false hope, hurried to Mr. Gowdy and gave him a welcoming hug. As she did so, she whispered in his ear. "No one knows what I'm hoping for. Since it's such a long shot, let's keep it quiet. Pretend you are here on personal business."

She had to give Mr. Gowdy credit. He nodded and returned the hug with such force that she thought her shoes might fall off. When she said "personal" business, he seemed to take it as very personal. For the rest of the evening, he escorted her around, alternating praises for her artistic talent and for her food.

"I'm *so* glad you invited me to this," he would say any time someone came close. "I wouldn't have missed it for anything."

By the end of the evening, though no one knew the relationship between them, they all assumed that Jane had invited Mr. Gowdy to the art showing. It was a great cover, Jane thought, but she dreaded having to untangle all the questions about him later. Unless—and her pulse quickened—he could actually find out something at Fairy Pond that could halt construction.

When the second batch of food had just about given out, the crowd started to dwindle. Justine had walked Josie home to put her to bed, and Louise had accompanied Mr. Gowdy to the inn to show him to his room. Only Jane, Alice, Viola, Sylvia, Lloyd and Ethel were left.

Viola, had she had any buttons, would have burst them. As it was, Jane thought she detected a proud puffing of the woman's chest. Either that or those neon giraffes and elephants were coming to life and beginning to move.

"My best party ever!" Viola exclaimed. "Jane, next time we do this we'll add a fund-raiser for my cats. You do paint cats, don't you? Wouldn't it be fun to have a showing of just cat paintings …?"

Next time? Cats? Jane knew she was in over her head now, but she chose to address the issue at a later time when Viola had calmed down.

"We'll help you clean up," Jane began.

"You most certainly will not!" Viola shooed Jane, Alice and Sylvia away from the table. "It is my honor to do this. Why, I sold sixteen art books tonight. Jane, you did me a huge favor. I can't ask another thing of you."

"You can ask it of *me*," Alice offered.

"Of course not. I also had the privilege of having

Mayor Tynan here on his first outing since his heart attack."
Viola grabbed Lloyd's hand and pumped it. "We are *so* glad
to have you back."

Jane peeked at Lloyd. He was beaming. He had more
color in his cheeks than Jane had seen since his heart
attack. And Ethel was standing proudly beside him, her
face finally relaxed, as if a huge burden had been taken
from her shoulders.

Just what the doctor ordered, Jane thought. *Thank You, God!*

Saturday morning, Jane's alarm rang at 4:30. She was rolling
to turn it off when she remembered why she had set it for
this ridiculous hour. She and Peter Gowdy had a date to go
to Fairy Pond before anyone was stirring.

She struggled to her feet and slipped into a light ther-
mal weave shirt and the bib overalls she sometimes used for
gardening. With a quick motion, she wrapped her hair into
a knot and held it with a claw clip. No use prettying up for
this. She hoped to be home again before anyone knew she
was missing.

Carrying her shoes, she tiptoed in stocking feet to
Mr. Gowdy's door and rapped lightly.

It glided open immediately. He, too, was in his stocking
feet and just as sensibly garbed.

"I need to stop in the kitchen," Jane whispered when

they reached the bottom of the stairs. "I've written a note to let my sisters know what I'm up to. Last night I set the timer on the coffeepot so we'd have fresh coffee, and I have some of those muffins you're fond of to keep us well nourished."

"Can't beat that kind of service," Mr. Gowdy said, pleased.

"You're the one doing me a favor. If there's nothing out there of interest, I've wasted a lot of your time."

"And if there is something there, you've helped me a great deal too. Let's go."

Walking at this time of day was lovely, Jane realized. The predawn hours had an atmosphere all their own. But they had to hurry. People got up early in Acorn Hill and she didn't want to be detected.

"I think we'll have to use flashlights here," Jane said as they stepped off the main road and onto the path that led to the pond. "I packed two. The sun will be up soon enough, but until then, I don't want either of us to trip."

"Good idea." Mr. Gowdy shifted his backpack and followed Jane down the trail that was so familiar to her.

The morning glow was beginning when they arrived. Mr. Gowdy stopped, looked around and whistled. "This is such a nice place. No wonder you don't want it destroyed."

"I think several people around Acorn Hill over the years have considered it their own little secret. Fortunately, no one has tried to cut anything down or littered." She looked at him hopefully. "Do you think there's any chance..."

"I won't know until I look, will I?" Mr. Gowdy said cheerfully. "Let's get started."

"What is it we're looking for?" Jane asked. She bent down beside him as he studied some of the flora and fauna at the edge of the opening.

"We're not likely to find anything that's actually endangered here, but there are several things on the threatened list that could possibly—though not very likely—be here."

"Such as?"

"There are several plants. Remember the small-whorled pogonia I mentioned once? And there's an eastern-prairie fringed orchid. Virgina spiraea and glade spurge qualify as well. Why don't you look for glade spurge? It has thick stems and three-inch leaves that are hairy, but they feel soft to the touch."

"I don't see how we could miss that," Jane murmured as she made her way deeper into the forest with an eye out for something with hairy leaves. Eventually she poked her head back into the clearing. "What's killing the glade spurge, anyway?"

"Mostly habitat destruction. Sometimes bad water. We humans aren't very good for nature."

Jane walked back into the clearing feeling useless. She went to a fallen tree by the pond and sat down. The sun was moving up in the sky, and Jane could see movement along the pond's edge and smiled. A colorful little turtle was making his way somewhere, slowly but steadily. Jane liked the concept of turtles. They weren't flighty or silly but persistent and diligent. She thought that perhaps if more people had those traits it would be a better world.

"Would you like a cup of coffee?" she asked.

Mr. Gowdy stood and stretched. "Sure. It might make me wake up a little. I could use one of the muffins too . . ." He paused. "Jane, what are you holding?"

She looked at the little turtle in the palm of her hand and then held it up to him. "Just a baby turtle. There are probably more around here somewhere. Isn't he cute? There used to be a lot of them around here when I was a child, but I guess they're disappearing too with all the encroaching 'progress.'"

"I should say so."

Something in his tone made her look up. He was staring at the turtle in her palm.

"Disappearing quite rapidly, in fact. Jane, did you know this is a bog turtle?"

"No, as kids we called them 'red-bellies,' a name that is obviously appropriate. Of course that was a long time ago, but I never had reason to know more than that about them. We stayed away from the big ones." Jane handed the turtle to Mr. Gowdy and put her hands about ten or twelve inches apart. "The adults get this big. Louise always made us scrub our hands if she thought we'd been playing with turtles. Of course, Louise always made us scrub our hands anyway—"

"Jane, do you realize what you've found?"

"Other than a turtle? Not much."

"No," Mr. Gowdy said patiently, "it *is* the turtle."

"What?"

"You said that there were many turtles here once and now you were surprised to discover one   as you should be, I might add. The *pseudemys rubiventris*, also called the red-bellied or bog turtle, is on the threatened list in Pennsylvania."

"You mean . . ." Jane stared at the little creature, dumbfounded. "You mean that they are threatened, and I've known they were here all along?"

"People know about bald eagles being endangered, but not many are likely to be familiar with the less famous creatures. Jane, you have stumbled onto something very important."

"I have?" Now that this was happening, she couldn't seem to take it all in.

"It makes sense, really. They like ponds and marshes as well as rivers and lakes. They love to bask in the sun and it looks like there's plenty of open space for that here. Usually they prefer—"

A sound drew their attention to the woods. Suddenly Jane hoped that they wouldn't find more than they had bargained for.

She was surprised and relieved to see Casper Jones break into the clearing.

He obviously didn't expect to see them there either.

"Oh!" He held a hand to his heart. "You scared an old man. Hello, Jane, what are you doing here this time of day?"

She explained and introduced the two men.

Then Casper looked at the baby turtle in Mr. Gowdy's hand.

"Is that a red-bellied turtle? A bog turtle?"

"You know about bog turtles?" Jane gasped.

"I didn't until just last night. I've been worrying something fierce about the stunt my nephew is pulling by putting up a building over this place. I'm not too pleased to have that sort of nonsense close to my property either. I'm a little," he chuckled, "solitary."

No understatement there, Jane thought.

"So I started trying to think of ways to stop Raymond. He's just doing it because he can, not because he needs the money. I know the only reason he wanted to put it here was because he wouldn't have to buy a scrap of land. Anyway, the only thing I could think of was endangered species. Why, I read once that someone had to stop building an entire highway because of some little critter that was threatened. That's when I started looking on the Internet to see what might be around here that could throw a wrench in Raymond's callous plan."

Casper looked startled when Jane and Mr. Gowdy both burst out laughing.

A half hour later, after they had all cleaned their hands with the wipes that Jane had packed, they were finishing the last of the coffee and muffins. Jane and Mr. Gowdy sat on one big log while Casper sat on another.

"Well, this has been a busy day and it's only six-thirty," Casper commented. "I suppose I'd better go home and do my chores. I have mouths to feed, you know." He shook hands with Mr. Gowdy.

The more Jane knew of Casper the more she liked him, she realized. What a charming man. Unthinkingly she blurted, "I wish you were out more. People would love to visit with you. You are so interesting."

Casper looked at her and chuckled. "You mean you wish I'd quit being 'that weird hermit'?"

Jane reddened. "I suppose that's what I meant."

"Well, I'll just have to think about that, Jane. That sounds very tempting sometimes."

"When you decide, I want you to come to Grace Chapel Inn for dinner."

Casper bowed with a courtly air. "Invitation accepted." And then he walked back the way he had come and disappeared.

Jane and Mr. Gowdy were almost back to the road when they heard the rumbling sound of big engines.

"What's that?" she asked.

"When did you say they were going to start working here?" Mr. Gowdy asked.

"Anytime. It's staked out. You don't think…"

But it was. The crew had arrived to start the destruction of Fairy Pond.

Chapter Twenty-Five

$\mathcal{J}$ ane felt drained by the time she and Mr. Gowdy returned to Grace Chapel Inn later that morning. They walked into the dining room and dropped into chairs at the dining room table where Louise and Alice were poring over the inn's books.

Alice had a pencil stuck behind her ear and another in her hand while Louise manned the adding machine. Both sisters sized up the new arrivals. The pair before them looked as though they had been tromping through both muck and brush, which, of course, they had.

"What is going on?" Louise asked first. "Jane, are you okay? You look exhausted. And whatever happened to your clothes?"

"And Mr. Gowdy," Alice added, "you seem not one bit better."

"Oh dear," Louise murmured. "I'll get the coffee." And she hurried to the kitchen.

"And some food," Alice added. "You two look like you must have been out for days."

Jane looked at Mr. Gowdy with a weary smile. "My sisters and I think food is the cure for most everything. That and prayer."

"I have a hunch that the prayer has been going on for some time around here. Perhaps it's time to bring out the food. I'm starving. I usually don't have such exciting mornings as this one has been. I actually consider my job quite sedate most of the time. I normally don't go toe-to-toe with construction workers, developers and the legal system all before noon."

"You were positively heroic," Jane said sincerely. "If it hadn't been for you standing in front of the bulldozer as you used your cell phone to call the powers that protect hapless turtles, the woods around Fairy Pond would be gone right now."

"You and I didn't make many friends this morning. In fact, we might have made a few enemies."

"No, not really. Those men were there to do a job. They know that things can change. In fact, while you were on the phone, I talked to one of the fellows standing around. He whispered to me, 'I hated to see this place come down. Guess I won't have to feel guilty for doing it after all.'"

It had been an emotional morning, but for the indefinite future, the destruction of Fairy Pond had been put on hold.

Louise and Alice returned with steaming mugs of coffee,

roast beef sandwiches piled high with tomatoes, lettuce and horseradish, apple pie and half a dozen other things they had pulled from the refrigerator—pickles, hard-boiled eggs and salads among them. Jane realized then how hungry she really was.

"Dear Lord," she prayed, "thank You for this bounty before us and for the prayers that You heard and honored. You are *awesome*. Amen."

They dug into the food with enthusiasm.

Louise and Alice waited until Jane and Peter Gowdy had devoured much of the food and they had slowed enough to ask for ice cream to go with their pie before starting to ask questions.

"What happened? You have to tell us everything," Louise demanded as she refilled their coffee cups. "And what time did you leave the house this morning?"

"Shortly after four-thirty. Now I am so glad I asked Peter to come here for one last shot at saving the pond. As you both know, I thought that if he could find a plant or snail or something that was on his threatened or endangered list, we could somehow stop Raymond Jones from bulldozing the place into oblivion. And he did it! Fairy Pond was saved by Peter Gowdy, Casper Jones and a turtle!"

Louise's eyes grew round. "Casper?"

Taking turns, Jane and Mr. Gowdy poured out the story of the morning, of sneaking out so that no one in the town would see them and of running into Casper, who had come up with an idea similar to Jane's. They related how Casper had been up half the night researching and had discovered that the red-bellied turtles that had once been so plentiful and now were so few were being threatened by industry and urbanization.

Then Mr. Gowdy told them of hearing the rumble of big machines and of having to confront the men with the news that they wouldn't be able to do anything with Fairy Pond until the situation had been investigated thoroughly and a decision made by the proper authorities as to what needed to happen to protect the turtles.

"It was a little like a showdown!" Jane said. "Peter and the foreman standing toe-to-toe with cell phones to their ears, each talking as fast as he could. But ultimately Peter won out. I could hear Sam Horton screaming on the other end of the foreman's line. He was furious."

"Why was he so upset?" Alice asked naively.

"He was yelling about how much money this was costing them, mostly. And he sounded afraid that he'd lose Ray Jones's business after this. He wanted to know why these things hadn't been discovered until now. And then he started talking about money again."

"Money is a great motivator," Louise said sadly. "More so than beauty or nature."

"But for once, it didn't win out," Alice said happily.

Suddenly they heard the porch screen door slam and shudder as Ethel hurried into the house.

She still had pink sponge curlers in her hair aiming this way and that, and she had not yet "put on her face" for the day. She wore an odd combination of the white blouse, now wrinkled, that Jane had seen her in yesterday, a skirt with large pockets that she usually wore when she was tidying her house and her gleaming white tennis shoes.

"Aunt Ethel, what's wrong?" All three sisters' minds went to Lloyd.

"Viola called me. Florence had called her. She was in the Coffee Shop with Fred and Vera Humbert when they heard big machines rumbling past. From the direction they were moving, they probably had come from Fairy Pond. Fred got in his pickup and drove out there to see what was going on."

Ethel looked down at her skirt as if noticing for the first time what she was wearing. "Of course, I pulled on the first clothes I could find and hurried over here. Florence sounded quite distraught, Viola said, and Viola was none too calm herself."

"And what was going on at the Coffee Shop?" Jane asked, delighted with the excitement in town.

"Well, Viola and Florence were both there, and the news spread like wildfire. Ned noticed the excitement and came over from the drugstore. Pastor Ley and the gentlemen from the men's early morning Bible study all walked over to see what was going on. Clarissa came down from the Good Apple. Why, it was like a town meeting.

"By the time Fred got back to the Coffee Shop, dozens of people were there waiting to find out what was going on. Apparently the machines had been at Fairy Pond to start tearing down the trees but something happened to stop them. No one knows what yet, but I'm sure we'll find out.

"And," Ethel said, finally drawing a breath and giving them a condemning look, "you lazybones slept through it all."

She was startled when her three nieces and their guest erupted into laughter.

When they had settled down, Jane pulled out the chair beside her and patted the seat. "Sit down, Aunt Ethel. We have something to tell you."

When they were done, Ethel sat slack-mouthed in her chair.

"You mean that Fairy Pond is safe?" She looked at Mr. Gowdy.

He grinned. "Certainly for the time being. The government will have to do a study. And you know how long a government study can take."

Ethel clapped her hands together as a child might.

"Praise God! I've been praying for something that would cheer Lloyd's spirits. Nothing could be better than this."

Suddenly she raised both hands to her head and started clawing at the curlers. "I have to get ready! I need to go to Lloyd's and tell him and Justine the news." Her jaw tightened a little. "And I'd better get there before that busybody Florence does. This is news I want him to hear from me."

After Ethel had hurried out of the house, the four at the table burst into laughter again.

Peter Gowdy pushed back on his chair. "Well, ladies, thank you for one of the most enjoyable mornings I've had in a long time. But now I think it's time for me to take a shower and spend some time on the telephone with my superiors. Please excuse me."

After Mr. Gowdy had left the table, the sisters remained seated.

A concerned look flitted across Alice's face. "You know, as delighted as I am that Fairy Pond will remain, I still feel somewhat bad for Raymond Jones. I'm sure he's already spent a lot of time and money on this project he'd planned."

"Ever the soft heart, aren't you, Alice?" Jane spoke tenderly, touched by her sister's compassion for the man who had nearly destroyed a local treasure.

"I suppose Alice is right," Louise agreed. "I wonder what he will do now."

"He should build something on the other side of town,"

Jane said logically. "Potterston is where the action is going to be in the near future. He'd make much more money if he were nearer to Potterston."

"You're absolutely right," Alice said.

Louise suddenly stood up and left the table, calling back, "I have an errand to take care of."

Jane and Alice exchanged looks.

"Where did she go in such a hurry?"

"I have no idea," Jane said wearily. "But I need to go upstairs and clean up. I think I might take a little nap too. It's already been a busy day."

Jane's nap turned into a sound, three-hour sleep. When she walked into the kitchen, clean and rested, Alice was chopping celery and tossing it into a pot.

"Soup for supper?" Jane inquired.

"I thought I'd start something. Louise hasn't come back, and I wasn't sure what time you'd wake up."

Jane picked a carrot from the counter and began to chew on it. "What's got into our sister?"

"I wish I knew."

"She certainly acted rather mysterious."

"Everyone has been acting a little odd around here."

"What have you heard from Aunt Ethel?"

"She called to say that Lloyd is beside himself with joy.

He even admitted to her that he's been a big baby and that he was a bit ashamed of himself."

Jane laughed out loud.

Louise didn't show up until after supper and when she did, she had a satisfied smile on her face.

"Where have *you* been, and what have you been up to?" Jane demanded.

"We were getting worried about you," Alice chimed in.

"I suppose that you think I've been a bit secretive."

"That's a fact," Jane said. "But we still want to know where you went."

"I went to see Casper."

"Louie!" Jane squealed as if she were thirteen. "Tell us everything."

"There is nothing to tell," Louise said primly, but her cheeks turned a rosy pink. "I just thought it might be nice to visit with Casper again. I called him and we met at the Coffee Shop."

"Were there lots of people there?" Alice asked, her eyes shining.

"No. It was practically empty."

"What did you talk about?"

"Life. Music. Books we have read. Things we have learned since we were foolish high school students."

"And?" Jane and Alice chimed together.

"And the rest of it is none of your business. Alice Howard, you are just as curious and as much of a busybody now as you were in high school. And," Louise turned a chastising eye toward Jane, "you are just as much of a pest. Do you know how hard Casper and I used to work to avoid having you see us and run back to tell Father that we were together?"

Maybe that was why I didn't remember Casper Jones, Jane thought. At least she wasn't going crazy after all.

Louise folded her hands in her lap and her younger sisters knew at that moment that not one more juicy thing was going to cross her lips.

Chapter Twenty-Six

*A*corn Hill was buzzing. Peter Gowdy, who had chosen to stay until Monday and make some more observations of his turtle find, had become an overnight local hero. He and Jane stopped at the Coffee Shop on Monday to find that everything was on the house, including an entire pie. Craig Tracy brought flowers to the inn from the Humberts. Even Wilhelm Wood, who had not seemed all that enthusiastic about the pond, sent a basket of teas and sundries with a note saying, "Thank you for bringing joy to our little community."

Jane, according to Sylvia, who was tracking the chatter around town, had become a heroine of sorts, and the story of the exchange she and Peter had conducted with the workmen had grown and expanded until it became an epic battle of words rather than a slightly heated discussion. Jane's bravery was reputed to be unparalleled in Acorn Hill's history.

"Next thing you know, I'll hear that I laid down on the ground and tried to stop the bulldozer with my own body," Jane said with a laugh. "Or single-handedly wrestled every one of those men to the ground and tied them like roped calves."

"I did hear that you and Peter had chains with you and had planned to lash yourself to the trees," Sylvia said.

"It's going to be a bit of a letdown to find out the truth," Jane chuckled. "The workmen were actually quite pleasant about the whole thing. Even they were disgusted with Sam Horton blaring on the other end of the line."

"It's interesting," Sylvia observed, "that whoever *didn't* care if the pond survived has somehow disappeared, and now everyone is rejoicing. Why, some had tears of joy in their eyes when they talked about it."

"I'm glad for everyone's sake—especially Lloyd's and the community. I do wish, though, that we knew for sure that no one who needed employment missed the opportunity for work."

"You did more than anyone expected," Sylvia pointed out.

"Not just me."

"You spearheaded the action."

Jane sat back in her chair on the porch of Grace Chapel Inn and stared out at the manicured lawn and shrubbery that Jose Morales had been so faithful about tending. "It's strange to say, but, looking back, I realize that I felt something bigger was at stake, something even more important than the pond or the community."

"What could that be?" Surprise was evident in Sylvia's voice.

"Stewardship, I think."

"What do you mean?"

"God gave us this earth and put us in charge of it. He gave us dominion over it, it says in Genesis. It occurs to me that we've been terrible stewards of His gifts. We've built and urbanized and destroyed natural habitats until some of His creatures are extinct. If Peter and I did find a way to protect something more helpless than ourselves, it feels right."

"You are remarkable, Jane. And I thought you were just worried about having a place to sketch."

Jane grinned at her friend. "That too."

Sylvia lifted a hand and pointed down the street. "Look who's coming."

Lloyd and Ethel were out for a stroll. Justine was following them with a concerned expression on her face. She looked as if she were ready to catch Lloyd if he fell over backward, but there seemed to be no danger of that. The spring was back in his step. In fact, he looked younger and healthier than he had *before* the heart attack. He was thinner now and truly needed suspenders to hold up his trousers.

Jane stood up and waved. "Hello there. Nice to see you out."

The threesome trundled toward the inn, and Jane and Sylvia pulled up more porch chairs.

When they were settled, Jane said, "Can I get you

something? I've been baking a lot lately, and Alice has politely suggested that she'd like some room in the freezer for ice cream."

"Sure," Lloyd said enthusiastically, but Ethel bumped him in the arm with her elbow.

"Remember your diet."

Lloyd's face crumpled. "Oh, that."

"Actually, I've been cooking for you, Lloyd. I have low-fat applesauce oatmeal cookies. Would that be okay?"

Lloyd's face showed his delight. "Jane, I owe you my gratitude in so many ways and now this. Why, no one's let me have a cookie since my heart attack."

Speculation ran rampant for the next two weeks. There was no activity at Fairy Pond, but there was no word either about what Ray Jones might do about his land. Jane went to the pond almost every day, thinking that she might run into Casper, but he had disappeared from sight. She was surprised to find herself so disappointed by his absence.

Louise—again inspiring intense curiosity in her sisters —had been walking around the house with a cat-that-ate-the-cream expression on her face and still refused to talk about whatever was pleasing her so.

Jane and Alice had made a game of trying to get her to spill the beans, but so far to no avail.

"Louie, you got a phone call today. It sounded important."

Louise straightened. "Who was it?"

"A man. On business."

"Did he say what kind of business?"

"What should he have said?"

Louise gave Jane a chastising look. "Do not try to trick me again. You two are incorrigible."

"Just tell us, Louise," Alice pleaded. "What have you got up your sleeve?"

"You'll find out soon enough ... I hope."

"So nothing's certain?" Alice pried.

"There's death and taxes," Louise retorted. "And now, if you'll excuse me, I have to go to the church to practice."

Pastor Thompson stopped by Grace Chapel Inn before going to the town meeting that Lloyd, in his first mayoral act since his heart attack, had called. The doctor had given him permission to return to his normal routine as long as he didn't get upset or overly excited.

"Are you ladies going to attend the meeting?" Pastor Ken asked. "If so, would you care to walk with me?"

"We were just going to start out," Jane said. Then she looked around. "Where's Louise?"

"She was here not long ago. Maybe she went ahead without us."

"She wouldn't do that, would she?" Pastor Ken asked.

"Normally not," Alice said with a sigh, "but Louise has been acting oddly for the past few days. We've both given up predicting what she'll do next."

Pastor Ken's eyebrows lifted in surprise. "She seems the same to me. I've talked to her half a dozen times this week and she's never said anything out of the ordinary."

"She's up to something," Jane said. "You can trust me about that."

"It's usually Jane who is up to something," Alice added. "Louise is normally so . . . *normal*."

As they walked toward the town hall, they watched people coming from all over town. Nancy and Zack Colwin were escorting Clarissa Cottrell, and Fred and Vera were walking with Nia Komonos. Dr. Bentley and his wife Kathy were strolling along with Craig and Sylvia, and Clara Horn had left Daisy at home and was walking with Florence Simpson toward the hall.

"I wonder what Lloyd has on his agenda," Jane commented.

"He's probably going to pin a medal on you," Pastor Ken joked, "for 'service above and beyond the call of duty' to Acorn Hill."

Jane groaned. "I wish this could all just die down and that people would forget about the uproar."

"That's not likely to happen until people know what's going to happen to the property," Alice pointed out. "Well, here we are."

They found seats near the front next to Sylvia and Craig. Jane noticed that Ethel and Louise had chairs in the first row. She turned to Alice.

"So she did come without us!"

Alice shook her head. "I don't know what's gotten into her."

There was no time for more speculation, however, because Lloyd stood, went to the podium and held his hand in the air for silence.

"May I have your attention, ladies and gentlemen? Your attention, please." Lloyd looked over the crowd as though he were looking at his own, much-loved children.

Jane felt a lump forming in her throat just watching him. And Ethel looked so proud.

"We've had a lot of turmoil here in our fair town in the past few weeks," he began, "and I thought perhaps the best way to address the issues that we've faced was to call a town meeting and give people the opportunity to ask questions about what's been going on and what the future holds. So I'd like to open this meeting to the floor."

A dozen hands went into the air immediately, and Lloyd was peppered with questions. Peter Gowdy, unbeknownst to Jane, had returned to town and gave a report on the current state of the bog turtle and the government's investigation into its habitat. Finally, the questions turned to what would happen to the property around Fairy Pond.

Lloyd smiled broadly. "Well, I can tell you that Fairy Pond is in good hands. And to explain what I mean, I will call on Louise Howard Smith, who has been instrumental in this process. Louise, could you come up here?"

Jane and Alice looked at each other. Were they finally going to hear what it was that Louise had been smirking about?

Louise, who had always been poised from long years of performing at the piano, made an impressive figure at the front of the room. She cleared her throat and placed some notes on the podium. Then she took the reading glasses on the chain around her neck and lifted them to the bridge of her nose.

"I have been asked by the parties involved to make an announcement. After much negotiation, my friend—and a friend to Acorn Hill—Mr. Nino Angelo has agreed to allow Raymond Jones to purchase property that Mr. Angelo owns near Potterston with clearance for Mr. Jones to build his convenience store and gas station on that same property. Therefore, both Potterston and Acorn Hill will benefit.

Both believe that it will be a mutually beneficial arrangement. Initially, Mr. Angelo had agreed to consider taking Mr. Jones's land surrounding Fairy Pond in exchange, but a third party, someone with a special, long-term interest in Fairy Pond, has stepped forward to purchase that land and has agreed to leave the land untouched."

A surge of interested, enthusiastic chatter spread throughout the room, and Jane and Alice beamed at what their sister had accomplished.

"So her meeting with Casper wasn't just for old times' sake," Alice whispered.

"Therefore, I am pleased to announce that all the land originally owned by the Jones family is now the possession of Mr. Casper Jones. Mr. Jones is interested in keeping a buffer between his home and the road and has also agreed to stipulate that upon his death, the land will be turned into a wildlife habitat. We hope, of course, that occurs in the far distant future."

Jane heard several people praising the neighborly deeds of Casper Jones. Then a round of clapping began and swelled throughout the hall. Soon everyone was laughing and cheering.

Smiling, Louise stepped away from the podium and returned to the seat beside her beaming aunt.

It was after ten o'clock by the time the sisters and some of their friends returned to the inn for tea, Lloyd insisting that he was feeling well enough to join the party.

"I can't believe it," Pastor Thompson said. "The first I heard of Casper Jones was just a few weeks ago."

"And now he's managed to do an extraordinarily good deed for the community." Ethel's expression made clear her appreciation.

"Louise, why didn't you tell us that you'd been dealing with Casper, Ray and Mr. Angelo?" Alice asked, perturbed at being left out of the fun. "And how did you know about Mr. Angelo's holdings?"

"Actually, Casper and Mr. Angelo spoke with Ray after I called Mr. Angelo and then visited with Casper at the Coffee Shop. But you know how Casper is—he doesn't like to leave home, so he asked me to do his leg work and establish contact with Mr. Angelo's office.

"As for Mr. Angelo's holdings, you may recall how pleased he was when we hosted the party for his son and daughter-in-law. Well, we chatted a good bit that day, and he told me that he had been investing in property near Potterston. You probably remember that he was adamant about wanting to be contacted if there was anything that he could do for us. Well, I finally saw how he could, and he couldn't have done better. Mr. Angelo is an angel."

"Sounds like one to me," Pastor Thompson responded.

"And Casper managed to do his part without leaving his land—except for that afternoon you *lured* him to the Coffee Shop." Jane's eyes twinkled with mischief after her last words, but Louise remained unruffled. "For someone who never leaves home, he's the least isolated person I've ever met."

"I don't get it," Justine said. She had come with Lloyd, determined to make him go home if she saw that he was getting tired. "If Mr. Jones never leaves his land, how can he work? Where does he earn his money?"

Every eye in the room turned to Louise. She obliged by providing the answer. "Casper's parents lived simply and left their sons quite well-to-do. Casper has never been much interested in material things, so he has always gotten along. He has, he told me, published some articles for which he has been paid and in the last few years has made a home-based business for himself buying and selling rare first-edition books online. He told me that he has become quite captivated by computer technology. It seems," Louise ended with a smile, "that Casper is a very up-to-date and contemporary recluse."

Epilogue

Nearly a month had passed since the night of the town meeting, and everything was settling back to normal. Fairy Pond and its bog turtles remained just as they had always been, only now they had the benefit of Peter Gowdy's watchful eye. Lloyd pleased his doctors with his rapid recovery, and he was given permission to go back to Justine's exercise class with Ethel for the stretching exercises. Calm again, Jane cut back on her baking, and the freezer was no longer filled to the brim.

"I think I can finally relax," Jane said to Sylvia and Louise as they sat at the dining room table, all hand stitching on one of Sylvia's quilts. "I have learned to appreciate peace and quiet in a whole new way."

"I know what you mean," Louise agreed. "Even the inn is running like clockwork. We have all return guests this week. My guess is that we will barely see them. It will be like a vacation."

"It will be lovely."

"I wouldn't count on that lasting very long." Alice walked into the house sorting the mail that had just been delivered. She had already opened one of the letters and was holding the notepaper in her hand.

"What do you mean?" Sylvia asked.

"We've received a request for reservations from two former guests who should enliven our days again."

Jane shifted uneasily in her chair. "Which guests?"

"Because they found our inn as 'adequate' as any in the area, Genevieve and Harold Thrumble are coming back for a longer visit." Alice lifted a second piece of paper out of the envelope. "She's sent a list of suggested breakfast menus for you, Jane, something more appropriate for her 'delicate palate.' And Louise, she's kindly enclosed a label from some of her favorite bedsheets, hoping you'll be making improvements in that area before they arrive."

Jane groaned as Alice laid the note on the table. Louise put her head in her hands as if praying for patience.

And Sylvia burst out laughing. "Serves you all right for thinking things could ever be serene here at Grace Chapel Inn."

Tales from Grace Chapel Inn

Back Home Again
by Melody Carlson

The Way We Were
by Judy Baer

Recipes & Wooden Spoons
by Judy Baer

The Spirit of the Season
by Dana Corbit

Hidden History
by Melody Carlson

The Start of Something Big
by Sunni Jeffers

Ready to Wed
by Melody Carlson

Spring Is in the Air
by Jane Orcutt

The Price of Fame
by Carolyne Aarsen

Home for the Holidays
by Rebecca Kelly

We Have This Moment
by Diann Hunt

Eyes on the Prize
by Sunni Jeffers

Summer Breezes
by Jane Orcutt

Once you visit the charming village of Acorn Hill, you'll never want to leave. Here, the three Howard sisters reunite after their father's death and turn the family home into a bed and breakfast. They rekindle old memories, rediscover the bonds of sisterhood, revel in the blessings of friendship and meet many fascinating guests along the way.

Judy Baer is the author of more than seventy books for adults and teens. She has won the Romance Writers of America Bronze Medallion and has twice been a RITA finalist. She lives in Elk River, Minnesota, with her husband.